THE ISLAND

MICHAEL BRAY

THE ISLAND

FAMILY TIES

LOMAR CORPORATION TOWER
NEW YORK CITY
SEPTEMBER 15TH 2018

The private Lear jet had flown him in from his business trip in Dubai, dropping him at the airport at the private terminal reserved for the wealthy. The trip had been cut short, something which still irked him hours after the event. He liked it there. He liked the heat. The wealth. It was like no place on earth, and about as far from his current location as it was possible to get.

Thirty-three-year-old Damien Lomar sat in the back of the limousine and stared out at a city which was dying around him. He sipped his bourbon, good quality stuff that cost more than a lot of the citizens of the broken city made in a year. He looked at the decaying bricks, the filthy windows, the garish neon signs advertising the latest snacks or soft drinks, and wasn't the least bit surprised at the mess it had become. The city had expanded far beyond its means and could no longer sustain its populous in either housing or employment. The official line was of course that there was nothing to worry about and that although unsettled, everything was under control. That was all the politicians could really say if they wanted to be voted into another year in office. Their slick lies and greasy handshakes would likely see them stuff their pockets for another year and give a little glimmer hope to those people who put their faith in them. Damien, however, knew the truth of just how serious the problem was. He played golf with the mayor's son every second Sunday. He was a snivelling brat who favoured pressed tennis shorts and polo shirts, and could always be

1

guaranteed to spill a few pertinent details once his tongue was loosened with a little alcohol. The truth was that the economy was broken and those in power knew it. They were just trying to squeeze a last few dollars out of what was left before fleeing to their big houses with their big wallets, and sitting by their big swimming pools and working out the next way to make themselves even richer. He sighed and sipped his drink, watching a woman lead her scruffy, wretch of a child down the side of the street, her face an expression of absolute hopelessness as she dragged the snotty brat along.

Yes. The city was going to shit alright.

He checked his watch, the forty-thousand-dollar Rolex telling him it was a little after three in the afternoon and he was late for the meeting, not that he cared. The beginning was always filled with the boring run of the mill shit he didn't care about. Share prices, stock flotation. All the things which gave him a headache if he thought about them too much. He stared out of the window, letting his eyes tune out of the pitiful wretches in the streets and focus on the ghostly image of his reflection. The golden hue of his tanned skin, the piercing blue of his eyes, the jet black hair swept into a side parting. He wondered how they, the poor and the destitute, the hungry and the desperate, would view him. He was sure it would be at first with hope that the rich man might give them something – food or money – then, when he refused their request, the mood would change. Anger. Hate. Frustration. All good reasons why he didn't mingle with the poor unless he could help it. And why should he? He had made something of himself. Scratched and clawed to get where he was, or at least, that's what he would tell them. The reality was that he was born into his wealth. Forget the silver spoon. The one he was born with wedged in his mouth was made of solid gold and encrusted with diamonds. He peered up the street, pushing his cheek towards the window. A snake of cars, mostly yellow taxis, had gridlocked the road as far as he could see. Ahead, he could see the edge of the building his father had built. Lomar Tower, which now proudly boasted the honour of being the tallest building in the city, glittered in the early morning sun. One beacon of light in a city of ruin. Prior to its construction, the second World Trade Center held that particular honour after its predecessors fell in two thousand and one. At just a shade over six hundred meters tall, Lomar Tower now stood head and shoulders above the rest, and rightly so. Damien sighed, growing impatient. For as much as he was vice president of the company and could afford to be late if he wanted to, he didn't want to completely piss off the rest of the board before he had shown them his proposal. His eyes went to the leather briefcase on the seat beside him. Even his miserable old fuck of a father couldn't fail to see its potential, as long as he could get to the building before the whole thing was over. He leaned forward in his seat, pressing the controls to roll down the divider between himself and the driver. "What's taking so long?"

"Traffic, Mr. Lomar. There's another protest about the state of healthcare. The city is gridlocked." The African American driver looked over his shoulder, nervous. He was young, and looked absolutely terrified of his powerful employer.

"Another one? Isn't that the third this month?" Lomar grunted.

"It is, sir," his driver said, staring at the traffic ahead of him.

"They should be out working for a living instead of holding up people like me who have things to do."

"Yes, sir."

Lomar knew his driver didn't agree. He was only slightly higher up the chain than the poor and the hungry, and knew well enough to keep his mouth shut and his job secure with it. Even so, Damien enjoyed teasing him about it, even if he was new. He knew people thought he was an asshole, which was fine with him. It was the truth. "Is it worth waiting in the car or should I just go the rest of the way on foot?"

"We might be here a while yet, sir," the driver said, cold and robotic, not wanting to offer an idea that might be wrong and could get him fired.

"Right, mingling with the peasants it is," Damien said, grabbing his briefcase and clambering out of the car. He walked briskly towards the steel and glass building, trying to ignore the acrid sting of the smog in his throat. It was becoming a real problem. Even as he looked up at the tower, the top of it was shrouded in a thick pollution-laced fog. It was little wonder the frequency of respiratory illnesses was on the up. He snaked through the endless throng of people, ignoring their envious stares, and arrived at the building. He strode across the expansive foyer, marble floor echoing underfoot as he made for the private express elevator tucked away at the rear of the building. He breathed in the clean, filtered air, trying to shake the feeling that he was dirty now that he had mingled with the poor. He inserted his special key into the slot in the elevator control panel and turned it, the doors closing and taking him towards the roof of the world. He tightened his grip on his briefcase, confident he would get what he wanted.

TWO

Jackson Lomar sat at the head of the boardroom table, listening to his director of finance go through the balance sheets. He wasn't really paying attention. He had already picked up on the fact that, all facts and figures stripped aside, they were still making a healthy profit year on year. He flicked his eyes, an almost translucent grey in colour, towards the vacant seat to his right which should have been occupied by his son and felt the familiar anger he had grown accustomed to where Damien was concerned. Jackson had worked his entire life to build their business from scratch, first in export, then in telecommunications. He was aware that as he was just a year shy of his seventieth birthday, he needed to make sure the company was in good hands when he decided to retire. The issue was that despite doing all he could to prepare him, Jackson wasn't entirely sure his son was the right man for the job. It was little things like this – the board meetings where none of them really wanted to attend but had to – which rubbed him up the wrong way. The ambition was there, that had never been an issue. His son had always had a competitive edge with anything he set his mind to, and the drive and determination to pull it off. It was just that if there was something he wasn't particularly interested in, he wouldn't show any aptitude for it. Jackson looked around the table, people he knew and trusted with the running of his multibillion dollar business, but could see it in their eyes all the same. The empty chair was an embarrassment, the elephant in the room which he was about to address when the boardroom door opened and his son walked in, his face showing the smug self-appreciation which was the root of all their issues.

"You're late," Jackson said, for the time being able to control his temper.

"Traffic is gridlocked. Another protest backing everything up for miles. I had to walk the last block," Damien said as he slumped down in his seat and brushed hair out of his eyes.

"That healthcare protest has been planned for weeks, which is why the rest of us left early enough to get here on time."

"Don't start with me, Dad, I've had a long day. Those pricks on the street are to blame. Not me."

"Those 'pricks' are people. They're just trying to get the assistance they deserve from the city," Jackson said, ignoring the awkward body language of the other board members as father and son conducted in their very public disagreement.

"They don't deserve anything. If they were too lazy to work for a living like the rest of us, there wouldn't be a problem."

"Work for a living? I was already a multi-millionaire by the time you were born. What do you know about work?" Jackson grunted, embarrassed at his son's behaviour.

"I work damn hard for this company, not that you've ever noticed i–" Damien cleared his throat and took a second to compose himself, remembering why he was there. "I actually have something I'd like to discuss."

"There's a first time for everything. What is it?" Jackson said, unsure if he was proud or surprised that his son wanted to do something other than just sit and go through the motions. Damien opened his briefcase and took out several identical laminated booklets. He walked around the table, giving each of the fifteen board members a copy the returning to his seat.

"I got the idea when I was over in Dubai on business."

"What is it? A theme park?" Jackson said, leafing through the booklet.

"An island," Damien replied, unable to help but grin. "A man-made structure, the biggest of its kind."

"The cost of this would be astronomical. Why would you want to even build it? For what purpose?"

Damien could feel it slipping away. The sour-faced old fucks around the table didn't get it. They didn't see his vision. It was going to take a bit of hard sell. "I have contacts," he said as he stood and walked around the side of the table. "Construction companies who specialise in this kind of work who are willing to do a deal. I can build the entire structure, including terraforming it in full for maybe, a billion five."

"A billion five?" Jackson repeated, tossing the booklet on the desk. "Have you any idea what that kind money could do to help the city? To fix some of the problems with it? We have a proposal in line to develop a new clean air filtration system as well as building low-cost housing for those in need over the next ten years. We don't have the resources for this pipe dream of yours. If you want to use your own money then that's fine. But you won't burn through the resources of this company on stupid pipe dreams. Not while I'm in charge."

Damien walked back towards his father, lowering his voice. "You always told me to think outside the box. To look at the bigger picture. This is exactly what I'm doing. Think about it. The jobs it will create. The positive business impact for the company."

"You still haven't said why you want to do this."

"It's all right there in the proposal. Our genetics research has started down some very exciting and ground breaking paths. Our telecommunications business is thriving. What if we combine the two? A nature reserve, untouched by man, a natural habitat for the creatures of the world to exist in peace. That's P.R. you can't buy and you know it."

"A billion and a half would buy a hell of a lot of P.R. son. You have to give me more than that. How would you expect to make our money back?"

"We can do tours, the world's biggest safari park. We could even go further. The Island hotel, a breath of fresh air away from the pollution of the city. It's perfect."

Jackson took a deep breath and put his palms flat on the table. "No."

It took a second to sink in. Damien had played it out in his head countless times and it always ended with his father agreeing to the project. Now, with this unexpected scenario, he had no idea how to react. "But it makes business sense. You must see it."

"I see nothing but a wild idea to do some kind of idiotic, poorly thought out publicity stunt. On one hand you're saying we should build this place as a sanctuary for local wildlife, in the next breath you see hotels and tours for the public. It's all just too wild. Too improbable. It would be a financial black hole and I think you know that."

"Father, please, how can I be expected to run the company one day if you won't even trust my judgement?"

"This isn't about judgement. This is about business. You're asking for a huge amount of money for something that is an outlandish pipe dream. The dimensions alone of this proposed structure would mean a construction unlike anything ever seen before. You say a billion five, but I know it would cost more. A lot more."

"Father, I–"

Jackson raised a hand. "Now I appreciate you trying to take the ball and run with it, but in this instance, you have it all wrong. True enough, one day you'll sit in this chair and make the decisions, and whatever you choose will be on you. It won't happen on my watch, though. That I can promise you."

"Just take some time to think it over, i–"

"I've heard enough. That money is going towards helping this city get back on its feet, not funding some stupid, half-assed idea. Now I won't hear another word about. Gentlemen, if we can move on to the next order of business, please."

Damien sat as the proposals were passed back down to him. Anger bubbled in his stomach, a molten ball of frustration and hatred. He couldn't understand why none of them could see he was a visionary, that the plan to try and save the city was even more doomed than the plans to build The Island. He suspected it was the old school mentality of the board. Not one of them was a day younger than sixty. All of them had their eyes on a cosy retirement and healthy bonus package. They didn't consider what kind of long-term direction the company would take, especially when he was holding the reigns. He made himself a promise as he shoved the proposals back into his briefcase. Even if it took until his dying day, he would prove the old man wrong and makes sure he apologised for ever doubting him.

DESPERATE TIMES

NEW YORK CITY
NOVEMBER 7TH 2043

The cough that had started as an irritating tickle in Chase Riley's throat had now transformed into a full blown rattle. He pulled his tattered jacket tighter in a half-hearted attempt to block out the bitter cold and pushed on. The city stretched above him, making him feel even smaller and insignificant than he already did. People pushed and shoved, those who could afford face masks to keep out the acrid smog wearing them, those who couldn't, suffered the bitter taste in the throat and the stinging eyes brought on by the conditions. At just twenty-eight, Chase had only known the world he had been born into. A world of poverty where unemployment was at an all-time high nationwide. He had lost his job as a delivery driver almost a year earlier, and the little savings he had put aside had soon dried up. With over two thousand applicants for the few scattered vacancies out there, it made the chances of finding work slim. He had taken to walking the streets and going business to business out of sheer desperation to get back on his feet. He was young and strong, and, as he told all of his prospective employers, willing to do any kind of work as long as there was a pay check at the end of it. He glanced around him at the immense skyscrapers which illustrated that not everyone was struggling to make ends meet. The towers stretched into the smog shrouded heavens, none higher than the three owned by the Lomar Corporation which graced the New York skyline. For them, the rich and the powerful, the quest to cram as much real estate into the city had become key, and as always it was the poor who suffered. Homes were being purchased and demolished to make way for bigger and better buildings and offices. The knock on effect for the poor was akin to a haphazardly constructed domino run. Without jobs, people couldn't afford homes, without homes, desperation turned to crime. Chase had seen pictures of the old city back before the Lomar Corporation took its stranglehold. The charm it once had was gone. The garish neon television screens, which were once exclusive to Times Square, now covered every building across the entire city as the Lomar Corporation sold advertising space to willing investors. The once lush green of central park was also gone, more than half of it now populated by large, ugly skyscrapers, the remainder a wasteland of rubble and earth. Darkness was starting to creep closer, bringing with it a bitter drizzle which would soon turn into snow. The coming dark would also bring out the criminals, the lowlifes and destitute, those hooked on cheap drugs, addictions that they had to feed no matter the cost. Those were the people who had given up on trying to fight against the horrors thrown at them by daily life and instead join the tidal wave of scum looking out for themselves at the expense of everyone else. Chase didn't hate them. He knew how easy it would be to fall into that particular way of life. The crowds were starting to thin now as he made his way home. The buildings in the neighbourhood where Chase lived were run down graffiti-covered shells riddled with damp and infested with rats and cockroaches, but it was the best people like him could afford. He walked down trash strewn sidewalks, keeping his eyes on the floor to avoid the hungry gazes of the gangs and desperate. They left him alone for the simple reason that they knew he had nothing of value worth stealing.

Brownwater Place was a block of two room apartments. The outside was an ugly red brown, and one of the glass panels in the entranceway had been boarded over. The rooms were cold in winter and overpoweringly hot in summer, but it was cheap and somewhere to live. He wrinkled his nose as he entered the building; the smell of mould and piss he would never get used to. He coughed, a brittle sound complimented by the creaking of the tired wood as he ascended the staircase to the fourth floor, passing a neighbour whose name he didn't know. He recognised the look though. The haunted expression of sheer hopelessness was more than familiar.

TWO

Chase went inside, closed and locked the door, then took off his jacket. Somehow, being home and a failure was worse than if he had been mugged or attacked. He tried to take a deep breath, almost lost it by starting to cough, and then swallowed it back down. He walked into the cosy sitting room, ignoring the damp and black mould which lingered in the corners. His wife, Ashley, smiled at him, the worry in her eyes cutting him deep.

"How did it go?" she asked, already knowing the answer.

"No luck today. I'll try again tomorrow. We'll get something soon."

"I know we will," she replied, this time unable to hold his gaze. She was a year younger than him, and a qualified nurse. Even for her there was no work. Nobody could afford healthcare, and so there was no need for an excess of staff. She had red hair and pale skin dotted with freckles. Her eyes were a deep jade.

He sat in the armchair and started to unfasten his boots. "How have things been here?"

"Fine. Nothing out of the ordinary. We've been worried about you. I wish you hadn't sold your phone."

"We needed the money. Besides, I can look after myself out there, don't worry. How's she been today?"

Ashley blinked and looked at her hands. She had chewed her nails down to the skin. "No change. She's awake if you want to go see her."

Chase wanted to tell his wife she would be okay, that they would be okay, but he wasn't certain it was true and didn't want to lie to her. Instead, he stared at her for a few seconds, hating himself for not being able to ease the burden he could see she was carrying. He wanted his old wife back, the one who wasn't pale and frowning, and who had lost so much weight because she was just too stressed to eat. It hurt him to even think about it. He got up and went to one of the two bedrooms, opening the door and stepping inside.

THREE

Elsie Riley was just five when the lung cancer was first diagnosed. Now aged nine, it had started to win the battle with its fragile host. Chase hated to see her the way she was. Tired and sick, frightened but trying to be strong for her parents. She had her mother's eyes and hair and his jawline and determination. Her room had been turned into a sanctuary. Soft toys lined the walls, and the portable electric heater – the only one in the house – was in here to keep the room warm against the bitter winter chill. Chase walked to the bed and sat at the foot of it, listening to the wet rasp of his daughter as she battled just to breathe.

"Did you get a job, Daddy?" she asked, turning to face him.

He hadn't realised she was awake, her words startling him. "No, not this time, sweetheart."

"You will. I know you will."

He held her hand, the skin so soft, so fragile that it looked as if it could break. "We'll get there, Elsie. I promise."

His daughter nodded, too weak to respond. He wanted to change the subject and turn her away from such a bleak line of questioning. "Hey, where's little Timmy from down the hall these days? I haven't seen him for a while."

A cloud of uncertainty passed over his daughters face. It was brief, but there all the same. "Timmy got sick."

"Oh, I didn't know," Chase replied, realising just how preoccupied with finding a job and setting them on the road to recovery he had been. "We'll have to get him a card. You can write it, how does that sound?"

That shadow passed over her face again, the uncertainty and this time, an unmistakable flicker of fear. "He's not here anymore, Daddy. He went to heaven."

It was a rare thing for Chase to be speechless, yet his daughter had managed to achieve that feat in a single sentence.

"What happened to him?" he asked, feeling as if he were having some kind of out of body experience. "He was here a few weeks ago. He seemed fine." Apart from that cough. The same one your daughter had before the cancer. The same one you have now.

Of course, he couldn't say any of that. His job was to protect his daughter. Instead, he held her hand. It was all he could do.

"He has the same thing I have, Daddy." She sat up then, and now there was no hiding the fear. He could feel it seeping out of her. "I don't want to go to heaven, Daddy. I don't want to die. Timmy said there was medicine, some that would make him better. Why can't we have that, Daddy? Why can't I get better?"

Although she didn't intend it, her words were like a one two punch and made him feel like an utter failure. There was no cure for the late stage lung cancer which ravaged her organs and ate her from the inside, but there were treatments which could ease her pain, even if they were only available to those who could afford the vaccine. The idea of it made him angry. His daughter, along with countless others like her, was dying a slow, pollution-related death because they couldn't afford the price put on it by the rich and powerful pharmaceutical companies. The idea that his daughter could die because they didn't have the financial means to stop it was almost too much to comprehend. Just affording to live week to week was hard enough, especially with both of them out of work and Ashley having to stay at home full time to look after Elsie. The welfare money only went so far, and with growing rumours that it was to be either cut or abolished in the next year depending on who you happened to ask, the future was bleak. He thought about the lowlifes, the criminals and the drug dealers, the armed robbers and the pimps. He was damn sure they were making money. Not cancer vaccine money, but money none the less. Although it was tempting, he wasn't prepared to make that step just yet.

"Will there be angels?"

He blinked and looked at her, his thoughts evaporating as he came back to the present.

"What was that?" he asked.

"Angels. When I die, will there be angels?" She was frowning, and he was struck by how much she looked like Ashley.

That figurative knife drove itself a little deeper, but somehow he managed to smile. "You're not going to die, Elsie. I promise."

She shook her head. "You shouldn't do that. Make promises you can't keep. It's wrong."

"I promise, you won't die. I'll do whatever we need to get you that medicine to need." He kissed her hand, somehow fighting back the tears.

"It's alright, Daddy. I know you're trying your best. You don't have to lie to me." There was no blame, no aggression in her voice. Just empathy and understanding that the young and innocent possess.

"I promise you, I'll get you the cure you need. Now you get some rest, okay?"

She nodded and lay back down. He tucked her in, still fighting the urge to cry. "You get some sleep, okay?"

"Okay," she repeated. He kissed her on the head and went out of the room. Before he closed the door, he took a last look at her, so small and fragile as she lay on her side, wheezing her breaths in great, wet, laboured motions. He closed the door and returned to his wife, who was watching for him. Without saying a word, he knelt in front of her, put his head in her lap and let the tears come as she stroked his hair.

A SEED IS SOWN
NEW YORK CITY
NOVEMBER 23rd 2043

Days blend into night and back to day, and the only thing that changes is the intensity of the cough and the deterioration of his daughter. Chase is in that place where the things he promised himself he would never do were looking like increasingly appealing options. He had never committed a crime in his life, but the idea of taking from someone who was better off than he was in order to provide at least a shred of hope to his family was starting to feel normal. It was this mind-set that had brought him to a part of the city which he never would have ordinarily visited. Formerly known as Little Italy, the lower Manhattan district had been hit particularly badly by the broken economy, and many of its Italian residents had long since moved on to pastures new. In their place, pop-up markets had been erected along with low-quality stores run by immigrants and those who had a product, however seedy, to sell. Here, the poor didn't try to hide what they were. Here they thrived in a seedy den of poverty and destitution. Chase walked through the stinking filthy streets, past the scammers and beggars, pushers and panhandlers. He passed garish neon stores selling everything from plastic bongs to exotic street food. His stomach quivered at the sight of rat meat kebabs being consumed by those who couldn't afford anything better. It wasn't rat or cockroach kebab he was looking for, nor low-grade amateur pornography which seemed to frequent every other stall and cater to every despicable taste imaginable. What Chase was looking for was tucked away in a dark recess, a stall set up to be as discreet as possible, the wares on it not the true product it was known to sell. Chase stood and looked at the array of lighters on the table top, many decorated with painted marijuana leaves or badly drawn skulls. He eyed the man behind the table with his filthy fingernails, scruffy birds nest hair and shallow features. His skin seemed to be stretched across his skull, the bluish veins visible beneath the skin.

"Anythin' you need?" the man said, grinning and showing an ocean of rotten, stumpy teeth. Although he was as white as white could be, he spoke with a bad fake Jamaican accent for reasons Chase couldn't comprehend.

"I'm not sure. What else do you sell?" Chase asked, careful with his words until he knew what was going on.

"What is it you need, brotha?" the wannabe Rasta said.

Chase looked around. Unsurprisingly, nobody was paying him the slightest bit of attention. "Not a lighter. I was looking for something with a bit more…impact."

The man made no reaction, which Chase saw as a sign he was at least in the right place. "Can you help me or not?"

The man behind the stall shrugged. "That depen' on exactly what you need."

"I think you know."

The scruffy man sucked his rotten teeth and placed his hands flat on the table. "You have to ask for it, brotha. Entrapment and all that. What are you lookin' for?"

Chase wanted to say it, but the three letter word that was so simple in principle just wouldn't project from brain to lips. He tried, swallowed, cleared his throat and tried again. "Gun. I need a gun."

A beat of silence, and Chase wondered if he had made a mistake. However, the man didn't tell him he was crazy or turn him away. He simply stared at him with those dead eyes and smiled at him with his stinking mouth.

"Can you help me or not?"

"Depends. Even if I knew someone who could get what you asked for, it would cost. The question is, do you have the money, mon?"

"How much would it be?" Chase asked, unable to believe he was indulging in such a conversation.

"Depends how big a shooter you need. Bigger costs more, obviously."

"How much for a small one?"

"Pistol will set you back three hundred."

Chase shook his head. "I can't afford that. You need to come lower."

"You don't make the prices here. Three hundred or you can get out of here, bumbaclat."

"I only have fifty, and I had to struggle to get that."

The stall holder shook his filthy head. "I can't do it. Best I can go to is two seventy five. Take it or leave it."

Chase felt it, the desperation and hopelessness. This was his one remaining plan, his one chance to maybe make something happen for his family. Now, it too was on the verge of being snatched away. "Look, please, you have to help me."

"I don't need to do nothin', mon. Come back when you have some green and we can talk."

"This is all I have. Don't you get it? It's all I can get. My daughter is sick, she–"

"Not my problem. Everyone is sick. If it's not the cancer, it's the cold. What makes you special? We're all scratchin' and fightin' to survive in this worl', mon. All of us."

Chase knew he was right. Nobody owed him or his family anything. A simple look around the city told him that they were just a small part of a machine that kept running no matter what happened to the Riley family. He supposed it might even have been for the best. He slinked away, losing himself in the crush of people in the markets. There was certain comfort to it. The noise, the smells, the desperation. He always thought he was above all that, but it was becoming obvious that he belonged with the scum in the streets. Even though he hadn't been able to go through with buying the gun, the intent had been there and that made him no better than those he had looked down his nose at for such a long time. He wasn't sure how long he walked. It started to drizzle, which then became sleet. Still, it didn't deter the crowds who continued to hustle and scheme and beg and borrow. He spotted a silver-panelled van, a mobile coffee shop with a line of stools under a tatty red awning at the side of the vehicle. Inside, the van owner flipped burgers and fried onions on the hot plate. Chase took a seat on one of the vacant stools and ordered a coffee from the money he had scraped together to buy the gun. It was watered down and served in a polystyrene cup, but it warmed his hands and tasted vaguely flavoursome. He sat, lost in his thoughts as he cradled his cup. Two stools down, two other customers were engaged in conversation. Without any intent or realising he was going to do it, Chase tuned into the conversation. One of the men, heavyset and in his forties with a little puff of hair on top of his otherwise shiny head, was called Earl. He had dark skin and a yellowish tint to his eyes. He nodded and listened as his friend, Roger, as slim as Earl was obese and a good fifteen years Earl's senior, tried to drive home his point.

"You know it makes sense, Earl. Things were never this bad before that son-of-a-bitch Lomar privatised everything. They all but own this damn city."

"Come on, Roger, you know better than to listen to those stories. I see that Lomar guy in the news. He does a lot of good stuff."

Earls shook his head. "That's all bullshit. Public relations, man. He stands there and smiles and lets them take his picture but he doesn't care about you or me."

"They don't owe us anything. It's easy to blame them for the mess."

"That's because it's their fault. They bought everything. The police. The hospitals. Who the hell do you think funded Mayor Wilson's campaign?"

"That doesn't mean a thing," Earl said, shaking his head.

"Bullshit it don't. You seen the pictures of them, smiling and playing golf in some fancy-ass club when people like you and me are scratchin' a living on the street."

"We're the forgotten generation," Earl muttered as he sipped his coffee. Chase thought it was a quite eloquent statement as he took a sip of his own drink.

"Forgotten nothing, man," Roger hissed. "Ignored maybe, but that son of a bitch knows we're here. Make no mistake about it."

"What about TV? They gave us free TV. All of us."

Chase glanced at the countless televisions high up on the walls of buildings. It was true, they were everywhere. He sipped his coffee, curious to see how the conversation would unfold.

Roger, it seemed, was not about to be swayed. "Don't get me started on that. Lomar Network. Oh yeah, you can have free TV as long as you watch what they choose to show. No, thank you. That's why I read books. I don't want to see what those assholes tell me I should be thinking."

"You're paranoid."

"And you're deluded."

The two men fell silent, and for a while, the only sound was the sizzle of cheap meat and onions. Roger drank from his cup, and then half turned towards his friend. "What about the island. Are you telling me that's normal?"

"Don't get me started on that, Roger. That's old school. A lot of these younger kids they don't know nothing' about it."

"Maybe that's for the best. Talk about dangling the carrot. What a cruel idea that was. And who thought it up? Lomar. That assholes name is on everything."

Earl sighed and took a battered pack of cigarettes from his jacket. He lit one and offered the pack to Roger, who took one. The two men lit up, then, after exhaling, Earl went on. "You know, the Lomar name used to mean something. Jackson Lomar was a good man. He had plans to help this city."

"I ain't talkin' about Jackson Lomar, I'm talkin' about Damien. Since he took over the business it's all gone to shit. Buy this, build there. Expand here, bulldoze there. That son of a bitch has killed this city."

"You don't know that. That's just guessin'." Roger didn't seem so convinced in his own words, and Chase could see why. Earl was making a great point.

"I ain't guessin' shit. My cousin used to work for Jackson back in the day. He had plans to fix this city up before he passed. As soon as that son of his took over, that idea went out of the window and he built his damn manmade island. What a waste of money it was too."

"Stupid idea anyway. Nobody who took part in that stupid game of his ever stood a chance of winning a damn thing."

"You think Lomar didn't know that? Why else would he give the prize of anything the winner wanted if they ever expected anyone to be able to win? Use your brain, goddamit."

Chase was now beyond curious. He knew about the Island of course, everyone knew of it. This was the first he had heard of any kind of game, never mind an outlandish prize. Before he could stop himself, he had turned to face Earl and Roger. "Excuse me, I couldn't help overhearing... What is this game you were talking about?"

Roger and Earl shared a look, one which Chase read as easily as they did with each other. It said: Be careful.

"How old are you, son?" Earl asked.

"Twenty eight."

"You know about The Island?"

"I know it's there. But nobody I know seems to know what it's there for."

Roger smiled and drank his coffee, letting Earl tell the rest of the story.

"Right now it ain't used for shit. Back when it was first built, it was supposed to be some kind of wildlife sanctuary or some shit like that. It never happened though, because Lomar changed his mind. He had walls built all around the perimeter of The Island and wouldn't tell anyone why." He paused for a sip of his drink. Chase realised his was going cold too and he drained his cup.

"So he builds these walls, and puts the place entirely off limits, as if anyone is gonna go out there to the middle of the ocean to his little patch of land. For ten years, nothing is mentioned about it again, and then out of the blue, Lomar runs a series of newspaper ads asking for volunteers to take part in a brand new game he had designed with the intention of airing it on his network."

"What was the game?" Chase asked.

"It was vague at first. Nobody knew much about it. Ten people volunteered and signed their waivers and all the rest of it, and then Lomar releases the information for the game. It was simple. Survive The Island. Cross from one side to the other and get out through the doors on the south wall. If you do that and win, you get anything you want. Money, fame. Prestige."

Chase couldn't quite believe what he was hearing. It was as if someone had gift wrapped the answers to all of their problems in the form of two grumpy and argumentative old men.

"Anything?" he asked, almost choking on the words.

"In theory," Roger cut in. "only problem was, nobody ever did it. Everyone who went in didn't come out."

"What do you mean?"

Roger ran a thumb across his throat. "What do you think?"

"How? I mean, what's in there?"

"Nobody knows," Earl said. "The whole area is a no-fly zone. Strictly off limits. Nobody knows what happens behind those walls."

"I don't understand. How does it work? I mean, how would a person apply?" Chase knew how desperate he sounded, but couldn't help himself. It seemed Earl and Roger could hear it too, the former turning on his stool and looking Chase in the eye. "Before you get any bright ideas, the game ain't running no more. Three seasons it ran for before complaints and lawsuits from the family of the contestants forced him to shut it down. Even Lomar, as powerful as he is, couldn't fight them off. For the last ten years, The Island has just sat there, whatever was behind its walls still a secret. Good riddance I say."

"Take it from me, son," Earl said. "You're better off not having it there to tempt you. God only knows, there are enough desperate people in the world that would jump at the chance to have a crack at that prize. If you ask me, it was no more than suicide to go in there."

He set his cup down, then shuffled off his stool. "Anyway, we better be on our way. You take care, son. And do yourself a favour. Forget all about that place. Shutting it down was the one good thing Damien Lomar has ever done."

With that, Earl and Roger disappeared, soon becoming lost in the crowd. Despite their warnings to forget it, the island throbbed in Chase's mind like a rotten tooth. The idea of what it could represent to him and his family would have been tempting had it been an active game. He wondered if perhaps the two old men were right, and playing Russian roulette with his own life was hardly the best way to help his family. Even so, as he started back through the crowd on the long walk back home, the words of the old men reverberated around his head and refused to go away.

REBOOT

NECKER ISLAND, BRITISH VIRGIN ISLES
DECEMBER 2nd 2043

Crystal clear waters lapped at the golden sand beach of the seventy-four-acre Necker Island located in the British Virgin Isles. Once purchased by Richard Branson for less than two hundred thousand pounds, it had later been sold to Lomar for almost nine million US dollars just a year after the merger between Branson's Virgin brand and Bill Gate's Microsoft. The new company, VIRSOFT was, for a long time the world's biggest brand until the Lomar corporation had in turn bought out VIRSOFT for a deal worth a staggering fifty billion dollars. For a short time, the three of them, Branson, Gates and Lomar were known as the biggest, most wealthy names in the world. Now, only Lomar remained following Branson's death when one of his low-earth-orbit commercial shuttles he was riding in exploded on re-entry into the atmosphere. Gates went via heart attack in 2022, leaving just Lomar behind.

Now aged fifty seven, Damien Lomar had aged well. He had retained much of his athletic build and although starting to go a little soft around the stomach (perfectly acceptable at such an age) he still had all of his own hair and teeth, the former dyed black, the latter bleached white twice a month. He couldn't complain, unlike some of the people he knew, rather than kick his ass, father time had eased him gently into the second phase of his life. He got out of bed, leaving the Brazilian model whose name he couldn't remember sleeping on her side, brown curls draped across the pillow. He pulled on his robe (finest silk), slipped into his loafers (Italian) crossed the room (custom marble with gold inlay) opened the balcony doors (hand carved) and breathed in the clean air and took in the spectacular view of the ocean. He squinted, pleased to see that the sky was completely cloudless. He reminded himself that those were the kind of views that made the price tag for The Island worthwhile.

To call the building a house would be a gross understatement. The decadent mansion in which Damien Lomar lived boasted fourteen bedrooms, an indoor and outdoor pool, a private dock and helicopter landing pad on the roof. It had been built from scratch and oozed modern luxury. Clean lines, shimmering chrome and crèmes and whites. The beauty of his surroundings aside, Lomar was agitated. He had dreamed of something spectacular, the vision so vivid that it had woken him with a mixture of agitation and excitement. He walked back through the huge bedroom, out of the double doors and made his way down the grand staircase to one of the open-plan reception rooms, this one housing a full-sized snooker table, the cloth blue and emblazoned with the Lomar corporation logo. He found what he was looking for. His jeans, which he had hastily stepped out of the previous evening when things with the model got a little heavy. He fished in the pocket and took out his phone, then perched on the edge of the snooker table and punched in the number for Maurice Gilbert, the chairman of the telecommunications arm of the Lomar Corporation. He waited for the line to connect, absently rolling one of the snooker balls around the table and catching it as it came back towards him. On the fifth ring, a tired and grumpy sounding Maurice answered.

"Maurice, it's Damien. Listen, I know it's early, but I have an idea that just can't wait."

"Of course, Mr. Lomar. What can I do for you?"

Lomar loved the way people feared him. He knew that if anyone else had called Maurice at home on his private line when it was five thirty in the morning would have received a hell of an ear bashing instead of the snivelling passiveness which he could hear on the other end of the line. "I was thinking about The Island."

Silence. The most obvious way to show caution. Lomar went on. "I was thinking more specifically about the game and how it wasn't the success it should have been."

The word he had wanted to use was failure, but Lomar would never saddle himself with such an admission of underachievement. Even so, Maurice still responded with silence. Lomar could imagine the fat fuck's shifty eyes dancing all over as he tried to think of something to say. "Are you there, Maurice? You haven't gone back to sleep have you?"

"No sir, I mean, yes sir, I'm here. I haven't fallen asleep."

"Good. Then you heard what I said? About The Island?"

"Yes sir, I did."

"What if we brought it back?"

This time, Maurice knew silence wouldn't cut it, and so settled for half formulating a word as he tried to figure out a way to respond to his employer.

"You can speak freely, Maurice, I'd like your honest opinion."

"Well sir, I don't think it's a good idea. With everything that happened last time, I think it would be better to leave it alone."

"We can do it better this time," Lomar said, rolling the ball across the table and sinking it in the corner pocket. "Things have changed."

"It's your company, sir, you can, of course, do whatever you like. It has nothing to do with me."

"Ahh but it does, Maurice because this time I want to televise it."

This time, Lomar let the silence hang, determined to give his spineless employee a chance to answer. To his credit, the radio silence lasted seven or eight seconds before Maurice spoke again, his voice high and shrill. Lomar thought to himself that if he had been half asleep before, Maurice was definitely wide awake now.

"Mr. Lomar, if we set aside the logistics for a second, which alone would make shooting on The Island difficult if not impossible, there is also the moral angle to consider. I'm not sure the company needs that kind of publicity again."

"Times have changed. The public has become far more desensitised to such things. The intrigue of what lurks behind The Island walls still holds strong. Imagine it. A group of contestants rigged with cameras, their every move tracked as they try to win the ultimate prize, knowing that failure will mean death. The public will be right there with them as they discover what lives out there."

Lomar stood and started to pace, making slow laps around the snooker table. "Reality television isn't what it used to be. People don't want to see people playing for money, or living in a house with strangers for three months at a time. They want danger. They want excitement. What if we could give it to them? What if we, the Lomar Corporation could guarantee a show that everyone would watch? The sponsorship alone would be worth billions."

"And what about the backlash from the families, sir? Of the ones who don't survive."

Maurice paused as the Brazilian model whose name still escaped him sauntered downstairs and disappeared into the kitchen, giving him a glimpse of her smooth thonged behind as she went. "The families won't complain. The world is a desperate place filled with desperate people who are looking for an opportunity to get out of the gutter. You think the families will have anything to say if we have the contestants on camera talking about why they are doing it or how much it means to their families? It would capture the imagination."

"I'm not so sure," Maurice said, which Lomar knew actually meant, I'm close to getting on board, sway me a little more.

"Think about this, Maurice. With ratings through the roof and billions of dollars in sponsorship in the bank, a media executive that was wily enough to take such a risk might be rewarded with a promotion. Say on to the board of directors of the entire company rather than just the media arm."

Lomar, of course, had the power and authority to demand the show be put into production no matter what Maurice thought; however, he also knew that having staff who worked with him rather than against him made all the difference, and even if it meant dangling the carrot of a promotion that probably wouldn't ever happen, so be it. "Well? Do I have you on board?" Lomar said, rolling another snooker ball across the table where it ricocheted off some of its companions.

"What about costs? I mean rigging the contestants up for TV will be easy enough, but The Island is huge. Not to mention the danger involved with the…things that are in there."

"Don't worry about that. I'm giving unlimited budget to this. I want it to be spectacular. I'll make sure we have camera coverage of the whole island, don't you worry."

Lomar expected Maurice to be excited, or, at least, a little enthusiastic. Instead, that annoying silence greeted Lomar from the other end of the phone. "What is it now, Maurice?"

"Sorry, sir, this is all a little bit much to take in. I was just thinking about the contestants. What if nobody applies for the show?"

"They will. You mark my words. People are desperate."

"Desperate I understand, especially with the poverty and unemployment so high. But desperate enough to risk their lives? That I'm not so sure about sir."

"Let me tell you something about people, Maurice," Lomar said, enjoying the irony that he was about to advise his employee about the same techniques just used against him. "You give them something they want or an opportunity to get something they want, and you would be shocked at how far they will go. Trust me, if they get desperate enough, and they want the chance to change their lives bad enough, they will do it no matter what the potential risks might be. Now what I need from you is to make it happen. Can you do it?"

"It's going to take time. Planning. When were you thinking of going to air with this?"

"Spring."

"Next spring?"

"This spring. Early summer at the latest."

"I'm not sure that's possible, Mr. Lomar."

"Make it possible. At all costs."

Lomar hung up the phone then basked in the quiet. He could hear the Brazilian model in the kitchen moving things around in the fridge. He wasn't sure if she was expecting to stay, but she was about to be disappointed if she did. He had used her for what he wanted, and now had more pressing matters at hand. The more he thought about it, The Island was an all-consuming idea, the perfect way to get the one blemish from his business history, to rectify the one thing he had got wrong and banish the ghost of his father's voice as it chastised him for it on a daily basis. He couldn't wait to get started.

PREPARATION
THE ISLAND, ATLANTIC OCEAN
JANUARY 19th 2044

The armoured truck cut through the undergrowth, the wet leaves of overhanging plants and trees leaving streaks on the bodywork as the cumbersome vehicle navigated the terrain. In the back, with only the light from the narrow post box windows high on the vehicle sides to illuminate them, sat the eight heavily armed mercenaries, five on one side of the truck and three on the other, each of them cradling their M16 machine guns as they prepared to disembark. They were guns for hire, paid to fight for whoever was the highest bidder. All, that was, but one of them.

Nicholas Ingleby was sweating as he sat on the bench in the corner furthest from the door, cradling the brown bag he had brought with him. Unlike the mercenaries, he was neither a fighter nor particularly brave and had no problem admitting that he was deathly afraid even after two weeks of following this same routine. He wiped sweat from his eyes, staining the blue boiler suit he wore a few shades darker. The truck came to a halt, wheels struggling for purchase as it skewed into a half turn. The second its forward motion had ceased, the rear doors opened, letting the light flood in as the mercenaries exited, fanning around in a protective half circle around the rear of the truck, weapons drawn and pointed away from the vehicle, all of them tense and ready.

Nicholas climbed out of the truck, the brown bag in tow. His eyes rattled around his skull as he stared into the dense undergrowth around him. He was still unsure if the tension within the soldiers was a good or bad thing, and then remembered why they are all there. Dropping the bag into the long grass next to the muddy gouges left by the trucks tyres, he returned to the rear of the truck. He dragged out a ladder, every scrape of metal on metal making him wince and grit his teeth as he slid it out into the open. He set it down beside the bag, then unfolded a map from his jumpsuit and studied it. He glanced around, then picked up the ladder and propped it against a tree, folding the map back into his pocket.

"Hurry up, fella," one of the mercs said, whispering over his shoulder. Nicholas complied. He hurried to the bag and reached in, taking out the small HD camera. He clipped it onto his belt and began to climb the ladder towards the upper branches of the tree, unable to resist the occasional glance over his shoulder as he told himself that every sound he heard was just birds or some other form of non-threatening wildlife, even if he had already seen something that told him he was probably way wrong. He reached the top of the tree and unclipped the camera from his belt. Equipped with infrared, night vision, and 10K hyper digital resolution, the all-weather, shockproof camera was attached to a thick strap reminiscent of a belt. Nicholas hooked the belt around the trunk of the tree, threading the loop back through the other side and attaching the camera to the trunk. He powered it up, adjusting the angle so that it pointed down towards the floor. Satisfied, he took the map out of his pocket and the stubby pencil from his breast pocket, when a roar, deep and powerful cut through the air, causing Nicholas to almost fall from the ladder. Below, the mercenaries moved a little closer together as Nicholas clung onto the tree and watched, staring out over the treetops to try and see what made the sound and knowing that it could have come from anywhere.

"Are you done up there?" one of the mercs half-whispered.

Nicholas nodded and then marked a cross on his map through one of the numerous red dots that covered it.

"Come on then, let's move," the merc said.

Nicholas didn't need to be told twice. He scampered down the ladder as quickly as he could, trying not to think too hard about the roar and what might have caused it. He folded the ladder down and slid it into the truck, then grabbed the bag, peering inside as the Mercenaries fell in around him.

One of them clapped him on the shoulder. "Just fifteen more like that and you can go home, fella."

Nicholas felt sick as he dragged the brown bag back into the van and took his seat. The mercenaries followed suit and closed the door. As the truck set off, they sat in silence, all wondering the same thing about the creature that had roared and if they were moving closer to it or further away. Either way, all of them wondered if the money they had been paid was worth the danger they were in. The vehicle lurched into gear and they moved onto their next destination where they would repeat the entire process again in the hope that they would remain undiscovered and get out alive.

THE SEED GROWS
NEW YORK CITY
FEBRUARY 20th 2044

Chase had woken up early and glanced out at the cold, bitter darkness as he pulled on his boots. His wife and daughter were still sleeping, for which he was grateful. The cough, the ever persistent cough, came and he was forced to press his mouth into the sleeve of his jacket until it had subsided so he didn't wake them. When he moved his face, there was a bloody smear on the sleeve where his lips had been. He stared at it for a few seconds, heart thundering and trying to convince himself it was something other than the same cancer that had already devastated his family so badly.

His tired brain started to drag him down the path which he was desperate to avoid, and it took a huge effort to keep focussed on the job at hand. He peered out of the window. Dirty snow was piled on the edges of sidewalks, and a light drizzle fell onto the streets, which looked almost beautiful under the dim glow of streetlights. He took the tattered flyer for the job fair out of his pocket and looked at it, knowing it was legitimately the last chance. He had exhausted every other option, chased down every lead that was there and tried to force some that weren't in the hunt for work, and all the while his daughter grew sicker as the cancer took a stronger hold on her fragile body. He turned away from the window, forcing himself not to think about such things. He needed to focus on getting a job, any job. A glance at his watch told him it was almost four thirty in the morning. Time to set off if he wanted to get close to the front of the line for when the fair opened at nine. He was sure that there would be others like him who were desperate for work no matter what it entailed, but he didn't care about them. To him, they were rivals, obstacles put in front of him with the sole purpose of stopping him providing for his family. He wouldn't allow it even if it meant taking a position that pride would have previously stopped him from accepting. He crossed the room, then as quietly as he could, set out on what he was sure would be the most important day of his life.

TWO

There was already a good-sized crowd at the fair when he and his friend, Shawn, arrived. Like Chase, Shawn was down on his luck and out of work. The difference was that Shawn had no children or family. Most of all Shawn didn't have cancer. The temptation to resent his friend was strong in Chase, but he couldn't bring himself to blame someone for not contracting a lethal disease. Either way, Shawn, like the other fifty or so that had already arrived early, was a rival. Shawn was slim, some might say skinny. His cheekbones were prominent and his eyes a pale grey. He had a fluff of patchy orange beard on his cheeks which, tie notwithstanding, made him look a little bit on the scruffy side. Chase scratched at his own clean, smooth cheeks and was glad his friend had either forgotten or not bothered to shave.

"Damn cold today," Shawn said, rubbing his hands together.

"What did you expect? It's February."

"No shit," Shawn replied, his breath fogging in the chill air. "Even so, I'll be glad when daylight comes."

Chase nodded and looked around. Since they had arrived, more people had shown up, arriving in groups of twos and threes.

"So uh, how you have been getting on, you and the family, I mean?" Shawn asked, unable to make eye contact with his friend because he knew what the answer would be.

"We're doing okay. You have to."

On the lie scale, it was a whopper, but some bizarre macho pride wouldn't allow him to admit to either weakness or failure in front of someone he considered, however bizarrely, his competition.

"You sure? If there's anything I can do..."

Chase shook his head. They all said that. Asking if there was something they could do, or wishing they could help when they knew the inevitable truth that short of a miracle, there was no help.

"No, we're fine. Elsie is strong."

"I, uh, was wondering about you. I noticed that cough. Plus you lost weight." Shawn stared at his shoes, then looked around at the growing crowd as the first hint of the coming day started to bleed into the horizon line.

"I'm not worried about me. Just my family, and don't you go telling those employers in there I'm not well," Chase snapped.

"Relax, I wouldn't do that man, I'm just worried that's all."

"I know, I appreciate it. I'm sorry, Shawn. I didn't mean to lose my cool. I'm just... It's hard, you know?"

"I get it, I really do. Times are hard enough as is without a sick family to think about. Have you had that cough of yours checked out?"

Chase shook his head. "Can't afford the doctor. Not with Elsie's medical bills to pay. Besides, I'm pretty sure I know what it is."

Shawn turned his face up to the sky and the hazy smog which hung in the fine drizzle which rather than fall, just seemed to hang. "It's this damn pollution. Making people sick, giving them the cancer. It's wrong. You should take the city to court."

"As if I could afford it," Chase grumbled. Despite his misgivings, it felt good to have it off his chest and share his secret with someone else. "Besides, nobody would listen to people like us. The city has already washed its hands of us. We're on our own."

"Yeah, well maybe we'll find something in here. A little positivity goes a long way."

"Yeah, maybe," Chase muttered, declining to tell his friend that his positivity went the way of his pride around the same time he tried to buy the handgun.

They waited and made small talk as the light bled into the day and the crowds continued to gather around the entrance. By the time eight thirty rolled around, they were all tired and cranky. Chase's cough had become progressively worse as the morning rolled on, earning him a few disapproving glances of the others who were waiting to get into the fair. He noticed as the crowds continued to gather, that his chances of finding work were dwindling with every new arrival. The unpaid medical bills, rent and bare food cupboards lingered in the back of his mind and increased his determination to succeed. He was about to turn to Shawn and tell him how he wished they had brought coffee when the big screen on the wall of the hall where the job's fair was being held sprang into activity, the bass notes deep and powerful as a slick introduction for the Lomar Corporation began to play. Chase looked around. All the others screens on the buildings he could see were playing the same thing. It seemed that whatever was about to be shown was something Damien Lomar wanted everyone to see. Chase turned his attention back to the screen as the logo faded and the man himself appeared on screen. Tanned, good looking for his age. Expensive tailored suit cut perfectly, gold signet ring glittering on his little finger.

"Good morning, citizens," his amplified voice said as the chatter died down and everyone tuned in to hear what he had to say. "The world has become a challenging place. We struggle against unemployment. Pollution is the highest it has ever been. Global warming has reached unstoppable levels. We struggle, and yet, the human spirit fights on."

Chase glanced around at the other people who were watching, wondering if anyone else was seeing the irony of a multi billionaire saying 'we' when referring to problems he would never have to face or deal with. He turned his attention back to the screen as Lomar went on.

"Here at the Lomar Corporation, we have been searching for a way to help. To give the people back some hope. To give them a way to flee from the trappings of daily life. We also want to instil inspiration and show that the bravery of the few can spur on the many to achieve great things. To this end, I present to you the return of The Island."

The screen melted into a drone shot of The Island, the two-hundred-foot concrete wall looming ahead. People in the crowd began to chatter through either nerves or excitement as Lomar's smooth voiceover accompanied the images on screen. "Who amongst you is willing to take the challenge? Who out there is willing to tread behind the walls of The Island and discover the secrets within? Who amongst you is prepared to risk your own mortality for the security of your friends and family?"

The image of The Island melted back to Lomar, who flashed his veneered smile into the camera. "I know what you're asking. What could possibly make it worthwhile? Why would anyone want to take part? What's in it for you?" He jabbed a finger at the screen as he said it.

"Go fuck yourself, Lomar," someone muttered from the crowd, which got a few chuckles. Chase didn't laugh. He was giving the screen his full attention and watched as the advertisement continued to play.

"A prize for something such as this is too weak a word. As most of you will know, The Island is a dangerous place. Nobody knows what lies behind its walls. That will all change. For the first time ever, the entire challenge will be televised live on the Lomar Network. You will see first hand why The Island is known as the most hostile, dangerous environment on earth, and why all who have tried to tame it have failed and paid for it with their lives."

"Tell us about the prize, numb nuts," another voice muttered. This time, there was no laughter. Everyone was staring at the screen.

"For those brave enough to take the challenge, for those lucky enough to be accepted, the prize is literally anything you want. Be it money or possessions, we at the Lomar Corporation are willing to provide it. The question is, are you prepared to take the risk in order to make a change? Applications are now being taken and spaces are limited. Visit the Lomar website or click through via your home touchscreens now for more information."

The screen faded and began to play another advertisement for some kind of soft drink. The crowds at the job fair had forgotten the cold and were chatting about the new announcement.

"Fools game," Shawn said, glaring at the screen. "I wouldn't go near that if you paid me."

You might if you had a sick family and no means to look after them. Chase didn't say it; instead, he shifted his weight and put his hands in his pockets.

"Don't tell me you're considering it?" Shawn said.

"No, of course not. It's insane. It's just…a tempting idea that's all."

"Tempting or not, you won't help your family by getting yourself killed for no reason. How will they cope then?"

"I know. I already told you, I'm not interested."

Shawn nodded, buying the lie. "Alright, I'm glad we're on the same page. Fucking Lomar. Did you see the look on his face? Arrogant piece of shit."

Chase nodded, only half-listening. His mind was swimming, racing with thousands of thoughts which all seemed to be gravitating towards the same idea which turned in his brain like a tornado. Shawn wouldn't understand. He didn't know how desperate things had become. At the same time, he wasn't convinced his wife would understand either, and unlike his friend, she would see right through any attempt to bullshit his way out of it if she knew the idea was in his head. He forced himself to stop thinking about it and refocused his energy on the job fair. With luck, he could get something. He had to get something. Although he had said it before, this really was his last chance. Or, at least his last sane chance. Wishing he had never seen the advertisement for The Island, Chase turned back towards the hall and waited for the fair to open.

THE EIGHT
NEW YORK CITY
FEBRUARY 28th 2044

Chase walked through the city streets, the anger finally simmering down from the initial overwhelming boil. It was rare for him and Ashley to argue at all, even less for them to have such a monumental explosion like the one that had occurred earlier that morning. He expected it to be bad when he had shown her the application form for The Island and he had seen a side to her he had never seen before. She had screamed at him, telling him he didn't care about them if he went through with it. How he wasn't cut out to do something so brutal and barbaric, how he would die and leave the two of them behind. He wanted to argue that she was wrong, but the words she had said were ones he had stewed on himself since he had made the decision to apply. Ashley had argued with him that he should wait, and he might yet hear from one of the jobs he had applied for at the fair. He told her that wasn't an option, that the number of applicants for The Island would likely be in the thousands and he had to ensure he was one of them. What he didn't tell her was that his experience at the fair had only hit home how difficult it was going to be. He had walked from booth to booth, sure they could smell the desperation as he tried to sell himself to whatever job was being advertised, and glad that the little thing called pride was no longer a factor. For the most part, the employers looked through him, eyes glazed as they listened to him reel off his skills and abilities, close to almost begging for a job. The issue was, he wasn't alone, and the employers knew they would be able to cherry pick those most suitable to work for them. Only The Island had seemed like a viable option. Somehow, deep down, he knew he could win it. He had an overwhelming belief that he loved his family so much that he would do anything to protect them.

Ashley didn't seem to care. She was screaming and crying, cheeks flushed and her eyes raw. She told him she had looked into what happened before the last time they had tried to get the show off the ground, how nobody to date had survived long enough to get to the end and tell the story about what was in there. He knew all this of course. He had researched it, becoming obsessed with finding out everything he could about the mysterious island. He had asked her why she had so little faith in him, to which she replied it wasn't a question of faith, but of stopping him from killing himself on live television. That one had hit home, and for a second, he almost considered forgetting the entire idea until he thought of the alternative, which was sitting and waiting until his daughter died.

Desperate, she had even turned on him, mentioning his own failing health. She asked how he expected to traverse The Island when the cancer was well on its way to ravaging his lungs. Again, he had no answer. Just that overwhelming self-belief that sat like a comforting ball of warmth in the pit of his stomach. He had grabbed her then by the arms, looking her in the eye and telling her he had to do it. There was no other choice. It was the first time he had admitted it, and it seemed to at least hit home. The way she had looked at him like he was already lost to her was one of the most painful things he had ever experienced. He knew she was just afraid and rightly so, and the things she was saying to him were born from frustration. He didn't hold it against her and hoped she knew. The change in her had been instant. It was as if she had been deflated. She had crumbled into his arms, head on his shoulder, whispering to him and begging him not to go through with it. He had let her for a while, feeling like absolute scum for keeping a certain coldness between them if only to make leaving her there easier. He had pulled away from her, holding her at arms distance. There was so much he wanted to say, so many things he wanted to do to reassure her, but no words would come. Instead, he had picked up the application form from the table and left without saying another word to her.

TWO

He had walked towards the Lomar Corporation building, the imposing tower seeming to pull him towards it by means of some kind of invisible rope. He felt somehow detached from his own body. Now that he was alone, he didn't feel the need to hide the bitter taste of fear in the back of his throat. He felt no shame in it, and although he had hope otherwise it didn't fill him with the kind of hardnosed determination he had expected to feel. He anticipated crowds, people in their hundreds, maybe even their thousands, clamouring to hand in their application forms and take a chance on making a change for the better.

Instead, to his surprise, there were no crowds as he made his way closer to the building. No groups of excited people trying to beg their way into the contest. The building, if anything looked deserted. He frowned as he walked towards the entrance, glass doors sliding open to accommodate him. Even the reception was quiet, and he walked across the marble floor to the counter, glancing at the steel LOMAR logo on the wall behind the harsh faced receptionist.

"I, uh, I'm here about The Island," he muttered. Still feeling detached, still able to feel that bitter taste in his mouth.

The receptionist, who had perfected the art of the snooty, down the glasses stare, glanced at him, then his application form. "Forty fourth floor. The elevator is at the end of the hall. Go right up." With that, she turned her attention back to the well-thumbed romance paperback he had pulled her from and continued to go on as if he didn't exist.

He looked around the cavernous reception, which, other than a janitor mopping the floor down the hall, was deserted. He walked towards the elevators, application form rolled up in one hand as the little voice in his head screamed at him to forget it and go home to his wife and family. He pushed the button by the steel doors, hoping he would get at least a few minutes to consider his options, but the doors opened immediately. He stepped inside, punching the number of the floor he wanted on the touchpad inlayed in the door, and waited as the reception was lost from view, and the journey to whatever awaited him on floor forty four began.

THREE

It took less than a minute for the doors to chime and open. A plush red carpet greeted him, immediately in front of which was another reception, this time manned by a slim man with a beak like nose. Unlike his sour-faced companion downstairs, he greeted Chase with a broad smile.

"Welcome to the Lomar Corporation. Are you here for The Island?"

He nodded. That bitter fear taste was growing stronger.

"Can I see your application form please?"

Chase looked at the form still clutched in his right hand. The persistent voice in his head reminded him that this was his last chance to change his mind and go home. Stubborn as ever, Chase ignored it and handed the paper over, feeling a sense of smug satisfaction that he had gone through with it. The receptionist looked over the form, keying in some details on his computer screen. He held out a small rectangular pad to Chase.

"Please place your palm on the scanner."

"What for?" Chase asked, giving the square pad a mistrustful glance.

"Standard health check," the receptionist fired back, flashing a polite smile. "Policy for all applicants."

This was something he hadn't anticipated. He had planned on there being no health checks of any kind, especially due to the nature of the programme. His health was bad, he knew he had cancer and suspected it wouldn't be long before it finished him off. He stared at the pad, then at the receptionist.

"Problem?" the receptionist asked.

"No, no problem, I just didn't expect this that's all."

"Nothing to worry about, sir, just standard procedure. Please place your palm on the scanner and hold it there."

Chase did as he was told, hoping he might be able to talk his way into the show when his symptoms flagged. The pad beeped as he placed his palm on it, and a digital bar started to fill as it scanned him. As the progress bar crept towards the one hundred percent mark, the receptionist started to ask him some questions, marking the answers on a yellow form.

"Full name?"

"Chase Riley."

"Age?"

"Twenty eight."

"Marital status?"

"Married." The receptionist marked his answers on the sheet at the progress bar on the scanner moved past sixty percent.

"Any long term illnesses? Diabetes? Epilepsy?"

Chase shook his head. "No." Just cancer, which you're about to find out I'm riddled with, he almost added, then decided to stay quiet and keep praying for his miracle.

The receptionist made another mark on the form just as the scanner pulsed as the bar reached one hundred percent.

"Thank you; you can remove your hand now."

Chase did so, heart thundering as he waited for the bad news to be delivered and him to be sent home.

"Did you receive and agree to the waiver form freeing The Lomar Corporation and its employees from any responsibility, legal or moral for anything that may or may not happen during the course of the show should you be accepted as a participant?"

"Yeah."

"Do you also agree that if selected, you will be taking part in the television show of your own free will and agree that The Lomar Corporation can use your name and likeness in any way they see fit including but not limited to any and all merchandising?"

"Yeah, it's all there on the form," Chase said, feeling like the whole thing was a waste of time now that they were due to find out about his cancer. As if in direct response, the receptionist frowned at something that popped up on his computer screen. He manipulated the keyboard, fingers dancing with lightning speed, then turned to Chase and smiled.

"Okay, please go on through the door to your right. You will be greeted inside."

Surprised, Chase choked on his words. "Yeah. Uh, thanks."

He did as he was told, struggling to grasp the reality of it all. He assumed he would be there just to drop off his form, not have medical exams and actually starting to go through the process. Suddenly, the advertisement for The Island which had been airing every hour every day seemed like a very real thing. He approached the door the receptionist had drawn his attention to, frosted glass with the Lomar logo cut out of it across the centre. It opened as he approached. Inside were bright, harsh white lights and cold steel appliances. Waiting there was a doctor, short and balding, eyes kind behind his thick-framed glasses.

"Mr. Riley, please come in," the doctor said, motioning to a chair beside a recliner bed. Chase remained standing. "I'm fine, I'll stand. What is this about?"

"I'm under the impression that you applied to take part in the show?"

"I did, but… I thought it was just dropping in my application form."

"Please, don't be alarmed. This is all a part of the application process. Please, take a seat."

Chase sat, curious as well as confused. The doctor sat opposite him, and picked up the digital tablet from his desk, scrolling through. "It says here your health scan came up with some irregularities."

Chase said nothing, averting his eyes and letting the doctor go on.

"In addition to slightly elevated blood pressure, we detected mid-to-late stage lung cancer. Terminal."

"Terminal?" Chase repeated, not quite comprehending what the doctor was saying.

"Are you telling me you didn't know?" the doctor asked, watching for a response.

"No, well, yes. I... had a suspicion. But I haven't seen a doctor or anything about it."

"I see. Your family medical records also show that your daughter is suffering the same illness. Life prognosis of fewer than three months without treatment."

"What? I didn't... nobody ever told us that. I mean, we knew she was sick, but..." He trailed off, trying to battle his emotions and keep them in check.

"No, I suspect nobody did. Usually, it's practice to hold such information back. In this instance, I feel it's pertinent to discuss it, if only because you are suffering the same illness. A very unlucky turn of events Mr. Riley, if you don't mind my saying so."

"Yeah, well, that's why I'm here. She needs medical help."

"As do you."

"I don't care about me. I'm fit to take part if that's what you brought me in here for. The cough I can handle. Don't worry about it." He knew how defensive he sounded, but that didn't matter. He suspected that without the say so of this doctor, he would be going straight home.

"Your lung capacity is reduced by thirty nine percent. Not to mention the advance state of some of the tumours. I assume you have been bringing up blood when you cough?"

"Look," Chase said, feeling yet another opportunity slip away from him. "I can do this. Please don't stop me from trying. Just give me the chance."

"I have no intention of stopping you, Mr. Riley. Frankly, it's not my decision."

"So why am I here?"

The doctor leaned back and smiled. "Nothing to worry about, just a standard assessment. All applicants have gone through the same process."

"So what happens now?"

"Now, you go on to the next room." The doctor motioned to another door beyond his office. Chase got up, keeping a wary eye on the doctor and moving towards the door. Like the others, it opened as he approached. Beyond was a corridor, at the end of which was another door. He walked towards it, pleased to be away from the harsh lights of the doctor's office. He wasn't sure what his cancer meant for his chances as far as The Island went, but he was still in the game, and that meant he still had a chance. He paused outside the door and took a deep breath, or at least, as deep a breath as he could manage with his mangled lungs. Composing himself for whatever came next, he pushed open the door and went inside.

FOUR

There were seven other people in the room, which looked to be some kind of waiting area. Moulded plastic seats were arranged around the outer perimeter of the room. A large TV screen on one wall was showing some kind of cookery show on the Lomar Network, an elaborate fish tank underneath it, its colourful occupants having no concept of the shitty world they existed within. Chase took a seat, feeling the eyes of the other people on him as he tried to get comfortable. There were four men and three women. One of the people, a dark-skinned man who looked to be somewhere in his fifties, nodded at Chase as he sat. Chase didn't return the gesture. Two seats down from him was another man. Young and strong. Broad shouldered and slim at the waist. He sat perched on the edge of his chair, tapping each finger in turn against his thumb as the network of nerves and muscles danced in unison in his forearms. He caught Chase staring, the latter quickly averting his gaze and staring at the floor. The third man in the room was pale and blond with a dashing of acne across his cheeks. He had the wide eyed appearance of a deer caught in headlights and was chewing his fingernails as his foot tapped rhythmically on the floor. Opposite him were what appeared to be a man and wife. Both dressed in army fatigues, their eyes were devoid of emotion as they glanced at Chase. He estimated them to be somewhere in their late forties, and as he looked at them holding hands, Chase wondered what would possess a couple to apply for The Island when only one of them would be able to win if they made it through.

The two women in the waiting room were of similar age, Chase guessed very early twenties. One was blonde and had a coldness in her eyes. She seemed completely relaxed, slumped on her chair, the top of a tattoo poking out from the neckline of her t-shirt. The other girl was different again. Black hair, blue eyes, slim build. She looked fragile, and Chase wondered what in her life could be so bad as to make her want to be a volunteer to take on The Island. He supposed they might think the same of him, and wondered what was about to happen next. One thing was for sure, the experience so far was a million miles away from the vision he had of dropping off his form and going back home. Something felt strange, not quite right. Maybe it was the fear; maybe it was just that it was now becoming more and more real as time went on. Maybe it was because these people in the room might well be his competition and if they were, there was every chance he might have to kill them in order to win.

Fifteen minutes passed, and although he expected more people to arrive, nobody else came through the door. Chase wasn't sure if that was a good or a bad sign and decided he didn't want to think about it. Instead, he stared at his feet at waited to see what would happen.

As if on cue, the lights dimmed and the screen cut to a view of a beautiful golden beach and a rolling blue ocean. The word 'LIVE' flicked up in the corner of the screen. As they watched, Damien Lomar walked into the shot. This time there was no suit, no expensive pinkie ring. He was wearing a loose-fitting cotton t-shirt and dark sunglasses. He turned to the camera and smiled.

"Hello from paradise," he said, the voice slightly out of sync with the images on the screen. "I'm sorry I couldn't be there to greet you personally, but as I'm sure you can understand, I'm a busy man. I'm sure the eight of you are wondering why you are here. I'm sure there are nerves and also a little apprehension. The truth is that despite our generous prize offer and extensive advertising campaign, we struggled to find suitable contestants. Some of you are here after a call back. Two of you are here for the first time after handing in your application forms during the last few weeks. One thing you have in common is that you all made the cut." Lomar grinned.

Despite what should be good news, the atmosphere in the waiting room was heavy.

"We were looking for a certain class of contestant. People who had a good story to tell, people who had a good reason to fight for what they believed in and who could win. The handprint scan you undertook on your first visit was designed to look for certain markers as well as search through your personal records, looking for certain key traits that we were looking for." Lomar smiled again, enjoying the sun, letting the news sink in. "In a moment, some of my colleagues will enter the room and further brief you on the next stage of the process. Paperwork will have to be completed, waivers and non-disclosure agreements signed. In three days, if you still wish to participate after signing said forms and getting a full rundown of what will take place, you will return here to this very room. By doing so, you will have passed the point when you can back out. For those who do, we have a reserve list of more than fifty contestants which we will draw from to ensure we have our full quota of bodies on The Island. Returning here will mean you will take part in the show and all that it entails. Use this time to spend time with your loved ones, to remind yourselves why you are taking part. Upon arrival, you will then be transported here, to my island, the place where I make my home. I will personally welcome you and give you a few days of luxury before the arduous task ahead of you."

Lomar paused for effect. Crashing surf, a breeze ruffling the microphone. "The reason for this is twofold. Firstly, it is to give you the last taste of comfort before what will be the most traumatic and difficult task you have ever undertaken. The second reason is to give you a taste of what could be, to give you a glimpse of the life you could have if you should win. The eight of you are the elite, the season one island contestants. I'm sure you will make for great television, and for one of you, live out the life you always wanted. Hopefully, I'll see you all in a few days. Congratulations again from everyone here at the Lomar Corporation."

The screen went dark and the lights came back on. There was a heavy silence in the room as the eight people inside came to terms with what they had just heard. Chase, too, was reeling. His day had started as a simple application drop off and had ended with him getting a pale on the show. As the door opened and Lomar's staff entered with said application forms and waivers, Chase's mind turned to his wife, and how he was going to tell her that not only had he gone through with posting his application, but was now a part of the deadliest show in the world.

LOMAR
THE SEA STAR
ATLANTIC OCEAN
MARCH 5th 2044

Chase stood on the deck of the boat, eyes half closed against the breeze as they cut through the water. It was cold, but he didn't mind. This was the first real ocean he had seen, and certainly the first that was blue instead of the garbage-filled brown of New York where he had lived all his life.

Of the eight of them who had been chosen to take part in the show, two had failed to return. Chase wondered if the couple in army fatigues were the wisest of all for taking the opportunity to back out. For a time, his return to the Lomar building had also been in doubt. He had gone back and told Ashley the news, and although he had expected her to be angry, he didn't anticipate the outright rage. She had screamed at him, eyes full of fear and betrayal. He let her vent, taking it in and soaking it up, his penance for putting her in such an impossible position. Reason was no longer an option. She knew as well as he did that it was really happening. Eventually, she calmed enough to stop screaming, but still she didn't speak to him, nor did she look at him. He knew why. The sooner she prepared for his death the better, and if that meant ignoring him in what could conceivably be the last days of his life, then she was prepared to do it. He thought she would come around, at least show her support eventually, but even with his bags packed and standing by the door on the morning he was due to leave, she still ignored him. Eyes down, not wanting to look, not wanting to acknowledge. He had gone into Elsie's room, but like she was most days, she was sleeping, skeletal and frail, breathing wet and ragged. He didn't want to wake her. Instead, he kissed her on the forehead, committing the image to memory as a reminder of why he was about to put himself through hell. Grabbing his bag by the door, he looked to Ashley, hoping she would, at least, look at him, or tell him she loved him, but she simply stared out of the window, eyes raw, cheeks wet. With nothing more to be said, he had left their apartment, possibly for the last time, and set out for whatever awaited him.

"Cold up here."

Chase blinked, and glanced towards the man. It was the African American man who had nodded at Chase when he had first arrived in the meeting room. His hair was a black and white shortly cropped afro, his beard trimmed into a goatee and sporting the same colour scheme. He had kind eyes, the crow's feet at the corners giving him a warm, fatherly appearance. Although it felt odd making small talk with a man who he might have to murder, Chase saw no harm in at least being polite.

"I don't mind it," he said, turning towards the man. "It feels good."

Chase looked at the man's shirt. Each of them had been given the same standard outfit. Boots and combat pants. Ration kit and sleeping bag. Khaki shirts each with their name stencilled both on the back and across the breast pocket in black. AWEYO the shirt read. To his surprise, the old man thrust out a hand.

"My name is Moses. I'd say I'm pleased to meet you, but under the circumstances, I'm not sure that's appropriate." He grinned.

Chase gave his own name and couldn't help but smile as he shook hands with the older man. "We must all be crazy," he said.

"Perhaps we are. Either us or the people who organise this barbaric game."

Chase nodded. He was about to respond by asking what Moses thought of Lomar when the cough came. There was no warning. Chase leaned onto the side of the boat, coughing and unable to catch his breath. When it subsided, Moses was watching him, Chase unsure if the look was predatory or concerned. "Are you alright?" Moses said, the African twang in his voice showing no hint of insincerity.

"I'm fine, just a cough, that's all."

Moses nodded. He didn't believe the lie but didn't pursue it either. For a moment, neither man spoke, both enjoying the wind in their face and the salt taste that came with it.

"Do you believe you will win?"

Chase was surprised by the directness of the question, and half turned towards Moses. "Do you?"

The older man shrugged. "Surely we all do, otherwise, why would we be here?"

Chase nodded. Moses was right. It was both ridiculous and frightening at the same time.

"What brings you to The Island?" Moses asked, jaundiced eyes watching carefully.

"That's my business. I don't see the relevance. I'm sure you wouldn't like to answer the same question."

"Fair enough. I meant no offence. For the record, I'm happy to discuss my reasons for being here."

"Go on," Chase said, not through any interest in Moses's story, but because he was starting to realise that any information, however small, might give him an advantage later.

Moses leaned on the barrier, Chase noticing how thick and muscular his forearms were. A small alarm started to ring in his head, telling him that there may be more to this man than met the eye.

"I was born in Burma. When I was a child, bandits raided our village. The women were rounded up, raped and murdered. The boys were taken prisoner and forced into servitude of the army. I was just seven when I was enlisted, a frightened orphan boy who had lost his entire family in one night. Over the next few years, I was trained to fight, to use weapons. To kill." He paused as he said it, staring at the white wake of the boat as it rolled away from them. "When I was ten, I killed my first man. Shot him, in the head. I wasn't proud. I cried myself to sleep. Never in front of my superiors. To show weakness was to die. When I realised no help was coming, I simply went on as normal. I returned to my duties, performing the same raids as those who had taken me. I became as cold and emotionless a killer as those who had taken me from my family. Ironic, don't you think?"

"Yeah."

Moses sighed and glanced at Chase. "I took no pleasure in these things. I did them because I knew that if I didn't, then I would be beaten and perhaps killed. After a time, even the atrocities I committed were distant to me. By the time I was twenty, I had killed more than two hundred innocent people. It was then when I realised what a monster I had become, that I decided to flee."

Despite his decision to keep himself distant from his fellow competitor, Chase was curious. "What happened?" he asked.

Moses sighed, linking his hands as he continued to stare at the ocean. "I left on foot with nothing but a few loaves of stolen bread. I walked for three weeks, frightened and alone. I contracted malaria and dysentery, but still I went on. Still I did whatever it took to get away. For three months, I scraped and begged, stole and borrowed to flee that life. Eventually, I made it to America."

"And you decided to do this? That seems like a strange decision."

"I was a young man then. After I spent all that time, scratching and clawing to make a new life in America, after I settled down, worked hard and tried to live quietly, a man came to see me. A man who found out what I used to be and threatened to have me arrested for war crimes if I didn't pay him."

Moses sighed, his eyes glazing over. "I don't have the money. This man says he will make my life hell. Has done for three years now. When times get desperate, a man will go to any lengths to survive."

Chase recalled the day he tried to buy the handgun. He knew all too well how that felt. "Can't you go to anyone? Ask someone for help?"

Moses shook his head. "I cannot. My papers are fraudulent. I can't risk anyone looking into me in too much detail. When I win this show, I will ask that all of my past indiscretions be forgotten, erased, then this man and his blackmail will go away."

"And what if you lose?" Chase didn't know why he even asked the question. The answer was an obvious one. Moses shrugged. "If I lose then it doesn't matter either way."

Cold cut through Chase, and not just because of the blustery conditions. There was certain finality to those words that applied to all of them. He looked again at Moses, perhaps seeing him for the first time. The man he had thought of as a harmless fatherly type was a killer. Maybe not for some time, but a killer nonetheless. Chase already felt woefully inadequate. Combined with the unforgiving cancer which was eating him alive, he was starting to think he had made a very big mistake.

TWO

The island first appeared on the south side of the boat. Not The Island, that would come later. This was Lomar's island. The temperature had climbed to such a level that not even the forward motion of the boat and the sea breeze could deter its baking heat. Chase had stayed on deck long after Moses had retreated back inside to enjoy the free bar. He wasn't there on some kind of pleasure cruise. He was there to save his daughter. As the boat turned towards its destination, and the island started to grow larger as they neared, the others came out on deck. Awkward, mistrustful glances were thrown. There were no greetings, no handshakes. Just a cold indifference. It seemed the game was already underway. Chase tried to assess each of them, hoping to discover where he sat in the pecking order as a potential winner or loser. The two girls (one was called Perrie, he didn't know the name of the other one) had already formed a bond, it had seemed. Their name-stencilled shirts had been removed and tied around waists, exposing slim bodies in matching black tank tops. Both looked to be half drunk already. Chase was curious if they were drinking to forget what was about to happen or having one last blowout before the inevitable shit storm to come. Moses he had already met, the older man hiding those yellow eyes behind reflective black sunglasses. The other two men were as far apart as it was possible to imagine. One of them, the one he recalled from the waiting room with the incessant finger to thumb routine, was called Ryder. He too had dispensed with his shirt, showing off a muscular torso which made Chase incredibly aware that he was out of shape. The girls seemed to be enjoying the view, and Ryder didn't seem to mind them watching. On his right shoulder was a black and grey tattoo, penned with incredible details. It shows a cobra coiled around a cracked human skull. Below it, in a scroll curling around the skull, were the words 'no fear of death'. Unlike the rest of them (half-cut girls aside) Ryder looked the most relaxed, and if Chase was honest, the most physically impressive. The other contestant, the one who Chase had seen chewing his fingernails and tapping his foot in the waiting room, was called Alex. The heat had brought out his acne in ugly blotches, and his eyes were still filled with fear as he flicked them to his rivals in turn.

There's a man who knows he's made a mistake. Chase found some comfort in that feeling. On the heels of it was another. In Alex, there was at least one person he thought he could definitely take out if he had to. The rest of the group could smell blood too and as such had already started to distance themselves from him. Based on his initial impressions, Chase suspected he could take all of them out if he needed to with the exception of Ryder and Moses, who he considered his most realistic threat.

The lush greens of The Island greeted them as they pulled up at the dock. They could see the sprawling house halfway up the hillside, a spectacular property with walkways and vast open spaces. They each got their bags and disembarked, waiting on the bright, hot dock and waiting to be told what to do next. As they watched, a figure approached from the house. Clad in brown loafers, crème flannel trousers and loose, white shirt, Damien Lomar jogged down the dock towards them, grin beaming behind tanned skin.

"You made it I see, welcome to my home."

All six of them gawped at the house, unable to believe that anyone could afford to live in such luxury. Lomar let them gawp for a while and then clapped his hands together. "Well, if you'll follow me, I'll show you around."

Lomar led them back the way he had come. Chase fell in behind Ryder, getting a close up look at the chiselled back and the muscles which continued to make him feel inadequate.

"For the next three days, you will stay here and go through your final preparations before you ship out to The Island. Think of this as your last taste of civilisation." Lomar grinned over his shoulder as he said it. Nobody else seemed to find it funny. He led them up the deck steps through a tidy garden filled with palm trees and flowers. "As you all know, the basis of the game is simple. Enter the northern gate as a group. Reach the opposite side of The Island and exit via the south gate. Only one of you can exit, and will only be allowed to do so when all of your rivals have been eliminated."

The wording wasn't lost on Chase. Eliminated sounded much better than killed or murdered. Lomar led them into the house, the cool blast of the air conditioning a welcome relief from the intense heat of the day. Lomar led them through a white marble reception room, past the pool table (the Brazilian model was long absent) and down another hallway. Stuffed animal heads watched over them as they passed, then moved into a large, spacious dining room of sorts. "Fan of hunting, Mr. Lomar?" Moses asked. Lomar nodded. "Occasionally. There is nothing more primal than man hunting beast one on one, don't you think?"

"I wouldn't know much about hunting," Moses replied. Chase knew that wasn't strictly true. The dining room had glass doors down one full length of the room leading out onto a sun drenched patio and swimming pool. A chef in pristine whites stood behind a barbecue, cooking burgers and sausages. Lomar turned to face his audience. Still grinning. "Before I let you enjoy the next few days, there are a few other things I wanted to talk to you about. This will be covered in greater detail tomorrow when you speak to our head of production. What I want you to remember is that this is a television show. Treat it as such."

"What does that mean?" Ryder asked.

"I mean keep in mind the entertainment aspect. You may go into The Island together but you don't have to remain that way. Go in groups or on your own, it really doesn't matter. What matters is that people keep watching."

"Isn't that out of our hands?" Perrie asked. Despite looking half cut earlier, she was calm and in control.

Lomar's grin widened. "Quite the opposite. It is all in your hands. The best television shows are filled with drama, twists and turns. Granted, there will be plenty of those when you get onto The Island itself, but I want more. A good double cross, a tasty argument. Maybe a bit of sexual tension between contestants." He looked at the two girls as he said it, raising one eyebrow for a split second. "Whatever you choose to do it up to you. Bonuses will be paid for those who are deemed to be making it more of a show."

"Isn't death enough to keep people watching?" Chase had no idea he was even going to speak until the words had left his mouth. Even so, the question was a valid one.

Lomar looked at him for a second, his grin faltering ever so slightly, and then he responded in the same conversational, jovial tone. "Of course, a person's mortality isn't something to be frowned at, and I mean no disrespect. But there is something to be said for the kind of dramas that only you, the season one contestants, can make. Be memorable, be controversial. Be ruthless. Remember, there can be only one winner. Your faces will be broadcast all over the world on live television. There are over three hundred thousand cameras rigged up through The Island to capture your every move. Each of you will be wearing cameras on your clothing too in order to capture everything that takes place. To capture the first glimpse of what lives behind those two hundred foot walls."

"And what does live there?"

It was Alex who had spoken. His foot was still, but his eyes still darted. His t-shirt was ringed under the arms with sweat and he looked completely uncomfortable. Lomar was still smiling, but now it was the smile of a crocodile rather than a friend telling a humorous story.

"I'm afraid to tell you that would spoil the very real reactions when you encounter what I have in store for you." Not so much the words themselves, but the delivery of them had brought everyone's mood down just a touch. The burgers still sizzled and smelled gorgeous, the pool still looked inviting and cool, but all any of them could think about was death. "Well," Lomar said, sensing the mood drop. "I have to leave on business later today, however, my staff have been instructed to give you anything you require until you leave for The Island. You will also be visited by our survival expert tomorrow who will show you a few basic survival tips. I believe one of you is former Special Forces, am I correct?"

Ryder raised his hand Lomar nodded. "For you, I'm afraid it might be a boring exercise, but the rest of you ought to pay strict attention. In closing, I will wish you all good luck. Pasquale is preparing food out on the grill, and the pool is gloriously cool. Enjoy these days of freedom. Soon, you will enter The Island. Now go ahead and relax, you've earned it. Leave your bags; they will be taken to your rooms which you will be shown to later."

The crowd was about to disperse, and Chase was about to head outside when Lomar put a hand on his shoulder. "Would you come with me, Mr. Riley?"

Chase's heart vaulted into his throat. He could feel the eyes of the other contestants on him, willing something to be wrong, hoping for their odds to improve at his expense. Chase suspected what it was about. It had to be the cancer. They had made a mistake in clearing him and now were about to kick him off the show. He followed Lomar to a small room off the dining area. It looked like a study or office of sorts. Immense oak bookcases lined the wall, the room itself dominated by the biggest desk he had ever seen. "Please, take a seat," Lomar said, motioning to the high backed chair. Chase sat, and Lomar walked around to the other side of the table, where he too sat. Folding his hands on the spotless table top, Chase tried his best not to appear nervous, but there was no way to deny that Lomar was an intimidating presence. Chase sat in the silence, listening to the monotonous tick of the clock as the seconds were eaten away.

"I understand you're not in the best of health."

With those words, Chase knew the game was up. He considered trying to fight it, to try and lie his way out of trouble, but Lomar's piercing gaze told him that any lie would be seen through, any excuse dismissed. "Yes. That's right," Chase said.

Lomar nodded. "Cancer of the lungs I believe. Terminal according to your medical scan."

Chase nodded. "Apparently. But your health scan cleared me to take part, if you intend to throw me off the show I–" A raised palm was enough to stop Chase in his tracks.

Lomar smiled a thin, toothless gesture. "Don't try to talk your way out of it. It's not necessary."

"I can still do it. I can still take part."

"Mr. Riley, please, let me speak." The slightest air of authority. Chase imagined Lomar would be terrifying during board meetings when he dialled that aggression all the way up to eleven if his staff wasn't getting the job done as he wanted it.

"I'm sorry," Chase muttered. "It's just that... This is important to me. You have no idea."

"Actually, I do. I selected you, remember? All of you. I know the motivations for you taking part. I know the situation, Mr. Riley. Make no mistake about it."

Chase nodded, folding his hands in his lap.

"Now I'm sure I don't have to tell you, that we can't have a contestant on our show that is already facing death regardless of if he wins or loses. The public would feel cheated. You see my dilemma?"

"If the public feel cheated that I'm already dying, then maybe it's them that are the problem, not me."

Lomar grinned, then stood and walked around the desk to the window, which gave him a spectacular view of the ocean. "I can't speak for the public, only myself. But you are of course right. That doesn't change the fact that the public will feel cheated. I can't have that."

"Then why bring me here? Why not just reject me at the application stage? Why give me false hope that I could do this?"

"Mr. Riley, please!" This time, the snap in his voice was clear. Sharp. This wasn't a man used to being questioned. "Let me finish."

Chase sat in silence, watching as Lomar opened a drawer and took a small silver device. It looked like a cross between a pistol and a tattoo gun. Smooth chrome, handle moulded for comfort. Chase felt fear bristle down his spine, wondering if he was about to be killed for trying to deceive a mega power like Lomar, for wasting his time and resources. He wondered if it would be quick, if they would put him out of his misery then take his body out to sea and dump it overboard. Panic was close to taking over. Lomar was approaching now, chrome device held loose and hanging at his side. Just as Chase had decided to try and make a run for it, Lomar placed the device on the table in front of Chase then returned to his seat. Chase looked at the device, confused and curious in equal measure. On closer inspection, the device was some kind of drug delivery device. The needle protruding out of its end covered in a rubber tip.

"What is this?" Chase asked. Lomar smiled. Crocodile this time like when he was asked about what was on The Island.

"Vaccine."

"For what?"

"Your cancer of course."

Chase stared at the needle gun, then at Lomar, looking for the joke, for the first hint that he was being tricked. He saw nothing but curiosity in the billionaire's face.

"I don't understand."

"Like I said, Mr. Riley. I can't have the public chastising me because one of our contestants is already dying."

"I don't think you understand. I have cancer."

"And there is the vaccine," Lomar said, slowly and patient as a man trying to explain something simple to a child. Lomar leaned on the desk, crocodile grin spreading. "When you reach The Island, you will learn that science has made many things possible that the public knows nothing about. The treatment for cancer has existed for at least twenty-five years. Only those rich or powerful enough can afford it. As you know, certain cancers can be treated with drugs. I believe that was your intention in coming here, correct, to get the treatment?"

Chase nodded.

"Well, here is something better. How will it feel to know that you can cure your daughter completely and immunise her from the disease if you win? Believe me, Mr. Riley, even I had to jump through a lot of hoops to get this vaccine. You have no idea how difficult it was to obtain."

"People are dying, my daughter... I mean... This isn't something you can hold back."

Lomar shrugged. "I've held nothing back. The decision not to release the vaccine is one made by people far more powerful than me. I would imagine the near eleven billion dollar turnover in the pharmaceutical trade each year has something to do with it. Frankly, none of that is our concern. What is my concern is making you fit and well for the show. So, if you want to take part in The Island, you will inject yourself with that in the left forearm. Within forty eight hours, your symptoms should have completely receded. By the time you set foot on The Island, you will be as healthy as you were before those deformed cells ever tried to invade your body."

Chase picked up the vaccine gun and stared at it. All his daughters suffering, all the suffering his family had gone through could have been resolved by that one little vaccine. A single jab then cured within two days He could barely comprehend it. There was so much he wanted to say, questions he wanted to ask, but his tongue was uncooperative and sat on the floor of his mouth, unable or unwilling to move. Lomar grinned, not crocodile, but friendly now. He was enjoying the show.

"Strange isn't it, how just a simple thing can have such a big impact?"

Chase nodded. "And you can get more of this? I mean, after the show, if I won, could you get this for my daughter?"

Crocodile grin was back. "Of course. The prize is anything the winner chooses after all. Why settle for giving her the best healthcare money can buy, when you could eliminate the problem and assure her of a happy and long life free of her disease?"

"If I win," Chase muttered, staring at the vaccine.

"If you win," Lomar repeated.

Chase stared at Lomar, then at the vaccine. He removed the rubber stopper from the end of the needle and touched it to his forearm. "Do I just jab it?"

Lomar shook his head. "Hold it there where you have it then pull the trigger."

Chase's palms were sweating. He couldn't bring himself to go through with it, knowing that he had the power to cure his daughter in his hands and was about to administer it to himself. He glanced back at Lomar, who seemed to be enjoying the mental struggle. It was then that Chase made a decision. He depressed the trigger, the sting as the needle fired into his arm and administered whatever miracle cure was inside a distant thing. One thought now cycled around his mind. No matter what it took, no matter how far he had to go to make it happen, he was going to survive The Island and cure his daughter.

"Congratulations," Lomar said with a smile. "You are now cancer free."

There was no joy. No excitement. Just an overwhelming desire to reach their destination so he could give his daughter the life she deserved. If that meant having to murder a few strangers he had just met, then so be it. He was more than prepared to do it.

FINAL PREPARATIONS
NECKER ISLAND, BRITISH VIRGIN ISLES
MARCH 8th 2044

Richard Glebe reminded Chase of a bug. A praying mantis maybe or some kind of stick insect. He was tall and skinny, his bulging eyes not complimented by his gaunt features. His hair was slicked down with a gallon of oil, and when he talked, he gestured with his hands, something that, for Chase, at least, had quickly become annoying.

The last two days had been anything but the luxurious relaxation that Lomar had suggested it would be before he had jetted off on whatever business he had (pausing to wave to them as his private helicopter transported him from The Island to the mainland). If anything, there was a sense of apprehension mingled with eagerness to get started. As Lomar had said, Chase's cough had subsided, and he felt better than he ever had before. The vaccine he had been administered was certainly potent. All of them had spent the last two days differently. Moses and Alex had been quiet and reflective, Alex the most as he continued to become more and more isolated from the group. The two girls, Ellie and Perrie were like chalk and cheese. Perrie was almost the stereotypical ditzy girl, a happy-go-lucky party animal who seemed oblivious to what they were about to undertake. Ellie, on the other hand, was an enigma. Although she was quiet, there was something about her that Chase couldn't quite place. Something between fierceness and a determination to succeed. She had spent the majority of the last two days sitting in the sun, earphones jammed in as she listened to music. Chase supposed that like him, she was assessing the competition, which was her right. The complete opposite again was Ryder. He was brash and cocky and took great delight in telling everyone that he was the favourite to win with the bookmakers, a fact that was impossible to verify the validity of. Chase watched him now, doing push ups by the pool, skin slick with sweat as he moved with piston like efficiency. Chase had tried to make conversation, but Ryder it seemed only wanted to talk about one subject, which was himself and how he was going to win. He had taken great delight in telling them how he had learned to live off the land and build shelters, start fires and survive in the most hostile environments on the planet. Chase wasn't certain how much of it was bullshit designed to intimidate or true. Either way, Ryder was confident of his chances. Chase decided he didn't want to think about Ryder or the rest of his competition anymore and turned his attention back to the mantis-like Glebe, who was gesticulating at the team of men who were setting up a green screen towards the rear of the pool area. It was rare for Chase to take an instant dislike to someone, but Glebe had all the qualities he hated in people. Smarmy and arrogant, he spoke like a man who was far superior to those around him as he buzzed from location to location checking everything was in order. As if hearing Chase's thoughts, he turned towards them and clapped his hands together.

"Contestants, to me, please. Stop what you are doing and come to me."

They all complied, Chase's heart rate increasing just a little. Every small event was now leading to the first tentative step onto The Island.

"Come on, a little closer so I don't have to shout," Glebe said, his patronising tone not going down too well with any of them. They all stepped closer, forming a semi-circle around him. Satisfied with their positioning, Glebe spoke, the insincerity of his friendliness easy to spot.

"Okay, as you can all see, we have a green screen set up here behind me. What I want to do is have each of you record little vignettes. For those of you who don't know what that means, we want to shoot little interviews, promotional segments where you tell the people at home a little bit about yourselves and why you applied for the show."

Chase switched from partly listening to giving his full attention. This was what he had been waiting for, to find out the motivations of the others. It seemed Glebe and Lomar didn't want to make it so easy. "You will do this one at a time in privacy. These vignettes will not air until you are already on The Island, so any attempts to glean a little information on your fellow competitors will be fruitless. If you would please wait in the reception room until my assistant calls each of you in turn, we can begin."

And so it went on. One by one, they went and stood in front of the green screen and told their stories about why they were there and why they thought they would win. When it was done, Glebe gathered them all back outside. The day was already hot, the sun unforgiving as it burned down on the concrete yard.

"Alright, if you would all gather your belongings, and report to the dock, we will be on our way."

"We're going now?" Perrie said.

"Of course."

"So soon?"

It occurred to Chase that Perrie was, at last, starting to understand what was going on. For a while, he had thought she was just a little bit shallow, but now he was starting to wonder if it wasn't a touch of denial.

"What did you expect?" Glebe said, reaching new levels of pomposity. "That you could stay here and sun yourselves on Mr. Lomar's island? No, the boat is waiting for you at the dock ready to take you to The Island. Remember that feeling of the beds you slept in last night. When you lay down this evening, it will be beyond the walls."

Although it was obviously delivered in a dramatic fashion for the television cameras which were all over the property, Chase thought it had done a good job of raising the drama. Even Ryder seemed a little quieter. Chase could see Glebe in some kind of amateur dramatics society, maybe Shakespeare or Macbeth. He suppressed a smile.

"Take all of your belongings with you," Glebe went on. "If you forget anything, or neglect to take it, you will have to survive without it. Once you have your belongings, please make your way down to the dock and board the boat. From there, you will be transported to The Island."

People started to move and gather their things. Chase's legs felt light as he moved around, that bitter fear taste he had first experienced in the Lomar building coming back. His stomach felt light and danced as the terror and adrenaline mingled to make a potent combination. His bag had been packed since the end of the survival course on day one, but he still double checked the straps, wondering if he had missed anything, if anything had been forgotten which would put him at a bigger disadvantage than he already felt he was. He shrugged into his backpack, the weight of it reminding him just how unfit he was compared to Ryder particularly, who was wearing his pack and bouncing from foot to foot like a tennis player waiting to receive a serve. Glebe led them to the boat, the three-man camera crew filming them. They each wore small cameras on the shoulders of their shirts which filmed everything as they saw it. For Chase, the walk down the dock was when it really hit home. Gone was the luxury boat with the free bar and the sun deck. In its place, a rough workman-like vessel complete with armed guards who waited on deck, watching them approach. This boat wasn't meant for them to relax on. It had an entirely functional purpose. There was no greeting, no warm welcome. It was now all business. One by one, they climbed on board. Perrie first, then Ryder, Moses and Ellie. Chase was fifth. As he approached, he wasn't sure he would be able to go through with it. He envisioned himself standing there on the dock, unable to step over as the others looked at him like a pack of hungry wolves. However, there was no hesitation. He stepped over the side, boots landing on the old boards with a finality that reminded him he was too far gone to back out. The disappointment on the faces of the others was welcome, and as much as he hated himself for it, he joined them and watched, curious to see if Alex would go through with it. He was skinny and looked positively ridiculous in his backpack, which seemed much too big for his slender frame. He was sweating, and Chase was sure they would be heading to The Island with five instead of six, but Alex too got on board, giving them all a cautious glance as he stood with them. Glebe stood on the dock, hands on hips, beaming his impossibly white grin. He waited for the cameras to get into position, one filming him, the other pointed at the six of them in the back of the boat.

"Alright, there you have it," Glebe said, addressing the viewer's rather than them. "Our first six contestants of the season one premiere of The Island are on board and ready to go. This is their last glimpse of the civilised world. Their next stop will be The Island and whatever secrets it holds." He waited, grin firmly in place. One second. Two. Three. One of the cameramen gave him the thumbs up to say they were off the air, and then moved to new positions ready to get shots of the boat as it left the dock.

With the cameras focused elsewhere, Glebe was his usual pompous self. "It's a twelve-hour ride out to The Island. Fifteen if you hit bad weather," he said, looking at them with contempt that was barely hidden. "Remember, only one of you can win, but that doesn't mean one of you has to win. If you all fall to The Island, then so be it. Just because this is a television show, don't make the mistake of thinking you will be protected. Once you reach The Island and go through the gates, you are on your own. Remember, one winner. Make the show good, make what might be your last hours memorable. Good luck."

Chase thought that was the speech they should have aired. He may have come across as a pompous prick, but at least he seemed like a real person. Either way, Glebe didn't stay to watch them leave. He made his way back up the dock, maybe to flit around the pool as the crews took down the cameras and returned Lomar's home back to its previous state. The six of them watched as lines were cast off, and the boat put into gear. They moved away from the dock towards open water. All of them watched as their last glimpse of the civilised world melted away into the horizon, and then thoughts turned to their destination, all of them aware that as of that moment, the game was underway.

ARRIVAL
THE DISCOVERY
ATLANTIC OCEAN
MARCH 8th 2044

One thing became apparent as the discovery and its boat full of contestants made for The Island, and that was that twelve hours wasn't as long as it seemed. It equated only to seven hundred and twenty minutes, or, broken down even further, just forty three thousand, two hundred seconds. Chase sat at the galley table, staring at his hands and wondering if everyone else could feel the relentless countdown as they neared what for all of one of them, would be their final destination as a living human being. The engines of the boat hummed as it powered them along. Chase half hoped for some kind of breakdown, something that might delay them just a little so he could fully come to terms with what was happening, but the old boat went on, driving them closer to their final destination.

His solitude was disturbed by Ryder, who sauntered into the kitchen, muscled arms swinging. He nodded at Chase, then went to the fridge and took out a carton of milk, drinking straight from it, and then putting it back. Rather than leave, Ryder sat opposite him across the table, a cocky half smile on his lips.

"You don't say much, do you?" Ryder said.

"I don't really have much to say."

"You think you can win?"

Chase looked at Ryder, trying to figure out if it was genuine curiosity or a sign that some people had already started to play the game. "Do you?" he replied.

"Oh, I'm going to win. It's inevitable." There was no arrogance in the statement. Just an unwavering self-belief in what he was saying.

"I wouldn't say it was inevitable. The way I see it, you have a one in six chance."

"Come on, you don't believe that. I see it in your eyes."

"You don't know me," Chase snapped, unsure why Ryder was getting so under his skin.

"No, but I know the type." He was doing that thing with his fingers again, each one touching his thumb in turn. His grin reminded Chase of the one Lomar wore, knowing and confident.

"I didn't realise I was a type."

"No offence, pal," Ryder said, standing and cracking his knuckles. "I'm sure you had good reasons for coming here. But I know for a fact, not one of you has thought about it and what you might have to do. I have. I've done it before, and I'll do it again. Not one of you means anything to me. I don't say that to be a dick, it's just a fact. When it comes to either me or you, I'll back myself every time."

Chase was still struggling to formulate some kind of an answer when Moses ducked into the door. He had a look on his face that told Chase everything he needed to know before he had even opened his mouth.

"We're almost there. You can see it from the deck."

Chase felt his stomach tighten, contracting into a tight ball of heat before relaxing and filling him with a chill. He glanced at Ryder, who was still grinning. "Well, let's go take a look, shall we?"

With that, he was gone, following Moses upstairs to the boat deck. Chase sat there for a moment, trying to compose himself before he let the others see him, then he got up and followed the others upstairs.

TWO

At first, it just looked like a smudge on the horizon. Only when they got closer did they see the true scale of The Island. The hilly terrain of lush greens was shrouded in a light mist beyond the immense concrete wall which ringed the entire island. All of them stared at it as the boat moved closer. Chase glanced at Alex, who was still wide eyed. His lips moved in silent prayer as he wrung his bony hands. Only Ryder was grinning, looking excitedly about the group. Nobody returned the gesture or shared his sentiment. The biggest reaction was from the armed guards who had accompanied them. As The Island loomed closer into view, they flicked off the safeties of their automatic weapons and stood ready. The two cameramen who had come with them were filming The Island, grinning as it loomed closer. Chase envied them. It was fine for them to grin. They were going back with the boat.

"Bigger than I thought."

Chase turned. Alex was standing next to him, Adam's apple bobbing in his skinny neck. It was the first time Chase recalled hearing his voice.

"Yeah," he agreed. "A lot bigger."

Alex turned to him, those blue eyes unable to hide how afraid he was. "Do you ever feel like you made a mistake by coming here? I do."

It was a valid question and one that Chase had asked himself with increasing frequency as the day drew closer for them to start the game. If anyone else had asked, he would have acted with bravado if only to keep up appearances, but he felt nothing insincere in Alex's questioning, and so decided to be honest.

"I thought about it, I mean, who wouldn't? Underneath all the posturing and showing off, I think everyone here would rather be somewhere else."

"Almost," Alex said, the faintest smile appearing on his thin, pale face as he nodded towards Ryder. "He loves every second of it. Best to keep a close eye on him."

Chase watched Ryder as he tried to talk to Perrie, chest out, muscles flexed as he pointed at The Island.

He turned back to Alex, surprised to find that he was looking right at him. "Why are you here?" Chase asked.

Alex shrugged. "Same as everyone else. Sometimes you have to do things just to try and make a difference."

"What do you think is in there? Behind the walls?"

"I have my suspicions, but I don't think it will help anyone for me to speculate on them. Besides which, it might be the one advantage I have."

"Do you think you can win?" Chase asked, only because it felt like the right thing to do.

"Oh, I'm going to win. There is no doubt about that at all."

Chase stared at him. For all of Ryder's posturing and posing, for some reason Alex was much more convincing.

"You seem pretty sure of yourself," Chase said.

"Oh, I am. I'll win, mark my words." Once again, Chase couldn't help but notice that there was more to Alex than he had initially thought, than he suspected any of them had thought. Behind the uncertainty and the fear, there was a certain determination, even if it was probably misguided. "You know what we might have to do in there don't you if we want to win?"

"Of course. I think I'm the only one who does." He flicked his eyes towards The Island, which was looming closer. "Once we're in there, it's going to be a war of attrition. Survival. Physical attributes are only the start of it. A lot of the battle is going to happen up here." He tapped his temple with a bony finger.

Chase nodded; part mesmerised and a little bit scared. He hadn't considered the psychological aspects of what was about to happen and felt completely unprepared.

"Well then," Alex said, shoving his hands into his pockets. "I suppose we better take a look and see how the land lies."

He walked away towards the side of the boat, shoulders hunched as he leaned over the side with the others who were staring at The Island.

THREE

Camera crews were on the dock filming them as they approached. The boat pulled in, the contestants paying no attention now to the television cameras or even each other. All they could do was stare at was the two-hundred-foot concrete and steel wall which loomed high above them. Beyond the dock was a short road and a series of port-a-cabins surrounded by thick vegetation. The contestants climbed off the boat and stared at the structure, craning their necks to see the top. Rain sat on the edge of the air, threatening to turn into a downpour at any time. The dock extended towards The Island, then down to a pebble beach, before ascending again. Beside it, an access ramp let to The Island proper. The wall was dirty and covered in moss. Other than a recessed section which contained a half dozen access doors, it was completely featureless. No windows. No texture. It was reminiscent of a dam wall, although instead of water housed something much more deadly. They stood on the dock, letting the cameras film their reactions, letting them savour the shock.

A sign, white and red was attached to the dock, one of many which were identical to it. It read:

ABSOLUTE SILENCE.

NO NOISE from this point forward.

A man approached. He was dressed in grey combat pants with black patches on the knees, and a black jumper, the sleeves rolled up to the elbows. Dark hair, sharp blue eyes. He walked down the dock, coming to a halt in front of them.

"Welcome to The Island," he said. He offered no introduction. Gave no name. He simply looked at them. "The waivers you signed prior to agreeing to take part on the show start from the moment you set foot through the gate there." He jammed his thumb over his shoulder to the small steel access door. "Your temporary HWLF licences will also be active the moment you step foot through the gates. For those of you who don't know, weren't listening, or thought this was some kind of a joke, HWLF stands for Hunting with Lethal Force licence. That means that anything you do when on The Island is not punishable by law, and I do mean anything. Inside the confines of The Island, anything goes. The only objective is survival."

The man stared at them each in turn, eyes cold. "Make no mistake; you will encounter things on The Island. Things that will want to kill you. Remember your basic survival lessons; remember your reasons for being in here. As a courtesy, the first mile beyond the wall is a designated safe zone, that's why we are able to converse beside these warning signs demanding silence. You will encounter nothing that will harm you until you reach the edge of the safe zone. This is clearly marked. After this point, you are in control of your own destiny. If any of you are thinking about backing out or changing your mind, the time for that is long gone. The six of you will enter The Island, and you will do it now. If you would make your way down the dock to the recessed area of the wall, you will receive your final camera checks then you will go inside. Good luck to you all, and to the eventual winner, I will see you on the other side. Remember, the exit is two hundred miles away as the crow flies. Depending on your pace and how determined you are you could reach there in just a matter of a few days. If you take one piece of advice with you, make it this. Do whatever it takes to win. Remember your motivations. Remember why you are doing this." He looked at them again, making sure his words had hit home, then nodded. "Alright, now if you would make your way to the wall, we can begin the game."

He stepped aside and waited. For a few seconds, everyone stood where they were, then Ryder started to walk down the dock. A little of the swagger had gone from his step, but he was still the most confident. One by one they all followed. Moses, Perrie, Ellie, Chase, and as always, Alex bringing up the rear. Hands still thrust in his pockets, head down as he stared at the dock. They went down the dock, crunched across the gravel beach, then up the ramp on the opposite side. The wind still threatened to bring rain, but so far it had held off. The recess was around ten feet deep, an angled depression cut out of the main wall. They gathered near an access door, one which was no bigger than a door which would be in any home anywhere in the world, except the ones at home tend not to be made from titanium and carry a warning on the front. Like the signs on the dock, it was printed in black on white with a thick red border.

STRICTLY NO ADMITTANCE.
RISK OF FATALITY

As far as signs went, it was short and got straight to the point, telling the reader exactly what could happen to anyone who chose to ignore such a warning. The cameras rolled, catching their reactions. Their unnamed guide saw them staring at the door and interjected, the words he said next doing nothing to reassure them.

"I suppose you were expecting something grander, maybe a giant gate like in the King Kong movies?"

"Actually, I was," Ryder said, grinning and winking at Perrie. Their guide didn't see the funny side.

"Well, unlike the movies, we keep the doors small for a reason. We don't want anything in there to be able to get out. Think of it as insurance."

There.

Chase had been waiting for it, to see the first crack in Ryder's armour. The grin faltered, and a moment of panic replaced it.

If he had been less afraid himself, he might have enjoyed it. As it was, he was struggling to retain a calm exterior. New York seemed like such a long way away, more so now that just a single door separated him from what could well be the end of his life. He looked at the other contestants. Some he had painted a half decent picture of, some he was no closer to knowing anything but a name. One thing was for sure. Soon enough, there would be no hiding their true intentions. Soon, the bullshit would stop.

A red beacon above the door started to flash. There was no accompanying sound. Their guide accessed a panel by the door beneath a black and yellow striped cover and punched in a number. The door opened, and instead of seeing lush greens of The Island, it was a narrow dark corridor, at the end of which was another door. Low wattage lighting ran across the roof of the tunnel.

"Alright," the guide said to them as the cameramen started to pack up their equipment and load it onto the boat, apparently having got the footage they needed and wanting to get as far away from The Island as possible. "Proceed to the end of the corridor and wait by the door there. It's automatic. As soon as this one is secured and locked, that one will open. As soon as you reach the other side, it's game on."

Now nobody was in a hurry to move on. Nervous glances were shot between competitors. Once again, it was Ryder who made the first move. He walked into the dark tunnel, footfalls echoing as he made his way deeper. Chase followed, the drop in temperature making his sweaty skin cold. He wasn't sure who was behind him. All he could see was the back of Ryder's head as they walked single file. He wondered where Alex was. He presumed he was at the back, hands thrust in pockets, head down and bobbing like a chicken as he walked. Chase realised he didn't like not being able to see him. They stopped, Ryder closest to the door, Chase just behind. He looked over his shoulder, expecting to see one of the girls, and surprised to see Alex. He was looking at the floor, shoulders hunched, hands in pockets, heart thundering, adrenaline making him agitated. Chase waited as the door behind them closed and locked, blocking out the civilised world, and the door ahead of them opened, spilling in the bright light of the hostile world which awaited them.

THE WORLD WATCHES
PRODUCTION OFFICE
LOMAR TOWER
NEW YORK CITY
MARCH 8th 2044

The production office was dominated by a vast array of television screens which stretched the entire length of one wall. Banks of production staff stay at consoles, each responsible for maintaining the live feed on The Island. Unofficially dubbed as mission control, it was a hive of activity. Biggest of all and surrounded by the smaller monitors was a larger screen showing a map of The Island, the digital representation penned in green on a black, six small yellow dots which represented the contestants flashed by the edge of the north wall entrance. Lomar approached Maurice, standing at his shoulder, knowing how intimidating his presence was.

"You've done well, Maurice. Really well. Everything looks good."

"Thank you, Mr. Lomar," Maurice said, not looking up from his console.

"And you have full coverage? Just like I asked?"

Maurice glanced Lomar's way and then turned his head back towards the dizzying array of controls in front of him. "Yes, sir. We have over three hundred thousand static cameras set up all through The Island, as well as roaming drone cameras which are able to go wherever we guide them. Each contestant is also wired for video and audio as well as vital sign monitoring. The static cameras are in hibernation now which is why all of the screens are blank. They are set to activate when they detect a signal from the GPS trackers so that they conserve battery power."

Lomar put a hand on Maurice's shoulder, squidgy flesh underneath his shirt moving slightly to accommodate. Maurice flinched. "You've done a fantastic job. Really, all of you should be proud." He made sure to say it loud enough for the rest of the production team to hear it. He wanted morale to be high.

"Thank you, sir. That means a lot."

"Can I trust you to do this, Maurice? I have urgent business as you know. I'm giving you a lot of responsibility here. You know how much is on the line here. This is a chance to prove yourself, Maurice. Run the production; make the show a success in my absence. I believe in you, Maurice. I know you can do this."

Lomar knew he sounded sincere, even if he could smell the fear coming of Maurice. Mingled with the slightly musty body odour smell, it wasn't pleasant. Even so, the words had the desired effect. Maurice straightened in his seat, renewing his attention.

"Yes, Mr. Lomar. You can count on me."

"I know it. I have to fly out this evening back to Necker. You have my personal number; I want you to call me if you have any issues. Any at all. Understood?"

"Yes, Mr. Lomar."

"Good," Lomar said as he looked at the array of screens on the wall, then at the large map of The Island. Yellow dots still blinking near the entrance. "Activate the GPS locators on our island residents. Let's see what they're up against."

Maurice glanced over his shoulder. Still a little uncertain. Lomar thought Maurice was probably still fighting with the moral implications of what was happening. He didn't care. He had already invested too much. He watched as Maurice's fat fingers danced over the computer console, showing surprising dexterity.

"GPS locators are coming online now, sir," Maurice said.

Lomar stared at the screen showing the outline of the map as the six yellow dots were joined by red. Lots of red. Some stationary, many moving. Red dots all over The Island. Lomar smiled. Six yellow dots and more than two hundred red. He liked those odds.

"All GPS trackers are online, Mr. Lomar," Maurice said.

Everybody in the production office stared at the screens, which had come to life now that the trackers had been active. He watched the reactions as they saw the things they revealed, things that until that moment had been a secret to all but Lomar and Maurice. He could imagine the public reacting in much the same way. How his contestants would react was another matter entirely. He couldn't wait to find out.

"Is the feed directed to my private jet?"

"Yes, Mr. Lomar. And to Necker Island as instructed."

"Good. I don't want to miss this. Call me when they reach the end of the safe zone. I really have to go. Good luck, Maurice. You and your team will be rewarded well for the work you do over these next days."

The next words he said loudly, addressing the stunned production team. "All of you will receive a hundred thousand dollar bonus on completion of the show as long as what you see remains secret. I want the public to discover the secrets of The Island at the same time as our contestants. As you all know, public excitement on this is high. Bets are being taken, favourites chosen. We collectively have captured their imagination. Now we need to deliver the best programming we can in the most professional way possible."

Nobody argued. Lomar had selected the best people. People he could trust. The financial incentive was just extra insurance, and something he could easily afford. Pocket change really. He took a last look at the map, imagining scenarios and how they would play out.

"Right, I have to go," Lomar said, tearing his eyes from the screen. "Give me regular updates. The first highlight show airs in a couple of hours. Make sure the editing is right. High production values. I want this to be the best it can be."

He could feel it now. The excitement in the air, the anticipation and determination to succeed. They were excited and ready to do what needed to be done. He left them to it, letting them work. As he made his way towards his office to get his travel bag, he knew now that the only thing that could let him down was the contestants, and he was sure that wouldn't be a factor. Fear was a good motivator too, and he was sure the six of them were already feeling it plenty.

THE GAME BEGINS
THE ISLAND – 4:44 pm

The heat was stifling. Chase suspected it was because the immense walls blocked out much of the breeze, which in turn made the atmosphere so humid. The group had stayed together, wordlessly walking in a line. The safe zone was marked by a dirt road which snaked into the distance. Immense trees and jungle terrain stretched ahead of them. In the distance, they could see tree covered hills. All of them became aware that the journey ahead was going to be a difficult one. Mosquitoes buzzed around, harassing the new arrivals. Birds sang, the surrounding jungle held back by wire fences set back on the edge of the road. It seemed that this area had been deliberately formed into a natural corridor of sorts leading them further inland. At least there, away from the walls, they might feel a little bit of breeze.

Nobody had said a word since the door to civilisation had closed behind them. Chase found it funny that the showboating and bravado didn't mean anything when the reality of the game took over. Chase glanced over his shoulder, the wall already starting to be swallowed from view by the overhanging trees. All of the contestants were dealing with the situation in their own way, but so far there was no panic. No overreaction. Chase thought of it as the opening moments of a boxing match or an MMA fight. They were all just feeling out the competition, testing the waters to see how to best move forward. He was sure that after the safe zone, things would take a very different turn. He assessed each of them in turn. Ryder was casual, thumbs hooked into the straps of his backpack, baseball cap pulled low as he assessed the terrain, keeping his eyes forward. Perrie stood beside him, keeping pace. The two had formed something of a bond over the last few days, probably physical more than anything else. He couldn't imagine any kind of intelligent conversation between them. Moses was walking close to the fence, looking at the fauna. He seemed calm and relaxed. He had tried a bandana over his head to catch the sweat which was already making his skin slick. Ellie was a little bit behind him. Silent as always, fiercely determined and wearing her earphones. Chase wasn't sure how wise it was to listen to music and mute one of the most important senses, but that was on her. As always, lagging behind, was Alex, hands in pockets, head down and walking with that bob of his head. For reasons he didn't understand, Chase was drawn to him. It was a slimy, uncomfortable feeling not unlike the sweat that ran down his spine. He was already tired and wondered if the others felt the same.

"First thing we need to do is find water," Ryder said. "That's essential."

Perrie took out a lip gloss and started to apply it. "I hope I look good on TV. My friends will be so jealous."

Chase couldn't believe what he was hearing. It was either a deliberate ploy to throw them off, or she was grossly out of her depth.

"You know what this is, don't you?" Moses asked.

"Of course I do. It's television show." She said it as if he had asked the most ridiculous question in the world. Chase realised that she wasn't playing a game. She literally had no clue.

"But you surely understand what we are here to do? The rules we're playing by."

She turned and grinned at him, a worry-free gesture.

She shouldn't be here. The thought came into Chase's mind again as he watched the exchange between her and Moses unfold.

"It's just for show," she said, falling back a little to keep pace with Moses. "My daddy works in TV. He says a lot of it is all for show. What happens off camera is nothing like the stuff they show. It's all edited together. This is a game."

"A game where five of us will end up dead," Moses fired back. "Surely you're not so naïve that you don't realise that?"

She smiled, although it wasn't quite so big a gesture this time. "But they won't actually have us die. That's all part of the show. For ratings."

Moses glanced at Chase. Even Ryder was paying attention now. "Did you even read the contract they gave you?" Moses asked.

"Not really. I've wanted to be on TV all my life. When I got picked for this, I was so excited. My friend Chelsea was so jealous."

Moses stopped walking, the rest of the group following suit and forming a rough circle.

"Wait, you're telling me you signed up to this, just so you could be on TV?" Moses was struggling to comprehend what Perrie was saying.

"Of course. I love celebrities. I've always wanted to be one."

Ryder chuckled and shook his head. "This is going to be easier than I thought," he muttered, then started walking again. The others followed suit.

"What's the problem? You think I'm shallow because I want to better myself?"

Moses looked over his shoulder as he walked away. "That's not it at all, girl."

"Then what is it?" she shouted after him.

"It's because you just killed yourself without even realising it. And I don't like to see a life wasted like that."

"You'll see, you'll all look stupid when I'm proved right," she snapped.

They walked on, and silence fell on the group again, leaving the world to the mosquitoes and birds and whatever else was waiting for them out there. The sun was starting to get lower in the sky, reddening the landscape with its fiery glow. The trees whispered in the light breeze as whatever secrets The Island held prepared to be shrouded in the coming dark.

"We need to make camp soon. I suggest here in the safe zone is a good idea considering how late it is." Ryder said, coming to rest and taking a sip from his water bottle.

"Makes it easier to slit out throats in the night," Moses said, calm and flat. He and Ryder locked eyes, neither willing to back down. Chase decided to speak up. He wasn't prepared to see blood spilled just yet.

"Look, I think it's a good idea too. We should be safe here. In the morning, we can decide what to do, either as a group or on our own. I think we can all agree that a night's rest will do us the world of good."

Moses and Ryder continued to stare each other down. Moses lowered his eyes first, shrugging his shoulders. "Works for me. Let's set up."

They worked together. Each of them had singular tents in their backpacks along with basic ration kits and a water bottle. If any exercise showed how prepared they were for survival, it was this one. Those who had experienced outdoor living were able to assemble their tents quickly. Ellie was finished first, closely followed by Ryder. Their tents were stable, taut and well put together. Moses was next to finish, then Chase and Alex, each of their tents functional, if not as good looking as those constructed by Ellie and Ryder. The canvas wasn't as tight, the support lines not as tight. But they were still functional. Perrie's tent was a mess. She had made a half-hearted effort to assemble it, moaning and complaining all the while about how dirty her hands were getting and how she had broken a nail, about how hungry she was and how tired. The constant whining was starting to grate on everyone so much so that Ryder helped her to get her tent up and secured. They had arranged them in a rough circle around the edge of the dusty road. Ryder had lit a fire using a few branches they had sourced from the trees at the edge of the safe zone, and they now sat around it, keeping warm and contemplating their next move. In the flickering glow of the firelight, shadows danced and warped their features into shifting, demonic faces of the beasts they would have to become to survive. Perrie had already started on her rations and was noisily chewing on an energy bar. The others watched her silently in either pity or absolute disbelief. It was way too early to be dipping into such finite resources. The sun had fallen beneath the horizon line, and only a pinkish orange smudge of colour remained in the sky, which was breathtakingly clear. Chase had never seen so many stars. His skyline had always been the smog covered skies of New York. This was simply breathtaking. He wished Ashley and Elsie were able to see it with him. He glanced across the fire and saw Alex looking at him, his expression, as always, impossible to read. He had a thin stick and was pushing the end into the base of the fire, letting it light, and then removing it until the embers died down. There was a certain calmness about the group, possibly because this was their last night of sleep and knowing they were safe.

"Has anyone heard about the last time they did this show?" Ellie said, addressing nobody in particular. She was staring into the flames, earphones finally removed.

"I've heard stories. Rumours mostly. Everyone knows them," Ryder said, looking about the group. "I heard they have people here, genetic mutations warped by nuclear radiation. I hear they're savages, brutal killing machines with a thirst for blood."

Moses snorted down his nose. "Bullshit. There's nothing like that out there."

"Then what is, old man?" Ryder shot back.

"Spirits of the dead. Supernatural things. Things that will make a man's blood freeze in his veins. This island is a place between worlds where those unholy things exist."

"Are you for real?" Ryder said, flashing a grin around the group. "You say mutants are impossible but ghosts are? You're out of your mind, old man."

Alex laughed. A single sharp bark of a sound. Everyone looked at him. In the glow of the fire, it was hard to tell if he was blushing, but Chase would have bet he was.

"What's so funny?" Ryder snapped.

"You two," Alex shot back. "Ghosts and mutants. It's funny."

"Like you know any better?"

"Actually, I know exactly what's out there." There was the faintest hint of a smile as he said it. Firelight danced in his eyes, making him impossible to read.

"Go on then, tell us," Ryder snapped.

"Why would I ever want to do that? It's the best advantage I have."

"Bullshit. You don't know anything." Ryder tried to smile again, but it came out more of a grimace. He was worried.

Alex shrugged. "You believe in your mutants. I know what I know and I'm happy with that."

"Until you die," Ryder snapped.

"Or until you do," Alex retorted, not missing a beat, showing no sign of fear. It was as if since arriving on The Island, he had grown where the others had shrunk back.

"Anyway, I've heard enough. I'm getting some sleep," Moses said, getting to his feet and dusting off his pants.

"Me too," Ellie agreed.

Perrie was next to go, complaining about mosquito bites and how bad she was starting to smell. Just Chase, Ryder and Alex remained. They sat in silence, the hiss and crackle of the fire filling the spaces where the conversation was absent. It was then that they heard it. A roar, a distant sound rolling towards them from somewhere far away. Chase and Ryder leapt up, staring down out into the darkness, the black hump of the hilly terrain ahead contrasting against the bluish-black hue of the sky. Chase had no idea how long he stood there, straining his senses and willing his heart to return to a more regular tempo. Ryder glanced at Chase, showing the real man behind the bravado. The whites of his eyes were showing, too much of them visible.

A whistle, a low happy tune. Something from an old show or an advertisement. Chase and Ryder turned to look at Alex. He hadn't stood or looked panicked. He was still sitting on the floor, poking the end of his stick into the flames just long enough for it to catch, then lifting it out again. He saw them watching, stopped whistling then smiled, looking Ryder dead in the eye. "So much for your mutants."

With that, he tossed the stick on the fire, stood and retreated to his tent, leaving Chase and Ryder staring out into the night.

TWO

The rain that had threatened came in overnight, barraging the tents. Chase couldn't sleep anyway. He was too agitated by the sound he had heard. He wondered if Ryder was the same, tossing and turning and trying to process. One thing he was sure of though, was that Alex would be sleeping without a care in the world. Deciding he had endured enough of the most sleepless night he could remember, he unzipped his sleeping bag, pulled on his boots and unzipped his tent, grateful to be doing something other than lie there and wait. He expected others to be awake, but he was the first. The fire was a smouldering pile of wet ash and branches, the rain having long extinguished it. He looked at the other tents, eyes drifting from one to the other.

You could kill one of them right now.

He wasn't sure where the little voice had come from and liked it even less. It was a part of him that he didn't know existed. He wondered if this was what survival instinct was, if this was that intangible thing that separates those who survive to those who curl up and die. Even so, the thought horrified him almost as much as the idea that he hadn't entirely dismissed it. He looked at Perrie's tent, a pale yellow dome of canvas set back a little from the rest. He had a knife in his bag. They were all given one, part of their survival kits. It was a big knife. Sharp. Serrated down one edge, and then curved at the tip into a sharp point. A real, honest to god hunting knife. He could do it quick, keep it painless. Slit her throat; cover her head with something so he didn't get blood on him. One in six becomes one in five, and in turn, the odds of his daughter's survival would increase. He had turned back towards his tent when he snapped out of it, feeling repulsed. Could he really be such an animal that he would kill an innocent girl in her sleep? He didn't think so. Not yet anyway. Shaken up, he walked a little way down the path, staring at the terrain ahead and knowing that whatever they had heard roar was out there somewhere. As he stared, unable to shake the dark direction his thoughts had just taken, he wondered if he might actually deserve to die.

THREE

The sun broke through the clouds and melted away the drizzle, resuming its punishing burn. They packed away the campsite and were on their way by seven. Subconsciously, Chase and Ryder walked together, bonded by what they had heard the night before. Neither of them mentioned it, but the look they gave each other before they set out said it all. As always, Alex brought up the rear, looking tiny in his backpack, head down, and hands in pockets. They walked for fifteen minutes, and then collectively stopped. Across the road in front of them was a concrete slab painted yellow and black. Across it in white, were the words none of them wanted to see.

SAFE ZONE ENDS BEYOND THIS POINT

Beyond the post, the road terminated, giving way to a vast valley with hip-high grass. At the end of the valley, dense jungle which seemed to stretch forever greeted them. To the right, an outcrop of impassive-looking terrain, grey shale which would be lethal to try and climb. To their left, the valley extended towards the wall, which was visible until it disappeared into the trees.

"What do we do now?" Perrie asked. She had groomed her hair, applied makeup and perfume. It was obvious she didn't belong, that she had no business there.

"The first thing we need to do is gather resources," Ryder said. "As a rule, always head downhill. Not only will the temperature increase for every few hundred meters, that's where you're most likely to find fresh water. My suggestion is we stay together for now until we know what we're dealing with out there."

"We have water," Chase argued. "I say we go that way, to the high ground. Get a look at the land."

Ryder shook his head. "Bad idea. The sun is coming up; it's going to be a hot day. Do you want to bake and waste all your energy by climbing up there for no reason?"

"No less of a reason than getting water when we already have full canteens for the most part."

"It's up to you," Ryder shrugged. "No offence, but I have experience in survival where you don't. You can do whatever the hell you want, I'm heading that way to try and find water and get under the cover for the tree canopy."

Just like that, it was decided. Ryder crossed the safe zone line and started down the valley, walking into the tall grass. The others followed, spacing out behind him. For a moment, Chase considered heading out on his own, but then remembered what he had heard the previous night. It was enough to help him decide that there was more safety in numbers for now. Reluctantly, he fell in with the group, keeping close to the back along with Alex, knowing that all bets were off and they were at the mercy of not only whatever lurked out there on The Island, but each other too.

FOUR

It was explosively hot under the jungle canopy, which made even walking a draining experience. Even breathing was a chore, each inhale of the hot air feeling like it sapped a little strength with it. Giant green leaves and thick roots blocked their way, making progress slow. The initial downhill gradient had changed, and Ryder now led them on an uphill trajectory. Chase was distantly grateful that he hadn't come here with his lungs in the state they were in before Lomar had cured his cancer. He would already be done. As it was, his body burned with the toil of exertion as he picked his way through the terrain. Although he was struggling, there were others who were struggling even more. Moses had fallen to the back, rasping as he struggled to keep up. Perrie too, with her whining and moaning, and constant sounds of disgust or disproval as she stepped in mud, or a mosquito touched her or she broke a nail, had also fallen behind. There would be no offer of help for her this time. Not now the game was in full flow. It was now about survival. Time lost its sense of meaning. With nothing to look at but foliage, it didn't matter anyway. After four and a half hours of walking, they reached a punishing hill, the ground carpeted in a loose covering of leaves which rustled as they ascended. Some electing to scramble on all fours, others, like Ryder traversing side on, muscular legs pumping as he made light work of the incline. Chase was in pain. He was struggling to breathe, his legs burned, his lower back was in agony from the weight of his backpack. He would need to take a break soon, and by the looks of the others, he wasn't alone. He finally reached the top of the rise where the others waited, all of them, even Ryder breathing heavily; sweat dripping from the ends of their noses.

"See... I told you," Ryder said as he pointed down the opposite side of the hill.

The forest opened up onto another natural valley, this one bathed in sunlight. At the bottom was a pool, a flowing river across which more jungle waited. Sunlight glittered on the surface of the water, which looked incredibly inviting.

Chase turned to Ryder, unable to help but smile. "This is one of the few times I'm glad I was wrong."

"Game or no game, I'm going' swimming," Moses said as he started down the other side. As far as ideas went, Chase thought it was about the best one he had heard. The idea was infectious, and they made their way down the valley, enjoying the sun, finally feeling like they could breathe.

Moses shook off his backpack and dived into the water fully clothed, boots and all, shaking his head as he resurfaced. "That's the best damn feeling I can remember in a long time," he said, a wide grin on his face. Ellie followed suit, dumping her backpack, removing her boots and shirt, and then diving in. Perrie straightened her hair, and then very deliberately took off her pack, her shirt, and her tank top, revealing a black bra which barely contained her. She knew she looked good and was showing her body to the world. She waded in, making sure she got said body wet and all but guaranteeing plenty of TV time. Ryder seemed to be enjoying the view as she suggestively flicked her hair around and washed, making sure she was visible from wherever the static cameras may be filming. Chase was about to join them, trying to imagine how good the water would feel when he noticed that neither Ryder nor Alex were making any attempt to get into the river. Ryder was hanging back at the tree line, sitting in the shade. Alex was a little further upstream and was on all fours by the water's edge filling up his water bottle, occasionally glancing at the others as he went about his business. Chase stood, torn as to what to do. The water did look good, but there must be a reason Ryder was hanging back. He didn't want to go back up the hill and look needy, and so he drifted towards where Alex knelt on the bank. His water bottles were now full and he was packing them away. Chase joined him, taking a long drink and then refilling his own water.

"Not going in?" he asked.

"No. In fact, you couldn't pay me to go in there," Alex said, as always his tone flat and emotionless. He flicked his head back the way they had come. "He's got the right idea. I would be up there too but I was getting low on water. Physically harder than I anticipated in this heat."

Chase nodded, and then looked further downstream towards the others who continued to splash in the water. The alarm bells inside started to ring, and he watched Alex as he stood, put on his backpack and started back up the hill.

"What do you mean Ryder has the right idea?" Chase said as he fell in beside him.

"He knows survival. He knows that it's not only people that are drawn to fresh water. It's much safer up there."

Chase stopped walking and half turned back towards the water in time to see it happen. From his vantage point halfway up the bank, it was all too clear. It came from the opposite side of the water, where the jungle was at its thickest. Chase was sure it must have been lying there in wait because there was no pre warning. A massive, reptilian head burst out of the trees, splintering wood as if it were kindling.

That's a dinosaur.

The thought was perfectly rational as it popped into Chase's mind as the twenty-two-foot Tyrannosaurus rex crashed through the trees and lurched into the water towards the others. Moses was almost out of the water when it happened, which is probably what saved his life. He screamed, the sound piercing the still air before he broke into a run, bag abandoned and forgotten, clothes sodden. Perrie too saw it in time and threw herself back away from the explosion of flesh and muscle as it charged into the water. This wasn't the animal Chase had read about in books or seen in countless television films. This was a living breathing creature of its environment. Its head and neck were covered in a soft down of feathers, which terminated into short spines. Ellie had been floating on her back directly where it had come from when the attack happened, and so stood no chance of escape. It bit down, popping her like a grape, blood and innards squirting out of her onto Perrie, who was less than ten feet away from its massive head. It stood upright with its prize, limbs hanging from its mouth as it shook its massive head from side to side, the water around it turning red. Perrie was out of the water now and sprinting up the hill. Chase was numb, unable to believe what he was looking at.

Dinosaur.

Dinosaur.

Dinosaur.

No matter how many times he said it, it still made no rational sense. He was looking at the impossible, and yet there it was taking place right in front of him. He had just watched a Tyrannosaurus rex decimate a girl right in front of his eyes. As he watched, the massive creature shook its head, and Ellie's severed arm fell into the water, landing with a hollow thud. That was enough. Chase turned and ran, making for the tree line where they might, at least, be safe. As he did so, he looked at Ryder, who had already scaled a tree and was perched in the upper branches, watching events unfold.

He knew, Chase's inner voice said. He knew what was going to happen and led us here to die.

He entered the cover of the trees, hiding in the undergrowth and watching as the dinosaur retreated back the way it had come with its meal.

The Island had claimed its first victim.

FIVE

"You knew that was going to happen," Chase said as Ryder climbed down from the tree. He, like the others, was in a state of total shock at what had happened. Moses was sitting on an overturned tree trunk, hands clasped in front of him, eyes wide as he let the heat dry his clothes. Perrie sat beside him, trembling, her eyes streaked with makeup.

"I didn't know anything was going to happen," Ryder said as he climbed down from the tree, going nose to nose with Chase. "If you want to make something of it, you do it."

Although Ryder was bigger and stronger than Chase, anger had become the great equaliser. "You led us here and knew that thing would attack us. That's why you stayed up here," Chase said, shoving Ryder in the chest.

"You think if I knew there would be those…things in the trees I'd willingly come here? You're out of your fucking mind."

"Dinosaurs. Just say it. We all know what we saw." Even to say the word sounded impossible, ridiculous, even. Even so, it seemed that Lomar had found a way to make it happen, and has inhabited his island with them.

"And you think I'd lead you here if I knew that thing was there?"

"Why not? All you've talked about is how you'll win and nobody else stands a chance. Well, congratulations. Your odds are down to one in five."

Ryder looked around the group, stepping back a touch when he found that all eyes were on him. "Alright look, I swear to you I had no idea what was down here. True enough, I hung back because I know animals are drawn to water sources too. After what we heard last night, I –"

"What did you hear last night?" Moses asked, looking up at them.

Chase and Ryder glanced at each other, then at Alex, who was staring at the floor and refused to make eye contact with them.

Chase cleared his throat. "Last night, after you all went to bed, we heard a noise, a roar, something big. Now we know what it was."

"And you didn't think to tell anyone?" Perrie screeched. She was panting and looked dishevelled. Ellie's blood was still on her and had started to dry onto her skin. "You should have told us, you had no right to keep it from us."

"Look, it wasn't intentional, it as a shock to us too."

"You knew there was something out there something big and close and you didn't tell us," she repeated. "This was supposed to be a TV show. Look at me. I've got blood on me. I have that other girl's blood all over me."

She was close to losing it, flipping out completely. Chase didn't want to get into any kind of argument with her. Firstly, he didn't have the energy to get into it; second, she had been hit hardest by what had happened. The rest of them knew what they were up against. For her, she had just realised that there was no director behind the camera, no stunt people of production teams writing their storylines. She now realised that her young life was very much in danger.

"Look," he said, trying to diffuse the situation. "Fair enough, we should have said something. That was a mistake. None of us here know what's in store for us. None of us expected to find these...things on The Island either." He turned back to Ryder, still angry and determined not to let him off the hook. "But you knew we were at risk. You led us here and now someone is dead."

"Oh, come on," Ryder said, pointing at Chase "This is because we didn't follow your lead and go climbing up into those hills."

"If we had we'd all still be alive."

"And without water, maybe suffering from sunstroke, and that's if we all made it to the top." He turned towards Moses. "No offence, old man, but I don't see you as the mountain climbing type. This walk to here almost had you on your knees."

"Well don't expect me to follow your lead anymore. We're done," Chase said.

Ryder picked up his backpack and put it on. "You know what, that's fine with me. If you assholes want to go off your own way and get yourselves killed, you go ahead and do it. Better for me. I'm happy to go out there on my own and win this thing."

"Fine with me," Chase snapped. "At least if we die now it will be of our own doing, not because you thought it would be fun to lead us somewhere you knew we might be at risk."

Ryder was angry now. His fists were clenched at his side. "You know what? I hope you die next. I mean that. I see you, watching everyone, trying to figure us out. You're nothing special, Riley. Nothing at all that says winner. It's only a matter of time before you make a mistake that will kill you. At least I know what I'm doing."

"And if that means picking us off one at a time, you're happy with that?"

Ryder shrugged. "We all knew what we came here for. We all knew what we would have to do. Trying the guilt trip thing won't work." He turned away, walking towards the deeper jungle. "See you around, Riley."

"Wait." Perrie grabbed her things and joined Ryder.

"You're going with him?" Chase asked. She nodded. She was clearly frightened and in shock. He couldn't blame her.

"I made a mistake coming here. I know that now. This… It's not what I thought. All I want to do now is go home. My best chance is with him. He knows what he's doing at least."

"He'll only help you for so long. When it comes down to him or you, he won't think twice about killing you if you stand in his way." Chase didn't mention that he had already contemplated killing Perrie earlier that morning, and although he hated himself for it, he didn't think Ryder would have the same moral issue.

"We're all going to die anyway," she said quietly. "Nobody can survive with those things out there."

Nobody had any sort of response for that. As young and unprepared as she was, she was absolutely right. The game had changed and they all knew it. It wasn't just each other they now had to be wary or. It was whatever else was lurking out there on The Island. Chase and the others watched as Ryder and Perrie disappeared into the jungle.

THE REALITY OF LEGEND
DAY TWO
THE ISLAND – 3:37 pm

They walked without purpose or direction deeper into the jungle. Chase now assuming the role of leader, Moses behind and Alex at the rear. The terrain was just as difficult as before, dipping and winding, their access blocked by rocks, roots and trees which were twisted and gnarled together as they reached for the sun. Chase had no idea where he was leading them. As a rough guide, he kept the sound of the river where they were attacked on his left, but there was no real thought in where they were going. As much as he didn't want to admit it, Ryder was the only one who had really known where he was going, how to read the land. Aside from a few documentaries on bush survival he had watched, it was the blind leading the blind. There had been little speaking since the incident at the water. Chase wondered how many of them were out there, and if they had been here last time The Island hosted people. He slowed his pace, dropping back to fall in with Moses. The old man was looking tired. His face was twisted into a grimace.

"You okay?" Chase asked.

"Blisters on my feet. Should have brought thicker socks," he grunted. Sweat clung to his face and a patchy white stubble was starting to form on his cheeks.

"If you want to stop for a while we can."

Moses glanced at him and carried on walking. "I don't need your sympathy or your pity. I'm fine."

"Fair enough."

They stopped talking for a while, saving their breath for a particularly steep section of jungle. At the brow of the crest, the terrain levelled off and became less densely clogged with trees.

"Do you know much about the last time they did this? The show I mean," Chase asked.

"No. I was never interested in it. If I didn't know, I wouldn't have come here."

Chase nodded, unclipping his canteen and taking a sip of water, forcing himself not to guzzle and throw up. "I was just wondering how long those things have been here on The Island. It's crazy to think something like that could have been kept secret for so long."

He waited for Moses to respond, but the older man seemed distracted. Maybe it was the sting on the blister in his sock, or just that he simply didn't know.

"They've been here for at least ten years."

Alex had pulled up alongside them so that they were now walking three abreast. He looked remarkably fresh. Still skinny, still bobbing his head, but not tired. He looked straight ahead, hands still in his pockets.

"How do you know?"

"How do you not?" Alex replied, glancing across at Chase and Moses. "Don't tell me you came here without doing your research."

"Of course I looked into it. I'm not stupid," Chase said, asking himself how much he really did try, how much he had actually tried to find out before signing the forms which were nothing more than a death warrant with fancy wording. "Anyway, what do you know about it?"

"The information is there if you dig hard enough. I'm good at stuff like that. Computers. Finding things out. Information is king."

Chase still couldn't figure Alex out. It seemed the assumption they had all made of him was nothing but the outer layers of whatever lay beneath. "What did you find out?"

He didn't immediately answer. Chase was about to ask him again when he started to speak. "The Lomar Corporation had been interested in cloning and actively pursuing it from right back when Jackson Lomar still ran the company. Of course, the assignment was different back then. Jackson wanted to see if it was possible to grow limbs for soldiers wounded in battle, things like that. When he died and Damien Lomar took the reins, all of that research was canned. Damien was hell bent on building his island and wanted a reason to do it, so he started looking into cloning at first. Did you ever see that movie, Jurassic Park?"

Chase shook his head. "Didn't see the movie, but I read the book."

"Damien did too. He always wanted to make it a reality. The problem was that the whole science behind the books and the movies was flawed, at least then."

"Even with new technology, where the hell would he find the raw materials to create one of these things? It's not like you can just get one like you can with sheep or an elephant."

Alex shook his head. "You didn't look into this too much at all, did you?"

Chase's silence confirmed that he hadn't. Not by a long shot. Alex went on.

"Do you remember in the mid two thousands, when the polar ice caps first started to melt?"

"Yeah, I read about that. Sea levels rose by ten feet in some places."

"Exactly. Underneath all that Antarctic ice was land. Quite a lot of it. There are documents out there that Lomar took particular interest in a certain partially melted glacier, and had a team go out and take something away. Several somethings according to the report."

He shrugged and glanced at them. "It stands to reason that what they took was some kind of carcass, maybe it had been locked in there for millions of years encased in ice. A complete body, flesh, skin. More importantly, useable DNA. Like that mammoth they found."

"And from that, they created living versions of these animals? That's a bit of a stretch."

"Actually, the science of creation would have been the easy part. The only difficulty would have been finding usable samples. It seems the Lomar Corporation hit the jackpot."

It was a lot of information to take in. It certainly seemed plausible. At any rate, it was the best explanation they had. "How do you know so much about it?" Chase asked.

Alex ducked under a low hanging tree root and then half turned towards Chase. "Like I said, it's all out there if you look hard enough."

"I have a question for you," Moses said, looking past Chase to Alex. "Knowing what you do about these things being here. Why the hell did you still apply to take part?"

"I have my reasons."

They waited for Alex to elaborate, but he said nothing. Chase checked his watch. "Alright, I suggest we maybe try to find a place to make camp."

"With those things out on the loose?" Moses replied.

"We can't walk all night. We need to rest up. It will be dark soon. For all we know, they might be more active then."

"Where do you suggest we camp?"

Chase stopped walking and looked around. The trees had thinned and they were walking through hip high ferns. Ahead, the ground sloped away into a natural valley, and then even further ahead was another rise with more rocky terrain. The water that had been beside them cut through the left side of the meadow, then opened up into a wide river of sorts. In the middle of the water was a rocky outcrop, a flat plateau of land with a natural formation of rock curving around the outer edge which the water surged around before heading down the valley. "What about there?" Chase said.

Moses nodded. "Looks okay. Should give us a little bit of protection from the land and warning if anything tries to get to us."

"What about you?" he said to Alex. "Are you okay with it?"

He shrugged. "I don't mind. Whatever works best, as long as we can cross the water. It's flowing pretty fast."

The shadows started to lengthen as the trio got to work. The water, although fast flowing, was only knee height, and getting to the plateau was fairly easy. The set up their tents against the rock formation facing out towards the water. They lit a small fire and opened their ration kits. It was then as their bodies started to rest that they realised just how fatigued they were. As far as temporary camps went, it was a good one. Protected on three sides with a wide view of both the water and the opposite bank. Conversation was sparse. Arrangements were made for a rotation of keeping watch, and attention turned to the next day. The terrain ahead was much rockier and would involve climbing down, possibly falling before they entered a maze of craggy rocks. It would be hot and difficult. They would also need to find food. There was no way their meagre rations could sustain them or replace the calories they were burning. Alex took the first watch, then Moses and finally Chase. He wasn't sure he would sleep before it was his turn, but he found as soon as he closed his eyes he fell into a fitful sleep until Moses woke him, gently shaking his shoulder. Still exhausted, he sat by the fire, looking out into the night and staring at the stars. He felt his eyes grow heavy just before dawn, his eyelids feeling as if they were weighted. He told himself he would close then, just for a second, his sin soon falling onto his chest. Had he stayed awake a little longer he would have seen two things. First, he would have spotted Ryder and Perrie as they skirted past their position, heading down into the craggy, rocky area beyond. He would also have seen the pack of velociraptors as they crossed the river, heads bobbing much like Alex when he walked. The six dinosaurs paid no attention to the camp. Or the sleeping Chase. They were on the scent of Ryder and Perrie and were in slow, stealthy pursuit. Much like everything on The Island, the velociraptors didn't care about prizes or game shows. All they cared about was survival and the hunt, one going hand in hand with the other. The six of them broke into two groups. One followed their prey directly; the others veered away and plunged into the forest. They knew these lands. Knew there was another way and would meet up with their brethren in good time.

When Chase woke twenty minutes later, he and the others were awake and preparing to leave. They broke down their camp and packed, then set out for the next leg of their journey. They crossed the river, weary and tired, unaware that they were following almost the exact path that their fellow contestants and the creatures which hunted them had used just an hour earlier.

BENDING THE RULES
DAY THREE
NECKER ISLAND – 8:12 AM

Lomar walked through the rooms of his house, enjoying the quiet. Enjoying the buzz of success. The launch show for The Island had been an amazing success. The sighting of the first dinosaur had sent the world into meltdown. Social media was buzzing, news networks the world over were covering the story, stating how the Lomar Corporation had managed to do the impossible. It was already the most-watched show in the history of television, and companies the world over were desperate to add their sponsorship, offering tens of millions of dollars. There were, of course, a few human rights groups who protested the show, but even they were in the minority and were unable to say much as the dinosaurs roamed free without boundaries or cages. The leading questions asked to the contestants when they recorded their green screen vignettes had been edited together to emphasise that they knew what they were getting into and the risks involved.

Not only was The Island the most watched show in history, it was also the most gambled on. Betting rings ranged from large to huge, as the people put their money on who they thought would survive. He wished his father could see him now, wished he could tell his father he had been wrong, and he would never reap the rewards for his lack of vision.

The house was silent, the staff already making their way to the mainland to enjoy their weekend away. Lomar liked this time. Liked the solitude. He was the only person around for miles, and it suited him fine. He walked into the dining room, then through into his office. At the back of the room was another door. Loma opened it and stepped inside. A spiral staircase led down into the dark. He descended, taking his time. Motion sensing lights flicked on as he reached the foot of the steps. He looked at the room, smiling, feeling the first surge of adrenaline.

It was an armoury of sorts. Weapons lined one wall, rack after rack of guns and knives of every conceivable type. To the right, was a large glass fronted wardrobe filled with clothing.

Camouflage pants and jackets, boots and other survival equipment. The room also functioned as a gym. There was a weight bench and running machine, equipment to train his body to be the best it could be. There were no windows. He didn't want them. He loved the private intimacy of the space. He loved how the room smelled. His secret place. He started to undress. Kicking off his Italian loafers, pulling off his jeans and unbuttoning his shirt. He glanced at the gym equipment, then turned away from it.

Not today.

Today he went to the glass-fronted wardrobe. He slid the door open and let his hand drift over the hanging clothes. He selected his favourites. Dark green with brown and black patches. Green vest. Jacket to match the pants. Brown boots. He dressed slowly, savouring the moment, enjoying the feel of the material on his skin. It wasn't like the expensive suits he wore my some of the finest designers in the world. These were functional clothes. Itchy and rough fitting. They served a purpose. He fastened the boots. They were heavy, but also durable. Not as flimsy as loafers or sandals. Next came the weapons. His hunting rifle, his beloved Angela, named after his first wife. He was a good shooter. He had paid for the very best training. He selected his favourite things and put them into the large carry bag on the floor. He was ready. He picked it up and went through another door. Down a short corridor. Into the elevator there, which took him to the roof. There, his helicopter waited, rotors spinning, charcoal bodywork sleek and dangerous looking. He tossed his bag into the back and climbed in, sliding the door shut. The helicopter took off, angling away from Necker Island, leaving Lomar's luxury home behind. In the back, Lomar closed his eyes, listening to the steady thump of the rotor blades and visualising what was about to happen. He couldn't wait to get started.

TWO

It was already hot. The terrain was rocky, but led mostly downhill, making progress easier than they could have hoped for. Unlike the jungle, it was dry and dusty. The river still accompanied them, although they could still hear the water somewhere off to their right. The rocky terrain was gradually growing on either side of them, forcing them into a natural channel of sorts, before winding away to the right, away from the sound of the river and putting the sun in front of them rather than behind. Chase led the way, Alex just behind them. Moses was in bad shape. He was at the back, limping along, wincing every time his left foot touched the ground. Chase wondered how much longer he would be able to last. The trail started to go uphill, a gentle curving natural path. It was hard going. Muscles burned with lactic acid, lungs sucked air, hearts thundered with the healthy beat of exertion. Chase checked his watch. They had been walking for four hours. It felt like at least double that. Ahead, the terrain seemed to level off. Chase glanced over his shoulder. "I say we stop up there and take a rest." He gasped the words rather than said them. Neither Alex nor Moses protested. The top of the hill was further away than they expected, and it took them twenty more minutes to reach it. When they did, they came out on a sparse flat plateau of brown rock. The river which they had initially curved away from had reappeared, dropping from the edge of the cliff in a cascading waterfall some sixty feet below before continuing on its journey. There was no way they could go straight down. The cliff face was too sheer, and none of them had any climbing experience. A scrub of trees to their right morphed back into jungle, the way down steep, but passable. Chase sat down, letting his tired muscles rest. He was hungry, his stomach grumbling in complaint. Alex walked to the edge, peering down the vertigo-inducing drop to the water below. He seemed to be remarkably fresh and least affected by the punishing conditions.

"What's the plan?" he asked, not turning away from the drop.

"How should I know? I'm no different to any of you." Chase was frustrated. He knew going back wasn't an option. They needed food, which meant they would have to find means to hunt sooner rather than later.

"I thought you were leading us somewhere," Alex replied. There was no accusation in his voice. No real emotion of any kind. Chase wasn't sure how to take it.

"I led us here. Now we need to decide where to go next. By all means, you make that call."

Alex grunted and turned back to look at the waterfall just as Moses limped up the hill. He sat down hard and started to unfasten his boot. Chase watched him, saying nothing as he took it off, exposing a white sock which was now red on the heel.

"Jesus," Chase said. Alex glanced at it and turned away again.

"It burst a mile or so back. Been walking in blood and pus ever since."

"Can you go on?"

Moses looked at him and then shrugged. "As long as you don't expect me to climb down any cliffs."

"It looks like we can go around. Through the trees there, although it looks pretty steep."

"Steep I can handle. I just ain't much of a climber. Arthritis in the hands." Moses gently touched the shredded skin on his heel, then looked at Chase, squinting against the sun. "What are we going to do for food? Surely I'm not the only one who's hungry."

"We need to find something to eat. Does anyone have any hunting experience?"

Moses shook his head, preoccupied with his wounded foot. Alex didn't acknowledge him. He had his binoculars out, scanning the terrain below them.

"What about you?" Chase said. Alex lowered his binoculars. "Someone's passed through that valley ahead of us."

Chase scrambled to his feet and stood beside Alex. "Where?"

"Down there," Alex said, handing Chase the binoculars. "There are fresh boot prints in the soft dirt by the river."

Chase looked, scanning over by the river bank. He could see footprints in the dirt, crossing back and forth. Two sets, one bigger than the other. "Ryder and Perrie," Chase muttered.

"Yeah."

"How did they get ahead of us?" Chase said, not really asking anyone.

"Probably went right past the camp in the tree line. We wouldn't have seen a thing as long as they were quiet. You see the other prints down there?"

"To the right, coming out of the forest."

Chase panned to the right. The prints were clear. Three-toed in the wet earth. Two sets coming out of the tree line which they were due to enter in order to get down. Chase lowered the binoculars and handed them back to Alex.

"Any idea what left those prints?"

Alex shrugged as he put the chord for the binoculars over his neck, letting them hang against his chest. "How would I know?"

"You seem to know a lot about this place."

"I don't know what species they were. Could be anything. It looks like they were on the hunt."

"Ryder and Perrie?"

"Who else," Alex muttered. "With any luck they found them," he added as he turned away from the edge and sat on a small rock near Moses.

"Why would you say that?" Chase asked.

"Why else? With them gone, that just leaves three of us. One in three is a lot better than one in five. I can handle those odds."

"You're still playing the game," Chase said, shaking his head.

"Everyone is playing the game. That's why we're here. That's why we're out here. It seems everyone but you is playing, unless you're just so good at it, you have the rest of us fooled. I'm not sure yet."

"Ryder I couldn't care less about. But that girl he's with shouldn't be here, she made a mistake."

Alex nodded, taking a swig from his water bottle. "She's a dumb bitch who made a mistake, and now will probably pay for it with her life. Seems like poetic justice to me. Anyway, since it seems the three of us are sticking together for the time being, we need to find food and a way to protect ourselves."

"What do you suggest?"

Alex flashed a thin smile. "Why do you keep asking me things like I know the answers?"

"Don't you?"

"To some things."

"Do you know the answer to this?"

"To what?"

"What we do next?"

Alex shrugged. "We need to get down from here that much is obvious. Going back would take too long, so it looks like we walk or slide down there and try not to fall, break any bones of cut ourselves up on the rocks. Once we get down, we follow those tracks and see where they go."

"There are...things down there," Chase said, still unable to bring himself to use the actual word.

"If you mean dinosaurs, I think it's safe to assume they're everywhere. Another reason we need to find some way to protect ourselves."

Chase turned to Moses. He wasn't looking so good. "You okay with that?"

He nodded. "Just give me a minute to get my boots on and I'm good to go."

As soon as Moses was ready, Chase led them into the scrub of trees. The downhill incline was steep, and they were forced to cling on to branches and trees as they half-walked, half-scrambled down the first part of the steep hillside. The ground levelled out a little, and they pushed through more thick trees, pushing aside leaves, swatting aside bugs and baking in the humidity. Chase was in the lead, trying to ignore his hunger when he pushed aside a huge green leaf and was in a clearing which glowed with sunlight. The others stood with him, none of them speaking. The trail sheared away into a sheer rock face reminiscent of the higher ground. It was smooth and without handholds. To their right. Half buried in the earth was a black maw, a cave entrance. They stared at it, then looked at each other. Their options were to either go back and try to climb back the way they had come, or venture into the cave. The entrance was huge, forty feet in diameter. Sunlight barely penetrated into the dark opening.

"I don't think I want to go in there," Alex mumbled. It was the first sign of weakness he had shown.

"We don't have a choice," Chase heard himself say, wanting no part of the cave system either. "Ryder and Perrie must have come this way and we know they made it."

"True," Alex said, staring into the dark. "Let's go then."

Although it was something he hadn't wanted or asked for, everyone was waiting for Chase to make the first move. Reluctantly and with his inner voice screaming at him about how big a mistake he was making, he led them into the dark to whatever lay beyond.

THREE

The day was quickly swallowed as they made their way deeper into the cave. Each of them had been issued with ultraviolet lamps, thin strips of plastic which were stitched into the shoulder of their shirts, just above where their names were stencilled. When activated, the lamp would glow a dull blue for up to five hours on a standard charge. Now activated, the lamps cast the cave into eerie, shadow-heavy shades of blue as they carefully made their way down the uneven slope which twisted down out of sight. Their boots scrabbled for purchase on the loose gravel, the trio moving in silence into the unknown apart from the occasional grunt from Moses as his blistered feet continued to trouble him.

"We seem to be moving away from the path of the slope, it doesn't make sense," Chase whispered, his voice still reverberating and rolling into the distance.

"You need to think outside the box a bit more," Alex replied. "Remember, this is a manmade island. It doesn't have to follow nature's rules. They can put things wherever they want to."

Chase almost slipped, grabbing at the wall to stabilise himself. "These are real rocks. This is a real cave."

Alex grinned, the expression ghastly in the harsh, artificial light. "But it's not. They might be real rocks, but this wasn't formed by nature. Just look at the walls. This was shaped by men with machines."

The cave narrowed as it curved away from where they wanted to go, the roof closing in on them and making their passage harder. They were forced to turn to the side as they continued to descend. Their path widened slightly, then Chase stopped moving.

"What is it?" Alex asked, the passage still too narrow for him to squeeze around to see for himself.

"Water," Chase replied, moving forward a little into the wider section to allow the others to see. The cave opened into a circular pool which was around fifteen feet in diameter, its surface black and impenetrable in the gloom. The cave surrounded it on all sides apart from small head high section immediately ahead just above the water line.

"Looks like we're going to have to swim for it," Chase muttered.

"We could go back," Alex said. Chase looked at him. There was no hiding it now, the fear. He was close to the edge.

"To what? There's no way to go without losing another day by going back to the river and crossing to the other side. Even if we did that, we know it terminates here. We have to move on."

"You don't understand, I... I'm not so good with enclosed spaces. We don't even know how deep the water is. Or what might be in there."

"I can't go back, my feet..." Moses looked exhausted. He seemed to have somehow shrunk over the last few hours, his face thrown into ghastly relief by their lights. "You two do what you want, but I'm going on ahead."

"Your call, Alex," Chase said as he took off his pack. "I'm going on with Moses."

"It could be a dead end. We might drown down there." His cheek was twitching, and his foot tapped against the ground as he struggled to decide what to do.

"Didn't we all come here knowing we might die anyway? Like you said, it's a man-made island. Chances are they left us a way out. Besides, Ryder and Perrie already came this way, remember?"

"I suppose so," Alex mumbled.

"Alright, let's do it," Chase said. He crouched and put his fingers into the water. It was frigid. He started to unfasten his boots.

"What are you doing?" Moses asked.

"That water is cold. I'm putting my boots and socks in my bag, my shirt too. When we get to the other side, I'll want something dry to wear. Our packs are waterproof. I'll put my dry clothes in there then change on the other side."

"Good idea," Alex said as he also started to remove his shoes.

Moses shook his head. "If I take my boots off, I'll never get them back on. My feet are in a bad way. Besides, I don't want to risk getting infected."

"You will be cold when we reach the other side. We won't have time to stop and light a fire."

Moses shrugged. "It's hot out there. As soon as we are in the sun, I'll dry before you know it."

Chase decided not to argue. He wanted to, then remembered that Moses was a rival, and in the way of him giving his daughter the life she deserved. He put his boots into his bag, then took off his shirt, removed the t-shirt from underneath and put that in with it, then sealed the waterproof backpack, ensuring the seals were completely closed. Finally, he put the shirt with his name stencilled on it back on so that he could use the light his UV torch provided. He waited as Alex did the same thing. Moses just stood by the edge of the water, face twisted into a grimace. Chase sat on the edge of the pool and dipped his bare feet into the water, gritting his teeth as the cold bit into him.

"I'm going to lower myself down and see how deep it is," Chase said as he rolled onto his front, bracing himself on his elbows on the edge as he lowered his legs into the water, it came up to his torso, then his chest before his feet found the floor. The cold was intense, sharpening his senses. He could feel the thunder of his heart in protest at the sudden temperature change as he pulled his backpack in after him, the buoyant material bobbing on the surface. "Alright, I'm touching the bottom."

Alex looked at him, still afraid. "How tall are you?" he asked.

"Six two. Why?" Chase replied.

"I'm five nine. That water will come up to my chin."

"Nothing I can do about that," Chase said. He no longer had the energy to play nice. Alex would either come along or he wouldn't. Either way, it was good to see him looking a little less confident. Moses was next. Like Chase, he lowered himself into the water, sucking air through his teeth as he too felt its frigid bite. Like Chase, the water went as high as his chest. The two of them bobbed there, waiting to see if Alex would join them.

"This feels great on my feet. Nice and cool," Moses said, even managing a smile.

Alex looked back the way they had come, knowing it wasn't on the cards. He looked from Chase to Moses, then rolled his bag into the water where it bobbed on the surface, waiting for him, then like Chase and Moses, he lowered himself into the pool. As he predicted, the water was much deeper for him and went up to his jaw. He breathed in large gasping breaths as he angled his head up towards the cave roof in order to keep it out of the water. He was panicking, but somehow able to keep control. Chase led them on, his hair brushing the cave roof as he made his way deeper, pulling his bag along my one of the straps. Moses was next in line, and seemed relaxed and at ease, still enjoying the relief as the chilly waters cooled his shredded feet. Alex kicked along at the rear, cheeks puffing in and out with each breath as he tried to keep his head above the water line. Every loose rock Chase's feet touched, he thought was something in the water waiting to drag him under. Still they moved on. The walls narrowed again, so that they could no longer move forward three abreast and had to go single file, then side on. Now the cave was barely wide enough for them to traverse. Sharp rocks dug into their fingers as they pulled themselves further into the dark. Very gradually, the ground started to fall away. The water that was chest high on Chase was now up to his chin. He glanced over his shoulder to see how Alex was doing. He was treading water, his face turned up to the roof as he pulled himself along. Movement was becoming more difficult, and they had to physically pull themselves through the passageway. Stone pressed against their chests as they went on, the cave seeming to never end. There was no concept of direction anymore. There was nothing to give them any sensory indication of where they were. All they could do was keep moving. They all understood just how easy it would be to die there. A slip underwater combined with a movement into an unfamiliar area could lead to being trapped and unable to reach the surface.

Ryder could win this.

For the first time, Chase had acknowledged that he might not survive. It was always there of course; sitting somewhere in the back of his mind, but it was the first time it had come to the fore. Death would be easy in such a hostile environment, and although he wasn't to Alex-levels of panic yet, he was close. He thought of Ashley and Elsie, how they would cope when he was gone, asking himself how they would live, how they would survive on their own. He knew then, as that moment as he pulled himself through the cave, that Ashley was right. He should never have signed up for this. Not when he was so unprepared nor had any concept of what the show would entail. He heard her voice, swimming out the place in his head where she lived. He recalled the day he had left the apartment; how she wouldn't look at him after telling him countless times that he was wrong to go. She had been right. So right. He got stuck, wedged between two jutting pieces of rock which pressed into his chest. He would have to go under. He ducked, his head plunging beneath the water line as he pulled himself along past the obstruction, then resurfacing for a lungful of air. He pulled his bag through, the material having more flexibility that his bones.

She would know now. What was here. What he was up against. The thoughts plagued him and refused to go away. She would have seen it on television. The dinosaur attack, the ruthless brutality in which it had decimated that other contestant. He searched for her name, but couldn't recall it, then, in turn, wondered if that made him a bad person. He had barely spoken to her. All he remembered was that she always had her earphones in. he thought about her now, what her family might be thinking. For them, there was no more need to watch the show. For them, the pain was over. Chase wondered why she was there. What her motivations had been for taking part in such a barbaric game.

Ellie.

Her name had been Ellie. She was a living, breathing human being with imperfections and problems the same as the rest of them. She had hopes of winning for reasons she believed in, just like the rest of them. And in the end, it wasn't enough because she had been crushed into pulp by something which had no right to exist in the modern world. Chase asked himself how arrogant the rest of them must be to think the outcome for the rest of them would be any different.

Panic was starting to creep in. Physically, he felt fine apart from the cold. It was the mental fatigue which was getting to him. He was tired and hungry and wanted to be out of this crushing coffin and breathing fresh air again. It felt like a lifetime since he had last seen daylight, and yet a check of his watch told him it had been less than an hour. Just when it felt as if he couldn't handle anymore, the walls started to widen, and his feet found the ground again.

"It's opening up again," he grunted over his shoulder, the elation he felt impossible to put into words. The cave sloped up and opened into a bowl again. After the time spent in such a confined space, the cave felt immense, like the church he had been married in back before things started to go wrong. Chase led them out of the water onto land, then fell to his knees, grateful to have solid ground under him again. Moses trudged out behind him, boots and clothes heavy with water. He walked a little closer and then sat on his pack, leaning against the wall, eyes closed as his lips moved in silent prayer. Alex came next. Scrambling out of the water, clawing at the rock as he pulled himself clear and fell in a heap next to Chase, breath ragged as he rolled onto his back and stared at the roof. They lay there for a while, grateful to still be alive, then Chase opened his backpack, took off his wet shirt and put the clothes he had taken off back on. Boots and socks, then his t-shirt. His outer shirt was sodden. He wrung it out, forearms flexing as he squeezed out the excess water. He then tied the shirt to the back of his backpack and put it back on. Whilst Moses chewed on the last of his ration bars, Alex did the same as Chase, replacing his dry clothes and tying his outer shirt to the back of his backpack. Sure enough, their combat trousers were still wet, but their feet and bodies were dry.

"Alright," Chase said. "Let's get the hell out of here." He led them further, the terrain now sloping back towards higher ground as the cave widened. He found his thoughts going back to his family and allowed his body to move forward on autopilot. He thought about all the things he would never see, all the things he would miss if he died on The Island. His pace slowed as he came to terms with it. The decision to join the show which he was sure was in the best interests of his family was looking increasingly selfish. He let his feet guide him through the narrow passageways as he became increasingly withdrawn. He barely noticed as the natural light started to increase. He was thinking of Elsie, and wondering if he would ever see her again when he was grabbed from behind. A powerful hand clamped over his mouth and yanked him to the ground. He struggled, kicking as Moses threw his other arm around Chase's chest.

He's desperate, Chase thought as he struggled against the surprisingly strong older man. He's been fading for a while and now he's desperate to win. I underestimated him.

Moses's voice in his ear, hot and hissed. "Be quiet, hold still."

Chase stopped struggling, realising that Moses wasn't trying to kill him, just restrain him.

"Look," Moses whispered.

Chase did as he was told. Ahead, the cave opened up into a larger space. White light bled from the outside world like liquid gold. Chase focussed on it. He had already seen the way out, and couldn't figure out why Moses was so spooked until he looked closer. Not outside the cave, but within it. There, by the entrance was a dinosaur. He didn't know the species. He wasn't too familiar with the different kinds of creatures Lomar had put on The Island; all he knew was that it was big. It lay on its side by the entrance, its massive belly moving in the rhythmic pattern of sleep. If Moses hadn't stopped him, he would have walked right towards it and likely wouldn't have seen it before it was too late. Alex crouched beside them and looked at the sleeping creature. It was greenish brown, its muscles lean and ready to attack. It looked like a smaller version of the tyrannosaurus rex. It appeared to be from the same family, sharing many of its characteristics.

"What is it?" Chase whispered as Moses released his grip.

"Majungasaurus. Carnivore. Incredibly dangerous," Alex replied.

"How do you know?" Moses said, eyeing Alex mistrustfully.

"I did my research."

"Yeah, I forgot you knew what they had here."

Alex didn't respond. Instead, he shifted position. "We should wait. It will go out to feed soon. Either it's resting or this is its lair. We're lucky it can't smell us. If we had been downwind and coming the other way, we'd all be dead."

"We might be yet," Moses said. "If it sees us, we have no way of escaping."

"Then we better hunker down until it decides to move on," Chase said.

"No. We don't have time. We need to find food and shelter before dark."

Moses and Chase looked at Alex, trying to decide if he was being serious or not. Seeing their uncertainty, he smiled in the gloom. "Relax, I'm not going mad. We know there is a lot of jungle out there. Chances are we can sneak past it and into the woods to safety."

"Screw that," Moses said, shaking his head for emphasis. "I saw what happened to that girl. You can forget it."

"You can do what you want to," Alex shrugged. "But trust me, I've researched these things and the last thing you want is to be out here and exposed after dark."

"What do you think?" Moses asked Chase, eyes like white pinpricks in the gloom. Chase didn't have a response. He had no idea what the best choice was, good or bad. All he knew was that every hour wasted was another hour his daughter was being ravaged by her illness. When he really thought about it, nothing else mattered. He glanced at the sleeping dinosaur, and then out at the blazing sunshine beyond, teasing them with how near and far it was away. It felt like he had been underground for an eternity, and longed to feel that warmth on his skin. He knew nothing about dinosaurs. He suspected Alex didn't know as much as he thought he did either. Nobody could be prepared enough for this. No matter. He wasn't prepared to stay there any longer.

"Alright, I'm in. we stick to the wall, move quietly." He turned to Moses. "How is that foot?"

"Don't concern yourself with that. It's fine," Moses snapped.

Chase next glanced at Alex. There was a defiance in his face. Something that was almost a sense of enjoyment rather than fear. Chase realised he was starting to find himself increasingly wary of the younger man, and seeing him as more of a contender as time went on. "Alright, let's move," he said as he led them out of the safety of the tunnels and into the wider section of the cave. As he had instructed, they hugged the wall, keeping it close to their right side. Alex was just behind, keeping close to his shoulder, a constant presence. Once again, Chase was struck with the ridiculous notion that he was more uncomfortable with Alex at his back than approaching the sleeping Majungasaurus. Moses was at the rear and seemed to Chase to be making a lot of noise, even if it wasn't his intention. Every few steps he wound grunt or suck air through his teeth as his damaged feet touched the ground. Both Chase and Alex were throwing regular glances at the older man, who was either ignoring them or oblivious, his brow furrowed as he concentrated on putting one foot in front of the other.

Up close, the Majungasaurus was much bigger than it had appeared from the rear of the cave. They were now thirty feet away from it and in turn only fifty away from the exit and the freedom that lay beyond. The one-ton dinosaur still lay on its side, eyes closed, tail curled up underneath its massive, muscular legs. Near the entrance in front of it were the remains of something none of them could identify. Shredded flesh. Blood. A few shafts of bone. It was clear that this was once another dinosaur, perhaps even one of its own kind and had since become the Majungasaurus's meal. Even as large as it was, the creature had been unable to finish its entire kill in one sitting.

For a man who had grown up in New York City and had never seen anything much larger than one of the many stray dogs which nosed around in the mountains of garbage cans on street corners, Chase was in awe of such an incredible creature. As terrifying as it was, the Majungasaurus was also a showcase for perfect evolutionary efficiency. Unlike the human species with its complicated web of emotions, the sleeping creature lived a beautifully simple existence. It slept when it was tired. Hunted when it was hungry, and killed when it felt threatened. There was nothing else. No society. No money to worry about. No pollution. No family. It was a perfect machine, evolved by nature to be efficient. Big powerful legs, each toe equipped with a seven-inch curved claw which was more than capable of disembowelling any of them with little effort. Its tail, large at the trunk then tapered to a point gave it balance for when it attacked. Its arms were non-descript. Similar to the T-rex in position, they were much smaller and completely useless. Anything it would ever need to grip was taken care of by the jaws. Slivers of white teeth visible as the creature slept. Like the clawed toes, the teeth were designed for maximum destruction. Alex tapped Chase on the shoulder, pointing to a spot on the side of the creature's neck. There, on the brownish green hue of its skin, Chase could see it clearly. A brand or tattoo of sorts. An identifying marker which reminded them all that they were part of a strange game.

PROPERTY OF THE LOMAR CORPORATION
SPECEMIN NO 79 – MAJUANGASAURUS
PRODUCT I.D – 154B-2585-SD00847A

A dry, teasing breeze pushed into the cave from outside, displacing gravel and teasing their hair. They froze as one as the creature stirred. Tail flicking, toe-claw twitching.

It's going to wake up.

Chase knew it was going to happen. He had never been surer of anything in his life. It would wake, see them and destroy them. There would be no hope of fighting back in such a confined space. One of them might survive; the odds were good of that. If Chase were a betting man he would say that Moses would be next. It stood to reason. He was the oldest. The slowest. He had blisters on his feet and would struggle to run. Unless…

He tried to change his train of thought, but it was already there. Unless it likes the hunt. Then it would chase one of the runners. And Chase knew that if it did stir, he would be one of the first to run. Not for his own life. He had already made peace with the idea of losing it, but for his daughter. That is all that kept him moving.

But the creature didn't wake. Its tail stopped flicking. The claw stopped twitching. It let out a throaty grunt, then was still, the rhythm of its sleep bringing them a little comfort.

Chase glanced over his shoulder at the others. Moses first, then Alex. The latter lingering a little. Chase wondered if there was some kind of shared idea there, some kind of momentary, telepathic bond where, for the briefest of seconds, he was sure they had shared the same idea without ever uttering a word. He could see how it would play out.

Moses is slow. Weak. Push him down, scream and shout, then run. Run as hard as these newly cancer free lungs will allow you whilst the creature feasts on its intruder. With luck, it will take both of the others. One in four is good odds. One in three would be spectacular.

Chase glanced towards the exit. He could see the way he would go. The cave broke into a clearing, then just ten feet beyond, the jungle. The heavy, twisted jungle. A place where it would be advantage human. Ten feet or so, plus the distance from where he stood. He did the calculations. Maybe, twenty five feet total. With his old lungs, a big ask. Now, though, he knew it would be easy.

One in three.

One in three.

One in three.

He knew it wasn't right. Morally it was out of the question. But the little voice, the one he had started to think of as the voice of his self-preservation, whispered in his ear, telling him what he needed to know to justify it. You signed an agreement, it said to him. These are the rules. This is how the game works. You think they won't do it to you if they get the chance? You think they care about Elsie?

It was hard to ignore, hard to argue when the opportunity was there in front of him.

This is the game. This is how it's played. No room for compassion. No room for doing the right thing. The only way to win this is to become an animal. A heartless, survival driven beast.

He turned away, heart thundering, torn as to what to do, heart saying one thing, and head another. The little voice wouldn't be deterred. They're just waiting for the right time. They will kill you without thinking twice, and then what? You'll have come out here and died for nothing. All because you don't have the guts enough to get a little blood on your hands.

"Shut up." He'd already said it before he could stop himself. He didn't turn back. He didn't have to. He could feel their eyes boring into the back of his skull.

Now. Now is the time. It will be easy. Just run. Put those lungs to good use. Make for the trees. Fuck these people. You don't owe them a damn thing.

He had never felt so tempted, nor had he wanted to do anything quite so desperately. The only thing that was stopping him as fear. Fear of being alone. He felt safer in a group. Could work better within a unit. At least this way he knew where they were. If they were to separate, the hunt was well and truly on. They would see him as a target, the man who had tried to kill them. Although a few days ago the idea had seemed ridiculous, he didn't particularly like the idea of Alex hunting him down. There was something in his eyes, a feral kind of aggression which he was trying to hide. For that reason, and for that reason alone, he didn't run. He ignored the nagging inner voice and led them on. One foot after the other, each step closer to the cave one he was sure would be their last and that the creature would surely wake up. Only when they had reached the heat of the day, the change in light making them screw up their eyes, did they run. As a unit, they sprinted for the tree line, Moses doing his best to keep up. As they crashed into the relative cool of the canopy, still in their trio, two thoughts came to Chase. The first was how long their fragile group would be able to stay together before somebody decided it was time to try and win. The second was if the others had gone through the same thought process in the cave that he had. He was pretty sure they had. With both thoughts swirling around his mind, he led them into the jungle and to whatever came next.

ODDS GET SHORTER
DAY THREE
NECKER ISLAND – 3:13PM

The sky had started to lose its unblemished shade of blue as the dark thunderheads started to build. The heat was still intense, but there was a light breeze now which told them that soon enough they would be facing the assault of the coming storm. Their encounter in the cave was still fresh in their minds as Chase, Alex and Moses toiled through the trees. Hunger was starting to become a real issue, even if none of them were quite prepared to admit it and show any kind of weakness in front of their rivals. Ignoring the moaning of his stomach, Chase led them on. He felt lighter like his skin was too big for his frame. He knew it had only been a couple of days, but he was already exhausted. He glanced over his shoulder at Alex, who was chewing on an energy bar from his ration kit. He was the only one with any food left. Moses was falling further behind. His brow was furrowed, and he was walking with a very definite limp. Chase felt unwell, Moses, however, looked terrible. At some point, he had acquired a gnarled, thick branch, and was using it as a support, a walking stick of sorts as he tried to keep up.

After escaping the cave, it became apparent that it had taken them off course and come out deeper into the jungle. They were backtracking now, Chase keeping the sun roughly ahead and to his right where it had been when they first came out on top of the cliff face. The shadows had elongated as the sun made its steady descent towards the horizon line. They needed food and water, but Chase had no idea where he might find the former. Water he would be able to get when they reached the gorge they had seen from the cliff top. The waterfall had plunged into a pool there, and he clearly recalled seeing Ryder and Perrie's footprints in the soft mud. Food wasn't going to be so easy. He couldn't begin to imagine how many calories they were burning, how much energy they were sweating out as they traversed the unforgiving landscape. He couldn't speak for the others, but he was feeling weaker and weaker with each passing hour.

Food.

A hamburger or a hotdog. Maybe a sandwich and a cold beer.

He started to salivate and wiped a forearm across his mouth. Thinking about it made things worse. He wondered if Ryder had any food. He suspected he might have. He was, after all, the only one of them with any survival experience. He would know where to look. Dinosaurs weren't the only creatures inhabiting The Island. Since they entered the jungle they had seen birds, spiders and snakes, rodents and even monkeys flitting high in the branches and safely out of reach of the dinosaurs. It was still so hard to comprehend. Two different evolutionary timelines had been thrust together by a man who had both the money and the vision to attempt it. Whether it was crazy or stupid was another matter entirely, and not something he cared enough about to consider. He ducked under and overhanging branch, and pushed aside a huge green leaf, then was blinded by the shimmer of sunlight on water, giving the pool the impression that it was on fire. The cliff face stretched high above them, the craggy gorge to their right, a thin trail cut through the hundred foot walls on either side.

Elation. Chase never expected to feel it at such a simple thing as the sight of fresh water, but even so he did. Water meant life. Life meant survival. Survival meant his chances of winning would increase. He hurried to the edge, dropping to his knees in the soft mud of the bank and cupping his hands, drinking the cool liquid, splashing it on his face, soaking his hair.

It was divine.

Even Alex seemed relieved. He filled his water bottle in between cupped double handfuls of water. Chase looked at Moses, who was sitting on a rock, staring at his dirt-covered feet. He had no interest in water. His expression told a different story. It was an expression which said his feet had let him down, and, as a result, had put him at risk. He caught Chase's eye.

"You cold?" he asked.

Chase glanced at the blue skies and burning sun. It must have been almost thirty degrees Celsius. He shook his head. "No, not at all."

"I'm cold," he replied. "Can't get warm."

Chase nodded, thinking back to the cave. How Moses hadn't taken off his shirt before getting into the water like he and Alex had. He could imagine how walking through the dark tunnels with wet clothes clinging to him could have brought on all kinds of problems. Hypothermia being the key potentially life-ending illness.

"Don't look at me like that."

"Like what?"

"Like I'm a dead man," Moses replied. "Don't count me out yet."

Chase was spared from having to reply by Alex, who stood stretching his arms out by his side. "We should make a move. We'll be losing daylight soon."

Chase looked at the gorge they were about to cross through, no more than a jagged eight foot cut through the sheer rock face. If they were to encounter anything inside it, there would be no running. No escape. They would have to face it, and with no weapons.

"Why don't we stay here tonight?" he suggested, not sure if he was mentally strong enough to go on any further.

Alex shook his head. "Do I need to remind you what happened last time we stayed for too long near a water source? If we stay here, it will be like putting up a sign saying the buffet is open."

"We're all tired and hungry. We don't know how long this passage goes on through the rock. Plus, we have no weapons."

Alex grinned, lighting a fire in Chase's gut. "Something funny?"

"No, not really. It's just that you seem to like to complain a lot."

"I thought I was raising a valid point."

Alex shook his head. "You're still not thinking straight. You have to see this for what it is. This isn't an island. Not in the truest sense. It's a set. We're the actors. Trust me, I think you'll find that passage ends right about when we need it to."

"What makes you so sure?"

Alex grinned, one eye squeezed shut against the sun which was turning everything orange as it fell slowly from the sky. "Because there are millions of people watching us right now. The powers that be are unlikely to want us to die because of the environment rather than the monsters." He walked towards the gorge entrance, sweat glistening on his forehead. "You coming or not?"

Chase didn't reply. They both knew that he was. As with everything, Alex had been right again. With more reluctance than he cared to admit, Chase and Moses followed Alex into the gorge and whatever awaited them within.

TWO

It was cooler and progression was easier as they made their way through the narrow path. The sun was kept off them by the high walls, and without tree roots to traverse, walking was easier. Alex led the way, still bobbing along with the awkward sloped-shouldered gait. Chase was in the middle, content not to have to either lead or talk to anyone. Moses was falling back, unable to keep up the pace. He was walking with a very definite and pronounced limp, his teeth gritted in half hopeless determination. He was unravelling before their eyes, each step further inland seeming to ebb a little more of his life force.

"You better come look at this," Alex called from ahead, his words rolling off the walls as he stopped walking. Chase jogged to meet him, wishing he hadn't seen what was waiting for him.

Blood.

It stood out against the sandstone. It spattered the walls and lay in clumpy drying pools on the floor. Perrie was lying against the wall, one arm bent up against the rock face. Her skin had already started to discolour and turn a purplish blue. Flies danced and buzzed around. Where her face had been was a mess, a bloody pulp of mangled flesh and white shafts of bone. Against the opposite wall, in the shade was the body of a velociraptor, its throat slit. It was obvious there had been some kind of struggle. Chase looked at the floor and tried to make sense of the animal and human footprints alike. He felt sick. When Ellie had been killed it was quick, and they had been forced to move on before they saw any of the aftermath. This was a different situation. Chase felt sick. Seeing what remained of her, nothing but an empty vessel left there as food or the flies, brought home how serious a situation they were involved with. This was the same fate that awaited all of them. There would be no ceremonious burial. No dignified send off. Just the harsh reality that was death. He glanced at Alex, his face unreadable as he stared at the carnage, his eyes focussed on the velociraptor rather than what remained of Perrie. Moses didn't look quite so shocked, and based on his past, Chase could understand. He had, after all, seen death. Dealt with it daily.

"Dinosaur must have gotten her, then she killed it and died as well," he said, just because he was desperate to break the silence.

"No," Alex said. "That's not what happened here."

Both Moses and Chase looked at him. Alex ignored them. His eyes were scanning the scene, flicking from corpse to corpse.

"What do you mean?" Moses asked.

Alex pointed to the floor. "There were at least three velociraptors in here according to the prints in the blood. Looks like they came the way we did, attacked from the rear."

He pointed to the dead raptor. "Ryder killed that one. Slit its throat. Left it for dead. At least one of the others attacked the girl. Look at the claw mark on her leg. It's sliced to the bone. After he'd killed the one by the wall there, he came over and fought them off. If you look at the tracks there by the wall, the footprints double back. They ran. Ryder did a good job."

"Not before they killed her," Chase said.

Alex shook his head. "They didn't do that. Ryder did."

Chase stared at Alex, then looked back at the body, trying to see whatever Alex did that told him the answers.

"The rock. By her head. See it? With the blood on it."

Chase nodded.

"Palm-sized. See the hair and skin on it?"

Chase nodded again.

"Now look above her, on the wall. See it?"

Chase complied. He could see it. A handprint in blood. A man's handprint. When it was all put together, it was all too easy to visualise. Perrie wounded badly, maybe begging for help. Ryder seeing an opportunity, a chance to shorten the odds. Straddling her, grabbing a good palm-sized rock. Holding her down with the right hand while he brought he rock down over and over again with his left, obliterating her face. When it was done, and the rock had been tossed aside, he had put a hand on the wall to push himself upright, leaving the bloody marker behind before he went on his way.

"Jesus, this is insane," Chase muttered.

"It's the game. We all knew we'd have to play it."

Chase glanced at Alex. "You think this is funny?"

"Isn't it?" Alex fired back. "A bunch of dead men arguing about morals. Surely you see the humour in it. Still, her loss is our gain. At least we have food now."

Chase took a step back, staring at Alex.

"Relax, not her," he said, nodding towards the dead velociraptor. "That. Plenty of meat on there that we can take with us. We can eat tonight."

"What about Ryder?"

Alex looked down the length of the canyon, then back the way they had come. "Not much we can do about him now. We just have to be ready. He's done the hard part now and has killed. The next time will be easier."

THREE

They camped there in the ravine, and as they sat around the crackling fire, eating the smoky dinosaur meat, they could almost believe in hope again. Chase was amazed at just how such a simple thing as having a full belly could boost morale. They had all been reluctant to eat the meat cut from the dinosaur, at least until they smelled it cooking, the fats hissing and dripping into the flames. Their stomachs quivered and growled, and even if the meat had been rancid, they would have still eaten it. As it was, it had been delicious. As relaxed as they were, they were also wary. They knew Ryder was out there, and could be watching them. Alex was sleeping, preparing for his night watch. Moses and Chase sat by the fire, staring into the orange glow, each of them contemplating both where they were and where they might be tomorrow. Moses had removed his boots and socks, getting some air to his feet. Chase could see why the older man was having so much trouble walking. The heel of his left foot wasn't too bad. It was pink and blistered but looked otherwise okay. His right, however, was shredded. The skin was bloody and raw all the way from the heel up the ankle. It was swollen and discoloured and was weeping clear pus from tiny ruptures. Although it had been masked by the cooking meats, now that they had eaten, the smell of his foot was impossible to ignore. It was bad, and they both knew it.

"Not looking good is it?"

Chase looked at Moses, who was watching him stare. Chase averted his gaze back to the glowing embers of the fire. "No, no it's not."

"Still can't get warm. Think I might be coming down with something."

Chase nodded. It was warm by the fire, hot even. But Moses was still shivering, his bottom lip trembling.

"How old are you?" Chase asked.

Moses didn't reply at first. He simply stared into the flames, watching them flicker and dance. "Fifty-seven."

Chase didn't say anything. He didn't want to push Moses into talking. To his surprise, the older man went on. "I wish I'd never got involved in all this. I knew I shouldn't keep pushing my luck."

"What do you mean?"

Moses sighed, and then nodded to his foot. "My body can't keep up anymore with what my brain wants to do. All part of growing old. Frustrating, you know? It only seems like five minutes ago that I was a young man with the world set out in front of me. Now look at me. A dying old man with a bad foot and maybe pneumonia to boot."

Chase glanced over his shoulder at Alex, making sure he wasn't listening. He was sleeping soundly, snoring lightly as he lay on his side. Chase turned back to Moses.

"Can I ask you something?"

Moses shrugged. Chase decided to read the expression as a yes.

"Why did you save me, back there in the cave?"

"I wasn't aware I had."

"You could have let me walk on right into the path of that dinosaur. It would have seen me, probably killed me. You didn't let it. You covered my mouth and stopped me from making a mistake. I'm curious as to why."

"Don't read too much into that. I didn't intend to do it. In fact, part of me regretted it. But a man can't completely ignore his instincts. Outside of here, I was a good man. I like to think I still am."

Now it was Chase's turn to be silent. He stared into the fire, unsure how to proceed. "Well, thanks. I appreciate it."

It wasn't perfect, but it was the best he could manage. Moses winced as he shifted position, moving his injured foot closer to the fire. "Besides," the old man said. "I didn't want to be left alone with that one."

He nodded towards Alex. "I don't walk at the back just because of my foot. I walk there because I like to see where he is at all times."

"You think he's dangerous?"

Moses shook his head. "No. Not in a physical way. He's clever, though. He's strong up here." He tapped his temple with a bony finger. "In a place like this, that can give someone an edge."

Chase half wanted to tell Moses his own thoughts about Alex but didn't want to risk being overheard. Instead, he stayed quiet, listening to the hiss and crackle of the fire and trying to ignore the old man's eyes on him.

"Anyway," Moses said eventually. "That's my burden to bear. Best I get some sleep before my watch begins."

"I'll shout if anything happens," Chase said, watching the old man as he struggled to his feet and then to where he had set up his small tent on the edge of the glow of the fire. Within ten minutes, the sound of Moses snoring joined that of Alex. Chase sat there alone, enjoying the quiet, staring at the stars and, like Moses, starting to think he had made a mistake.

A FIGHTING CHANCE
DAY FOUR
6:37AM

Ryder was tired, but the adrenaline still surged through him and spurred him on. He was filthy and still covered in Perrie's blood. He was still trying to convince himself that he was just playing the game, and this was exactly what had been expected of them when they came in, but he couldn't deny that he had made a conscious decision to kill her when she was at her most weak and vulnerable. As he ran, skirting around a herd of Ankylosaurs as they drank at a watering hole, armoured backs low, huge ball-ended tails swaying, spiny ridges lining each side of their mammoth frames. Their heads were small, legs short and wide. There would be no survival from them if they chose to attack. He tried to reason with himself that he had saved her. The velociraptors had attacked without warning. Much smaller than their TV and movie interpretations, they were quick, pack hunters, and had come at them from behind. He had managed to fight them off, killing one and wounding another before the group realised this was a fight they weren't going to win. Even though he had fought them off, they had still wounded Perrie, slicing her across the leg. He wasn't sure what they had cut, but there was a lot of blood. It was certainly beyond his ability to stitch. A voice in his head told him to stop lying to himself, that he never had any intention of saving her. It reminded him how tired he had grown of hearing her whine and moan as she finally understood that they weren't on a set, or in a studio with actors and a director dictating the action. He had been managing to ignore it, but if he was honest with himself (and, as he was alone, why not?) he had been thinking about either ditching her or ending her life for a while. He thought about how it would come across on television, and of the first time wondered if what he had done to her had been caught on camera. He was sure people would hate him, misjudge him for it.

He paused for breath on the opposite side of the watering hole, the herd of Ankylosaurs keeping a wary eye on him. He took his canteen, which was almost empty. He drank from it, sucking in air, then trudged in the soft mud on the edge and filling up the bottle, sure to keep an eye on the nine-meter-long beasts on the opposite side of the water.

As much as he had tried to convince himself that he didn't care what people thought, the truth was that he did. He hid it behind his tough, confident exterior, but he was no different to the others. He had his reasons for being there.

He looked into the water, which rippled and warped his reflection. If he looked hard enough, he could see his reason for being there.

His father.

The worst part wasn't that his father was a womaniser and an alcoholic, or a man who, no matter how hard Ryder tried, was never pleased; it wasn't even the fact that he was a strict disciplinarian who ruled his household with an iron fist, usually in the literal sense when the booze had been flowing. The worse was that when he looked at his reflection, he could see the bitter old man he had grown to hate staring back.

Not wanting to see it anymore, and wary of the attention of the dinosaurs across the water, he retreated into the trees, unable to shake his disturbing train of thought.

As bad as it was, the constant put downs, the sly comments about how he would never amount to anything, or how he would be the one to let the family name down (his two brothers were both serving in the army, a fact that Ryder's father used against him at every opportunity). Ryder saw The Island as a way to prove his father wrong. He had been brought up with the survival skills he thought he would need, and was sure that it would be enough to win. Of course, that was before he knew what they were facing, before the rules were changed and everything stopped being about trying to get one up on his father and about actual survival. He wasn't a killer. That wasn't his intention. It also wasn't something he thought he would be able to do until he had gone through with it. Even so, the thought of Perrie's terrified face as he stood over her, rock in hand, when she had realised that he wasn't there to help her, but to hurt her, the sound of the rock connecting with her skull, the hot, bitter taste of blood, the wet crunch as her skull softened, were things he knew he would never forget.

The ultimate irony of it all was that the one act that had repulsed him, the one thing he would have done anything to avoid having to do, was probably the thing his father was most proud of. Ryder could see him in his mind's eye, sitting in the armchair in the den, TV turned up way too loud due to his hearing not being so good anymore. He would have a beer in his hand, a Miller or a Bud, and would be perched on the edge of his seat, dirty burgundy baseball cap pushed back on his head, smiling at his son's actions. Proud at last that little Ryder had finally grown a set of balls.

It was because of this particularly grim train of thought that he lost concentration, and snagged his foot on a tree root as he tried to step over it. His heart lurched as he pinwheeled, desperately trying to right his balance as he pitched forward, losing the brief battle against gravity. He fell, tumbling and rolling down the steep embankment, grunting as stones dug into him, a loose rooster tail of dust and leaves accompanying him as he fell. Even though it was a sudden incident, he was still aware enough to remember his survival training.

Tuck the elbows, protect the head. Stay loose and don't try to fight the fall.

It seemed like it lasted forever. His world finally came to a stop, leaving him face down, legs angled back up the hill the way he had come. He lay there for a moment, quiet and letting the loose leaves and stones settle around him.

Silence.

He assessed his body, knowing that a broken leg or foot would spell disaster. He waited, forcing himself to be thorough. He moved his fingers and arms, then his ankles and knees. Finally, he sat up. It was then, when he took in his surroundings, that he realised that there were more secrets to The Island than just the dinosaurs. He stared, unable to comprehend what he was seeing. Had he stayed on the trail, he would have walked straight past it, as this was something not meant for the eyes of the contestants. It was a game changer.

He stood and brushed himself off, then turned and scrambled back up the hill, wanting to get as far away from what he had seen as possible.

TWO

The gorge opened up into a large open valley, which all circumstances aside, was stunning. It was still early, and a light morning mist hovered over the ground. The sun, just rising, was a deep, fiery red, and had just begun to illuminate their world. The ground sloped away into a natural bowl of sorts. The water source which had been their constant companion ended here in a large watering hole. Around its edges, a herd of large dinosaurs grazed beyond them, more forest awaited, the trees sloping uphill. On the horizon, barely visible, was the south wall.

"Those things are big," Moses said, still catching his breath. "They look dangerous."

"Ankylosaurs," Alex said, cupping his hands to see against the rising sun.

"They dangerous?"

"You don't want to get hit by one of those tails, put it that way. Imagine a big, angry, carnivorous rhino and you'll be somewhere close. Best we avoid them if we can."

"We need water," Chase said. "In this heat, hydration is important."

"I ain't going down there," Moses grunted.

"If we give them a wide berth, we should be okay." Alex tore his eyes away from the grazing dinosaurs and looked at Moses. "What's the matter, old man? You starting to lose your nerve?"

Moses met his stare. "There's no shame in being scared."

"Well, I'm not filling that canteen for you. You either come with us and stock up on water, or you don't. Just don't be asking me to share later."

Moses grunted but said nothing. He was still shivering and was covered with sweat.

"Alright, let's do it. Slow and quiet," Chase said, leading the way down the scrub bank. Alex fell in behind him, Moses a reluctant rear guard.

What had seemed like a good idea from the top of the hill seemed borderline insane as the approached the water hole. The Ankylosaurs herd were huge and no less agitated. They positioned their three-ton frames to face the approaching trio, tails swishing from side to side.

Chase stopped moving around twenty feet from the water. He couldn't go on. He knew he was once again staring death right in the face. He looked at the creatures, again riding the line between terror and wonder. They were beautiful, almost regal. He was once again struck by the fact that these were real living breathing things. He could see the way their muscles bunched as they dipped their heads to drink. He could see how they blinked, how they breathed. How flies landed on their thick bodies for respite. He could see their tails, the huge, bulky, ball-end of them more than capable of shattering ribs, breaking bones, pulverising flesh. All were things which would snuff them out in an instant. He flicked his eyes to the water, the precious water which they needed.

"What's the hold up?" Alex said, irritated and curious as to why they had stopped.

"What if they attack us?"

"If we hurry up and get out of here, they won't. Come on, we're wasting time."

It was another chink in the armour of Alex, another glimpse into the fear that bubbled and morphed just beneath the calm exterior mask he wore.

"Nobody's stopping you. Be my guest."

There was no expectation that he would do it, Chase said it because he was hoping to frighten Alex off. To his surprise, Alex pushed past him, walked to the water's edge and started to fill his water bottle. Feeling stupid, Chase followed, keeping a wary eye on the giant creatures less than twenty feet away. Moses hung back, still shivering and grimacing. He had no interest in approaching the water and kept glancing towards the relative safety of the trees.

Chase filled his bottle, unaware that he was in the exact same spot Ryder had been just a couple of hours earlier. He thought they might just get away with it and avoid a confrontation. He turned to Alex, to tell him that he thought they had all been riding their luck and froze. Alex was grinning, a wide, white wedge of a smile. In his left hand was his full water bottle; in his right, a large palm sized rock.

"Don't," Chase grunted, just as Alex threw it overarm at the nearest Ankylosaurs, the rock glancing off its armoured back. Chase drew breath as the ground started to rumble, and the Ankylosaurs charged in retaliation.

Chase was frozen, unable to move as the lumbering animal charged with more speed than he expected. He knew it was over, his time had come. He was about to die.

He was tackled to the ground; Moses crashing into him and knocking him into the soft mud as the huge dinosaur charged through the water and straight through where just seconds earlier Chase had been standing. Both he had Moses started to get up, just as the ankylosaurus half turned and swung its huge tail towards them. They both flattened, pushing themselves into the dirt as the huge tail swung inches over their heads.

"Come on, go now," Moses screamed in his ear. Chase scrambled to his feet, pulling Moses with him, but the dinosaur wasn't to be denied. It lurched towards them, driving them back towards the rest of their herd, who were pacing on the opposite side of the water, spreading out to cut off any escape.

"Can you run?" Chase screamed, wiping wet dirt from his face.

Moses nodded. The two men ran into the shallow water, skirting away from the agitated dinosaur. Ahead, just about at the tree line, Alex waited, watching them from a distance. The ankylosaurs lurched after them, thundering into the water in pursuit. Chase knew he could escape on his own, but Moses was slow, his ravaged feet unable to carry him at any sort of speed that would help them escape. There was no forethought, he simply acted on his human instincts. He shoved Moses away from him.

"Get to the trees," he screamed, then turned and charged towards the ankylosaurs. There was no time to think about how crazy the situation was. He simply acted. Game or no game, Moses had saved his life twice now, and he wasn't about to go on without at least trying to repay the favour. He charged at the ankylosaurus, meeting it head on, then at the last second changing direction, relying on his smaller size and speed. The ankylosaurus let out a frustrated grunt, and in a single fluid motion swung its lethal tail towards Chase.

He dived, slamming hard into the ground, knocking the wind out of himself as the tail swung over his head, and then he was up, sprinting towards the tree line. Moses had just reached them, Alex standing beside him. The ankylosaurus gave chase for a few seconds, earth shaking with each footfall, then gave up, realising that it could never keep up. It retreated back to the rest of the herd. Chase slowed to a jog, heart thundering, and adrenaline making him aware of everything going on around him. He saw Moses, hunched over, hands on knees, coughing and spluttering. He saw Alex, still grinning, still amused. Chase didn't slow or hesitate. He threw a punch. It was sloppy, but it hit the target. Alex went down, clutching his nose.

"You tried to kill us," Chase grunted as Moses leapt in to stop him from doing any more damage.

Alex sat on the floor, holding his nose, blood gushing out and down his clothing. "I didn't mean to, it was supposed to be a joke."

"A joke? You think this is funny?"

"I didn't think they would charge. I thought it might spook you."

He tried to get up, but Moses shook his head. "I'd stay down there unless you wanna be knocked on your ass again."

Alex took the warning and stayed where he was, gingerly touching his bloody nose. "I was right there too. You think I wanted to put myself at risk?"

"You were well clear before they attacked, you made sure of that," Chase grunted, pulling away from Moses and walking away, trying to calm himself down.

"I'm sorry, I don't know why I did that. I made a mistake, okay?" Alex said, spitting blood onto the dirt between his feet then scrambling up. "I was just trying to lighten the mood."

"By putting our lives at risk? Nobody does that, nobody sane would do that."

"Whatever," Alex said pushing past them and into the trees. "Think what you want."

Moses looked Chase up and down. Both of them were covered in mud. "You alright?"

"I'm fine," Chase grunted. "That makes us even." He followed Alex into the trees, Moses falling in behind him.

THREE

The atmosphere was tense as they delved deeper into the trees. Alex had forged on ahead, walking with the familiar sloped, shouldered head bobbing motion. Chase was thirty feet further back, still angry and trying to decide what to make of Alex. It seemed like an attempt to have him and Moses die so that he could go on. Such a thing shouldn't have bothered him, as it was part of the game and why they were all there. They walked in line, the punishing heat of the day not making their progress any smoother. Chase was aware that he had lost weight. The rations had long since gone and they had eaten only once in what was now their fourth day. His clothes had started to feel loose, something which didn't surprise him. The calories they were burning were far outweighing their intake. He suspected they might be nearing the point where the alliance they had formed would have to end. Moses looked to be fading fast; his feet were a mess, his body breaking down with each mile. He reminded himself that Ryder was still out there somewhere, maybe watching from the trees. He didn't like that idea. Ryder was dangerous and had already done what none of them had so far managed to find the guts to.

He had killed, and done so in a brutal fashion. Chase wondered if it would be easy. He thought about how Moses had saved his life twice now, and he wasn't sure if he could go through with ending his life when the time came.

"Hey, come take a look at this." Alex was out of sight, somewhere ahead in the curving, dense tangle of trees. Chase broke into a jog, weaving around the dense undergrowth towards where Alex had headed. He squinted as the dim light of the canopy exploded into sunlight.

The jungle had opened onto a large, green valley. Birds, disturbed by Chase's sudden presence, took flight, squawking as they made their leave. Alex was standing there, hands planted on hips, breathing heavily from the exertion of the walk. Chase stood beside him, both of them some way ahead of Moses who was still toiling up the hill.

Chase had no need to ask what Alex had seen. It was plain enough to them both.

The truck had been abandoned, driver and passenger doors open. Dirt and dry leaves covered the jeep, its wheels half buried in the dirt. Dry smudges of blood spattered the bodywork on the outside, the rear doors mangled and pushed closed. Alex and Chase shared a glance as Moses hobbled to join them. The three of the stood silent on the edge of the valley, staring at the truck as if it were some kind of magician's illusion.

"Looks like it's been here a while," Alex muttered.

Chase glanced at him, his nose crusted with blood, an ugly cut in his top lip. His punch had landed well. Even so, he still looked fresh and full of energy and vitality. Chase felt a pang of envy.

"Why would there be a truck here. Why would nobody recover it?" Chase said, glancing around.

"Maybe it was too dangerous to come out here for it," Moses said around his permanent grimace. All three of them looked around. They seemed to be in no immediate danger. The truck looked to have been abandoned. The tree line ahead of them looked clear.

"Look at the long grass around it," Chase said. "It's been flattened. Someone was here recently."

"Ryder?" Alex said.

Chase gave the merest of nods.

"We should check it out. See if there's anything that can help us."

"Just wait a second," Chase said, putting a hand on Alex's shoulder.

He studied the grass, the way it had been flattened around the truck. That greasy, uneasy feeling rolled in his gut. "Look at the grass around the truck. Whatever he did, he did in a hurry."

"So?" Alex said.

"So, the trail doesn't lead anywhere. It doesn't go off in any direction."

"You think he's still here?" Alex whispered.

Chase nodded to the mangled rear doors of the truck. They were closed, hiding whatever lay in the rear. "Maybe he heard you coming and was searching it and had nowhere else to go. Maybe he's hiding in there."

"Shit, shit, shit. What do we do?"

There was a moment of absolute silence. They stood and stared at the truck, light, warm breeze ruffling their hair. It was Moses who spoke next, and Chase saw a glimpse of the man he said he used to be some years earlier.

"We have to end him." As he said it, he pulled the hunting knife from the sheath on his belt. He looked comfortable with it, and like with Alex, Chase saw another man beneath the mask Moses was wearing. One which maybe wasn't as run down and close to the end as he first thought.

"He's dangerous," Chase whispered. "He's probably seen us now, he'll be ready."

"I agree with the old man," Alex said, taking out his knife. "We need to put an end to him now. Besides, we can use that truck. Maybe we don't have to spend as much time on foot."

Chase glanced over at Alex, wondering where the timid, shy kid who had been on the boat coming in had gone. He stood now, knife in hand, brow furrowed. He didn't look afraid, which Chase didn't understand. After all, he was afraid. It stood to reason that Alex should be too. "Alright," he said, joining them in taking out his knife. It felt heavy and cumbersome and he wondered why the others seemed much more comfortable holding them. "We outnumber him, which is good. Let's see if we can get him to come out on his own before we charge in there and end up stabbing each other in the excitement, okay?"

Two nods. Both Moses and Alex were psyching themselves up for the confrontation. Chase just felt sick. The trio approached the rear of the truck, stopping ten feet away from it. There was no sense of any motion or movement. The small gap where the mangled door hung open a few inches was a black void betraying none of its secrets.

"Alright," Chase whispered. "I'm going to call out to him. See if we can get him out of there. Just be ready."

Two more nods. Alex and Moses were ready, the tension already unbearable.

"Ryder, we know you're in there. Just come out."

His voice rolled across the valley, swallowed up by the environment. They waited, listening. No movement, no response.

"Come on, Ryder. Just come out of there. We want the truck. We won't hurt you. We're all armed."

He felt like an idiot saying it, wondering if he sounded at least a little bit convincing. Still no movement, no response.

"What now?" Moses whispered.

"We go take a look. No choice," Chase replied, unable to shake the sick feeling in his stomach.

"We should make use of our numbers advantage," Alex said. He was still determined, knife swaying as he held it at his side. "One each of us should grab one of the rear doors, the other be ready to see what's inside. Play the numbers."

"That sounds good unless you're not one of the door guys. I take it you don't want to be the one waiting to face him in the back?" Chase grunted.

Alex sighed. "Look, I know you're still pissed at me. I'm not as weak as you think I am. You and the old man get a door each. I'll be ready at the back."

A glance towards Moses said he was as surprised as Chase was at this latest turn of events. He wasn't about to argue, though, and hoped this was a sign of the mental fatigue starting to take the same toll on Alex as it was him.

"Alright," Chase said, the nauseous feeling seeming to hang in his throat. "Let's do this."

They approached the rear of the van, fanning out. Moses towards the door which was intact, Chase towards the mangled one which was rocking against the frame. Alex approached centrally, knife held out in front of him. Chase couldn't figure out why he wasn't scared. Even Moses, a man who had seen more death in his life than perhaps any of them was showing signs of fear as he hobbled towards the rear door of the truck. They took their positions, then waited. Chase strained to listen, to get any sense of movement. He glanced at Moses directly opposite him. The old man nodded, hand on the door handle ready to open it. Alex next, defiant and ready, feet parted, knife held up in front of his bloody face. A nod said that he too was ready. Chase reached out to the mangled door, grasping the twisted remains of the handle. He mouthed his silent countdown to the others.

One...

Two...

On three, both he and Moses pulled the rear doors open, as Alex planted his feet, ready for whatever was inside.

Silence.

No movement, just the smell. Moses threw up, Chase and Alex just stared. There was no sign of Ryder in the back of the truck. Nobody sane would have climbed in there with the mess that was left. There were three bodies, dried up and partially skeletal remains which were putrid and stinking. An army of flies, disturbed by the doors opening, took flight, buzzing around the corpses, which were swarmed with maggots. The bodies had been there for some time. One was just an upper torso, the legs and innards missing, one arm twisted and mangled into shapes no human was ever meant to make. He was dressed in army fatigues, the bloated body pushing against the material. Something had eaten the rest of him.

The other corpse was complete apart from having no legs. The white shafts of bone terminated below the knees. They had been chewed on. The soldiers bloated hand still held the gun he had used to kill himself with, the remains of his head thrown back, mouth agape, a halo of dried blood and brain matter from the exit wound splattered against the rear wall of the truck.

"Holy Mary mother of god," Moses muttered.

The three of them stared, unable to take their eyes from the gruesome scene in front of them. It was almost artistic.

"Looks like they were attacked," Alex said. "See those on the floor? The same cameras they have up in the trees. They must have been rigging this area up when…"

There was no need to finish the sentence. They all knew. The mangled door, the chewed up remains. Something had found them and caught them unaware.

"Where are the rest of them? The driver? There were more people in here," Moses said.

They looked at the scattered equipment littering the floor of the truck.

"Maybe whatever attacked was too full to finish these two. That guy with the gun knows there's no hope, managed to pull the doors closed, drags himself over there and offs himself," Alex said. He was so cold, so emotionless with his words.

"So where did Ryder go?" Moses asked.

"He was definitely here. This grass was flattened recently. Maybe he was going to take the van and something spooked him," Chase replied, walking around towards the driver's side.

"No, he didn't want the truck. Look at the tyres," Alex said, crouching by the rearmost wheel. Chase and Moses joined him. There was a long cut in the tyre. From a distance, Chase had thought the wheels were buried in the soft earth. He could see now that it was just the illusion of the tyres being flat.

"Shit," he grunted, standing and going to the front of the vehicle and crouching by the front wheels. "He did these ones too. Seems he didn't want us driving anywhere."

"Why?" Moses said.

"Because he wants to hunt us down on foot. It's obvious."

As was becoming the norm, Alex was cold and emotionless as he said it. Chase wondered if he was finally starting to break.

"Whatever he intended, he missed a trick," Chase said, standing up as his knees groaned in protest. "He must have seen the truck, cut the tyres, had a quick glance in the back then moved on. Probably flattened the grass so we'd stop and take a look. The thing he missed is the back. There is at least one weapon in there. Probably more. As well as other things we might be able to use."

"You don't think that if he moved on, we should too? He was the survival expert after all."

Chase considered it, but couldn't stop thinking about the handgun grasped by the dead man.

"I think we should at least look. See what we might be able to use."

"I don't like it here," Moses said, glancing towards the tree line where they had just come from. "It feels…wrong."

"I agree, but this could be an opportunity we might not get again. Remember before we left? Glebe said we need to take advantage of any scenario that presents itself." Chase was trying to be diplomatic, but the simple truth of it was that he wanted the gun. He was pretty sure he couldn't kill a man with his bare hands or by something as intimate as stabbing, but pointing a gun at someone and shooting them was another matter entirely.

"No," Alex said, stepping between Chase and the rear of the truck. "I don't think I'm comfortable with that."

"With what?"

"With you having a gun. This is still a game. Remember why we're all here. If you have that, then you have a huge advantage."

"I'm taking it," Chase said, stepping towards the back of the truck. Moses stepped in, standing beside Alex.

"He's right," the older man said. He still held his knife, forearm muscles bunching. "No one should have the gun. It's too tempting."

"So you just want to leave it here? We're trying to survive for god's sake."

"You really think this is a team effort, don't you?" Alex said, the grin transforming into a wince as his damaged lip protested the gesture. "You do know we're not friends, not colleagues or a team. This is a game. The end result being that all but one of us has to die."

"We made an agreement to stick together."

"On an even playing field. If you get a gun, that changes the odds." Alex also now had his hand on the top of his knife. Chase flicked his eyes to it, then back at Moses and Alex.

"That gun could save our lives."

"It could end it too," Moses said. "I don't want to have to put a knife in your back while you sleep. I'd drop this if I were you."

Chase shook his head. "This is crazy. Can you hear what you're saying?"

"If this were a team game, I'd agree with you," Alex said. "But the old man is right. We either go on with a level playing field, or we can make sure you don't get it here and now and then he and I go on towards the end."

"You're threatening to kill me?" Chase said, taking a step back.

"Nobody said that," Alex fired back.

"But you would. I get it. Fine, leave the fucking gun where it is. Let's give Ryder every chance to pick us off on at a time from wherever the hell he's hiding. If not him, one of the animals, the dinosaurs that are, unless you've missed it, thriving on The Island and could kill us at any time."

They didn't give him any response. They simply stood there, guarding the back of the truck from him. The point was made. If he tried to get the gun, they would kill him. "Fine. Let's go, but together. I don't want either of you two coming back to get it later."

"No, that's not going to happen. By the time we camp tonight, we will be miles away from here. No way any of us is coming back later and wasting another day. Besides, have you seen that sky? Looks like rain."

Chase glanced in the direction they were going. Unlike the blue skies which they were currently under, ugly, tropical thunderheads were starting to build in the distance. It was likely they would see rain by the end of the day.

"Right, in that case, we better go," Chase grunted.

They walked in line, away from the truck and the handgun and towards the growing storm and whatever else waited for them ahead. As much as he was tempted, Chase didn't look back at the truck. He knew the others were watching him now and had begun to understand that unless he started to play the game, he was likely to die.

FOUR

The rain came just after three in the afternoon. The heat of the day had started to dissipate, a fresh breeze bringing some much-needed respite to their exhausted bodies. Their progress had been good. They had travelled around twelve miles and were now in an area of open savannah. In the distance, a herd of triceratops were grazing in the long yellow grasses, the three-horned beasts far enough away for the group to feel safe. The tension amongst them had been almost unbearable. They hadn't spoken to each other for much of the journey, and when they did it was in either grunts or one word answers. As they had moved south, they had seen an increasing number of dinosaur species, but unsurprisingly, none that had paid them much attention. They seemed oblivious to their presence for the most part, which if anything made them more uneasy. It was when they were midway across the savannah plain, their shadows long since gone as the cloud cover had rolled in and darkened the day, that the rains arrived. It was akin to somebody switching on a warm shower. There had been at first a few large single drops, each leaving a stain the size of a coin on the arid ground, then it arrived, a deluge of biblical proportions. They did the best they could to keep themselves dry, but it was no good. The rain drove don with a furious urgency as dull rumbles of thunder heralded the coming storm.

Chase glanced over his shoulder. Moses was falling back again, limping along as fast as he could. He had found a stick from somewhere which he was using as a walking stick. He had produced an oversized hat from somewhere, which looked almost comical, the brim waterlogged and sagging around his ears.

Ahead of Chase, Alex had pulled some of his waterproof tent material out of his backpack and fashioned a poncho of sorts. It was a genius idea which he copied without apology, managing to keep his upper body, for the most part, dry. The dusty ground at their feet became a thick, sludgy mud which coated their boots and made their progress both slow and hard. Their old friend fatigue had started to make his presence known, and each heavy, mud-laden step seemed to take more and more of a toll.

Another hour passed, and the rain which had initially been a welcome and pleasurable respite from the heat had turned cold. Chase picked up his pace to catch up to Alex, falling in beside him. They walked in tandem for a while, neither speaking to the other.

"What is it, Riley?"

"We'll need to stop soon. It's getting dark."

"I'm aware of that." He turned and smiled, filling Chase with more of that unease which seemed to be ever present. He didn't seem particularly tired or concerned with the situation. Chase got the impression that he was enjoying every second of it. "Good luck lighting a fire in this. All the water in the world is being dumped on us at once, or so it seems."

"We can't stay out in this. We need to get dry."

"I take it you have a suggestion?"

Chase nodded the way they were going. The terrain changed again, the flat savannah transforming into a craggy, hilly landscape.

"We might find a cave up there. Somewhere we can hole up and make a fire."

"Maybe. But again, I don't know what you intend to burn. Everything is pretty wet in case you didn't notice."

"We'll also need food… I–"

Alex stopped and turned to Chase. "You don't get it, do you?"

"What?"

"All this teamwork and survival stuff. Pretty soon it's going to have to stop. Soon it's going to come down to why we came here."

"I know that," Chase grunted.

"Then please, for the love of god, stop trying to be my friend. Stop trying to lead this little expedition. It's going to be hard enough for you to do what you have to as it is without attaching yourself to me or the old man."

"What do you mean?"

"You're not as smart as you think you are, Riley. I've got you all figured out. I know as well as you do that when the time comes, you won't have the guts to kill someone. You came here thinking you could do it, but when it comes down to it, you're too nice. Too much like the rest of society. You play by the rules. I came here thinking I was the only one who understood what it would take to win this. I was wrong about that because Ryder seems to get it too. But you…" He shook his head. "You don't see it. It's going to hit you hard when the time comes and it's down to either you or someone else. Something tells me you'll roll over and die just like the old man back there. But then again, I was wrong about Ryder, so who knows. Just stop trying to be the voice of reason. This isn't your show. This isn't your team and you don't have any sway or influence over me. We'll stop when there is a place to stop. If we can find food, we'll eat. If not, we won't. If we can light a fire, we'll be warm. If not, we'll be cold and maybe the old man will die. Just leave me alone, Riley. I'm done with you."

Alex walked away, leaving Chase standing there in shock and unsure how to react. Eventually, he started to walk again, hands thrust in his pockets against the cold and trying to ignore how true Alex's words had been.

FIVE

The hilly area was dangerous. In dry conditions, it would have been no more difficult than any other terrain they had encountered.

With the deluge, it had become a mud bath of sorts. They slipped and scrambled as they climbed higher, all the time the storm raged, the combination of driving rain and thunder proving just how potent a force Mother Nature was and how insignificant they were in the bigger picture. As they climbed higher, the ground underfoot became more solid, the loose mud giving way to solid rock. They found what they were looking for around two-thirds of the way up the hill. It wasn't a cave, the rock didn't cut back deeply enough. Instead, they saw a jutting slab of rock with a deep recessed hollow underneath. It was almost perfect. Sheltered from the elements and dry, it also gave a spectacular view of the valley they had just crossed, which stretched away into the distance.

They were too wet and exhausted to do anything at first but rest, sitting in a line with their backs to the wall, watching the fury of the rain as it continued to drive down. It was so intense it was almost like they were sitting under a waterfall.

Alex had taken off his backpack and was removing some things from it. Chase watched, their conversation still fresh in his mind. Alex had branches in the bottom of his bag, along with dry grasses and a slab of the dinosaur meat from the previous day's meal. He glanced over at Chase, flashing a warm smile.

"Good job one of us prepared for the rain. You want to give me a hand with this? The old man looks in a bad way."

It was as if their argument had never happened. For a moment, Chase considered questioning it, but then he glanced at Moses and saw that Alex was right. He had deteriorated further. His breathing was a wet wheeze, and he trembled all over, his sodden clothes sticking to his body. His eyes were glassy and staring into the distance, not focused on anything other than the death he knew was on its way. Either hypothermia or pneumonia, whichever it was, Moses didn't look like he would last much longer.

Chase decided it was better to just work and keep quiet, so he helped Alex to construct the fire, his eyes drifting every few seconds towards the dinosaur meat. He was ravenous.

"It always pays to keep some dry wood and tinder in the bottom of your bag," Alex said, smiling again. "I remember from this TV show I used to watch about this guy who puts himself in the wilderness and has to survive. He was named after a bear. English guy. He was good."

Chase nodded and said nothing, still confused about the sudden shift in personality.

"We'll get this lit, warm this place up. It's been a long day."

They managed to get the fire lit. Chase never ceased to be surprised about how something so simple could boost morale so completely. The cold seemed to have seeped through to the bone. He sat in front of the fire, letting its warmth radiate through him. Alex sat opposite, turning the meat which sizzled as it cooked. He had a wistful, half-smile on his face. He looked content.

Even with the warmth from the fire, Moses was getting worse. He lay on his side, shivering by the fire, mumbling semi-incoherently. Chase wondered if Alex could smell it too. It was the smell of pending death.

"This reminds me of when I was a boy," Alex said, his voice echoing around the small space. "My father used to take me camping. We'd go out into the woods in Oregon and hunt deer. If we caught one, we'd cook it over a fire just like this."

Chase didn't say anything. He watched the younger man across the flames as the rain continued to pummel the earth. Alex went on.

"One day, we caught this big buck. I shot it, but I was young, and it wasn't a clean kill. We found it on its side in the snow. It's a strange sight you know, that contrast of red on white. The blood was thawing the snow around the deer, still warm, still hot, you know? Anyway, it was lying there on its side, just panting and waiting to die. It had this look in its eyes, a look that said it didn't understand what was happening to it. I pointed the gun at it, intending to finish it off, but I couldn't do it. I just stood there and watched as its breathing got more and more shallow and eventually stopped."

"Did you still eat it?" Chase asked.

"Of course. No point killing it otherwise. It was the best venison I've ever tasted. I've often wondered if the fact that it was afraid at the end made it taste better. You ever heard that? How the way an animal is treated in life can change the way the meat tastes?"

"No, I can't say I have," Chase muttered.

"There is a brand of beef where the farmers massage the cows every day until they are taken to the slaughterhouse. Apparently, it makes the meat taste nicer. I often wondered if the way something feels before it dies has the same effect."

"I can't say I've ever thought about it," Chase muttered.

Alex shrugged. "Just one of those weird memories I guess."

He removed the meat from the makeshift skewer and cut it into three pieces. "This is the last of it. We'll need to get more if we want to eat tomorrow. Pass me your knife."

Chase handed the weapon over the fire, aware that he had just unarmed himself in front of a rival. Alex, however, didn't seem to realise. He skewered the dinosaur meat onto the knife and handed it back to Chase. He broke the skewer stick in half and stabbed it through the other piece of meat, and also passed it over to Chase. "For the old man," he said.

Chase shuffled over to Moses where he lay on his side.

"Penny, is that you?" he mumbled, eyes closed.

"No, it's me. It's Chase. I brought you some food."

The old man blinked, and looked at it, then shook his head. "Give it to the grandkids. I'm not hungry."

"You have to eat, Moses. You need to keep your strength up."

"There's money in my wallet if they want an ice cream. The van will be here soon."

Chase glanced over his shoulder at Alex. He was watching, an indifferent look on his face as he ate.

"Please, try to eat something," Chase said again, putting a hand on the old man's shoulder. He snapped awake, still in a place far away from reality. "Damn you, why can't you just leave me alone? You said this was the last time. You said I wouldn't have to do this again. I just want to retire. Please, just let me retire."

"It's okay, Moses. You try to get some sleep. You can eat later, okay?"

The old man grumbled and closed his eyes. He was still trembling and mumbling. Chase shuffled back to the fire and started to eat. Suddenly, it didn't taste so good.

"It won't be long now," Alex said.

"What won't?"

Alex nodded towards Moses. "Now the hallucinations have started, it's only going to be a matter of time. We should leave him here."

Chase didn't say anything. He took another bite of his meat, waiting for Alex to elaborate.

"He might have a day or two left tops before he dies. We could do it humanely. Finish him in his sleep. We would be doing him a favour."

Still Chase said nothing. He took another bite of the meat which was suddenly bland. There was something sinister about him. Chase couldn't decide if it was the lighting or the way his tone was so flat and conversational. Even the rain had stopped, bringing an eerie silence to the hollow.

"Besides," Alex went on, "this is the last of the meat. Remember how we were told to make the most of any situation that presented us? This could help us."

Chase paused, the dinosaur meat halfway towards his mouth. He was no longer hungry. He tried to figure out some way of convincing himself he had misheard or misinterpreted, but there was no denying it. Alex was talking about cannibalism.

"You think you could do that? Eat another human's flesh?" Chase felt detached from himself as he asked. It almost felt like it was someone else in charge of his body.

"I wouldn't want to," Alex said, correcting himself. "I'm talking about last resort survival. Look at it in a purely black and white way. He's dying anyway. Plus we need food to keep our strength up. Unless you feel like hunting down some dinosaurs, or have some other suggestion, I don't see what choice we have. Plus it will lower the odds."

"One in three," Chase muttered.

"Exactly. One in three. Surely it's better than letting him suffer. I think that's why the story of that buck came back to me. The old man is like that deer. He's just lying there, already dying. It's now down to if we intend to stand here and watch him die or do the right thing and put him out of his misery."

Chase hated himself for it, but Alex's plan seemed viable. Not so much from the humane perspective, but the odds.

One in three.

Much better than one in four, no matter how he tried to look at it. Much better odds of being able to help his daughter.

"I need some time with this," he said.

"I get that. It's a big decision."

Chase stood, and stretched, his head almost touching the roof of the rock. "I need to go take a leak. Don't do anything until I get back," he said.

"No, of course," Alex said.

Chase ducked out of the cave, trudging away out of site and towards a scrub of trees. As he urinated, he looked down over the valley. Night was drawing in, and although there was a half moon, it was shrouded in cloud. He felt nauseous at the thought of what he was about to agree to, but also knew that sooner or later it would have to be done. It was all part of the game. He turned to head back to the cave, when a dirt-smeared hand grabbed him and pulled him off his feet, dragging him back into the scrub of trees. Chase kicked and squirmed until the point of the knife was touched to his throat. He flicked his eyes to the man who had taken him. Ryder was covered in a thick layer of mud. He had deliberately covered himself to help him remain invisible. His eyes were wild and white, glaring at Chase as he pushed the blade closer to his throat.

"Make a noise and I'll cut you," he whispered in Chase's ear.

Chase stopped struggling.

"Good. Now come with me. Don't fight," Ryder said. Chase did as he was told, allowing Ryder to drag him further away from the cave and into the darkness.

THE GAME CHANGES
DAY FOUR
8:29PM

"Alright, I'm going to uncover your mouth. Just relax, alright?" Ryder whispered.

Chase nodded. Ryder released his grip. Chase stepped away, glaring at Ryder and wondering what was about to happen.

"Take those cameras off. All of them."

Chase did as he was told, unhooking the camera from his shoulder and handing it to Ryder. He dropped it to the floor and stamped on it, then tossed it down into the ravine. Chase saw that Ryder had at some point dumped all his own recording equipment.

"You can take that look off your face; I'm not here to hurt you."

Chase looked at him, covered in mud, dirt and leaves stuck to his skin. It was no surprise they hadn't seen him. They could have walked right past him and he would have been invisible.

"What do you want with me?"

"Just shut up and look. Down there." Ryder pointed through the gap in the trees. Below them were the valley and the hilly terrain they had just negotiated. Night had rolled in, and the entire plain was bathed in pale moonlight.

"I don't see anything. What the hell am I supposed to be looking for?"

Ryder pointed. "Watch there. That rocky outcrop."

Chase watched and was about to tell Ryder he still couldn't see anything when something moved. Not a dinosaur, or a creature, but a person. It was too dark, and they were too far away to see any details, but Chase clearly saw the figure scramble from behind one rock outcrop to another, then crouch.

"What the hell? Who is that?" Chase said. Ryder crouched, pulling Chase to the floor with him. His eyes were wild and showing too much white as he spoke.

"This game isn't what we think it is."

"What do you mean?"

"It's all different, so different."

"You're not making any sense."

"We got it all wrong. This isn't about the dinosaurs. They're incidental. This is about man hunting man." He pointed at the tiny figure down by the rocky outcrop. "We're part of something bigger. He's been following you for the last two days."

"Who is it?" Chase asked.

"Our friend Lomar."

Chase glanced at Ryder. He was still staring down into the valley. "You really think the CEO of a multi-billion dollar company is running around out here?"

"I know he is. I've seen him. I was twenty feet away from where he was camped."

"This is stupid. You know how this is all recorded in real time? I don't think it would impress Lomar's investors if they saw him running around out here in the dark."

Ryder grinned. For a moment, white eyes and white teeth shone through the dark. "Don't be so naive. You know how easily stuff can be faked, doctored. I'll tell you what I think. I think they're showing us exactly what they want us to see."

"Sounds like you're clutching at straws," Chase grumbled, even though part of him believed what Ryder was saying.

"I saw something else. Down in the forest there, I was heading this way and I lost my footing, fell down this fucking hill, knocked myself around pretty badly. There were no tree cameras down there, and with good reason."

"What did you see?"

"There was a pit dug into the ground. It was full of bodies, man. People. Must have been a hundred of them."

"Impossible. We're the first ones to do this," Chase said.

"No, that's what I'm trying to tell you. We're not. We're just the first ones that have been put here in the public eye. Those bodies... They had been executed. They hadn't been attacked by the dinosaurs, they had bullet wounds. They'd been shot."

"Shot? By who?"

"Fucking Lomar," Ryder hissed. "This is his own personal playground."

"Why would he? He's a high-profile man. A celebrity almost."

"He's a fucking killer," Ryder said, eyes still wide.

"I could say the same thing about you."

Ryder lowered his eyes and cleared this throat. "Yeah, believe me, I regret that. But I didn't know. That was when I still thought we were playing the game. If I could go back... God, I would do it in a heartbeat."

"I just don't see the connection. Why would there be bodies out here?"

"Think about it. Rich people need to get their kicks somewhere, right? He doesn't need money; he can buy anything he wants. My theory is that he sets people loose on The Island, gives them a head start, then goes in and hunts them down."

"I don't know, it sounds implausible," Chase said, although Ryder was making him consider the idea.

"Remember when we were at his house? What did he have all over the walls?"

"Hunting trophies," Chase muttered. He remembered it well. His stomach tightened as he started to see the pieces fall into place.

"Exactly," Ryder said. "Hunting trophies. Is it too far a stretch to think he's got tired of hunting animals and wants a bigger challenge?"

"But the bodies, why leave them here? Anyone could find them."

"How?" Ryder said, flashing that grin again. "This place is off limits. Plus it's full of fucking dinosaurs. Nobody is going to find those bodies that will live to tell anyone about it."

"Doesn't bode well for us," Chase muttered.

"Yeah, why do you think I ditched the cameras? I also took the tree cams down near here so we could talk without them hearing."

"So what do we do now?"

"Now we get back to that camp of yours and move on. I could see your fire lighting you up like a beacon. You can bet Lomar can too."

"It's not safe to travel at night. We were told before we came out here," Chase said.

"Forget everything they told you. It's too dangerous to stay. We keep moving. It's the only way to give ourselves the advantage."

He didn't wait for a response. He made his way back towards the way they had come, Chase following behind and still trying to come to terms with the information he had just been given. Seeing his family again seemed like it was even further away.

TWO

Down in the Valley, Damien Lomar paused to rest. He realised that he wasn't as young as he used to be, and the hunt wasn't getting any easier. He took a sip of water, keeping a wary eye on his surroundings and enjoying the heady mixture of fear and adrenaline that came with his chosen hobby. The communicator he wore in his ear crackled to life, and the worried voice of Maurice Gilbert filtered through.

"You there, Mr. Lomar?"

"I told you not to bother me when I was hunting, Maurice. This better be good," Lomar whispered, again checking his surroundings.

"Actually, it's bad. They know you're out there."

Lomar paused, unsure if he had misheard. "Who knows? The public?"

"No, them. The contestants. Ryder took a fall and landed in the pit. I told you we should have disposed of the bodies properly."

"Where is he now?" Lomar asked, feeling his body tense.

"We didn't know for a while. He dumped all his camera equipment. His GPS tracker too. He's good. He turned up out of the blue and pulled Riley away from the group."

"Shit."

"He made Riley dump all of his gear and had killed most of the tree cams, but he missed one. We picked up their conversation.

They both know now. I don't need to remind you what this could mean for us."

"No, you don't," Lomar grunted. "Where are they now?"

"Back at the camp. They're getting ready to move."

Lomar took his binoculars from his belt and fixed them on the flickering orange glow of the campfire up the hill. He could see them getting their equipment together, Ryder talking animatedly to Alex. "Where's Moses?"

"He's there. Just not in a good way. Looks like he's coming down with pneumonia or something. You need to finish this and do it now. No more games."

Lomar wasn't listening. He looked beyond the campsite. Further up the hill, it became increasingly steep and impassable. A few years ago, he would have relished the climb. Now his tired bones weren't so keen.

"Mr. Lomar? Did you hear me?" Maurice said, the fear and urgency in his voice reminding Lomar what a spineless prick he was.

"I hear you. Don't worry, I'll take care of it. Is Station Thirty Two online?"

Lomar waited, the anger simmering in his gut.

"Yes. It's active and online."

"I'm heading there. I'm going to prep the pheromone sensors. It's time to give the people their grand finale."

"You know if you do that it will put you in danger too, sir."

"I know that," he snapped, clipping the binoculars back to his belt. "At this point, I don't see what choice we have. Keep me in the loop, Maurice. I want to know everything as it happens, understood?"

"Yes, sir. I'll keep you in the loop."

"How are you handling this for the TV feed?"

"We have a one hour delay. The live stream that people think they are seeing is old footage. I had to authorise overtime to the editing suite. They're doing a great job of making sure nothing gets out to the public that could harm us."

"Good. No matter how many hours overtime they need, I'll sign off on it. We can't have any mistakes here Maurice. That footage needs to be perfect. One slip, one oversight that lets some dirty little fuck from the world sniff even the smallest hint that something isn't as it seems, and we're dead men."

"We?"

"You know as much as I know, Maurice. Keep that in mind."

Silence. Lomar thought it would be easier to tolerate Maurice if he took that approach more often. "Yes, sir," he said. Sharp, tense. Lomar smiled. The message had been received.

"Good. Remember, Maurice, regular updates. I'm making my way to station thirty-two now. For god's sake, put those editing guys under pressure. No mistakes. I want strict control over what goes out."

"We're doing the best we can, sir, but with the constant stream of data to work on–"

"I'm not interested in how. Just get it done. I'm holding you responsible for making sure that it happens. Perks of having a higher position with the company."

"Are you talking about a promotion, sir?"

"As we discussed. But for obvious reasons, not until this ugly little situation is resolved. Can I trust you with this?"

Another pause. Maurice waited, letting the fat fuck think.

"Yes, sir. I can do that."

As if you had a choice Lomar thought, and smiled to himself in the dark. "Good. I knew I could count on you. Keep in touch."

He ducked out of cover, pausing to check the GPS tracker attached to the wrist of his army fatigues. A smaller version of the one in the production office, it showed the locations of the contestants in yellow (now minus Ryder and Chase) as well as the dinosaurs which inhabited The Island. It couldn't have worked out better. There was nothing close to him that could interfere before he reached his destination. He broke into a loping run, heading on a diagonal towards the base of the hill where the others had climbed. He didn't follow. He knew another way. He skirted around the bottom of the hill towards another large outcrop of rocks, pausing to check his GPS to verify his safety. Satisfied, he moved towards the outcrop, searching for a specific location, one he had designed himself. He saw it, a narrow crack between two large slabs of rock. He turned side on, pushing his skinny frame between the two rocks. It was an optical illusion, designed to look like a dead end. Instead, it veered off to the right and opened up into an interior cave, completely shielded from the rest of The Island. Set back against the wall was a steel door. He walked over to it, heart thundering. Waiting for his father to die so he could run the company properly was frustrating, and he was sure he wasn't about to let a group of street scum take away everything he had worked so hard to build. For as much as he enjoyed the thrill of the hunt, business was business and it was time to end this game before he paid the ultimate price.

Lomar opened the door, white artificial light spilling out and making a pool around him. Nobody was going to take what was his. He wouldn't allow it. He grinned and went inside, closing the door behind him.

THE CLIMB
DAY FOUR
9:02 PM

Convincing the others to believe Ryder wasn't as difficult as Chase thought. Moses was incoherent and babbling and didn't seem to care either way. Alex, although surprised initially, believed the story. They had all dumped their cameras and GPS trackers in the overhanging cave, and put out the fire, removing the one thing which had brought them comfort to such a bleak day. Even though the rain had passed, the night was chilly and their breath fogged in the night air.

"So what do we do now?" Alex asked as he put his backpack on. "I'm not sure it's a good idea to travel at night."

"No choice," Ryder said. He was agitated, keeping his weight on the balls of his feet, eyes darting everywhere. "He's close. Maybe a half mile away. He's in shooting range."

"What about him?" Alex jabbed a thumb over his shoulder to where Moses was sitting, head slumped.

"If he can walk, he can come. If he can't, we have to move on anyway."

"I'm comin'," he slurred, lifting his head, eyes rolling in his skull. "I'm not dead yet."

"Alright then let's move," Ryder said, slipping into the leader role with ease.

"Which way?"

"Up. We have no choice. We can't go back, we'll run into Lomar. It might be a bit of a tough climb. We have no other option, though."

"Climb?" Alex repeated, glancing up the hill.

"Yeah. Is there a problem?"

"Well no, it's just... I don't do heights, that's all."

"Well, you better get used to it. It's either climb or eat a bullet to the face from Lomar. Your choice."

"What choice do I have when you put it like that?" Alex grunted, that flicker of anger visible for a second.

"Then let's stop talking about it and move," Ryder replied, turning and making his way further up the hill.

For a while, the going was manageable. Sure enough, it was exhausting, their tired calves burning at the extended punishment and not getting the rest they deserved. Ryder led the way, Chase just behind. Alex was a little further back and starting to look a little dishevelled. At the back and falling further behind was Moses. Climbing with feet that just ached was hard. For Moses, trying to navigate the tough, steep terrain with feet that were shredded, was becoming nigh on impossible. He could feel them sliding around inside his socks, and knew it was because they were swimming in a combination of pus and blood. Every breath was now a wheeze, and he had taken to almost scrambling on all fours in an effort to keep up. Ahead of them, the cliff face loomed, the moon high and pale behind it, as if presenting them their next challenge in a milky spotlight.

Chase picked up his pace and joined Ryder at the front. Although he was exhausted and just breathing was hard, there were questions he wanted answers to.

"Whatever you want to know, now isn't the time," Ryder said between deep breaths.

"Now is the only time I might get to ask," Chase replied, marvelling at how well his cancer free lungs were performing, and reminding himself that without the vaccine he was given, there was no way he would have survived so long.

"Well go ahead and ask, unless it's about the girl. I don't want to talk about that."

"No, it's not about her."

"Then what is it?"

Chase paused, taking a second to try and catch a breath. "The truck. Why did you cut the tyres? We could have used that to help us."

Ryder glanced at him. "Truck?"

"Back there in the valley. The one with the bodies. All the tyres were slashed."

He shook his head. "I didn't see a truck. I skirted around the valley. Stayed in the cover of the trees. Did you walk straight through?"

"Yeah, we did...so you're saying you didn't see it or sabotage it?"

"Fuck no. If I'd known there was a truck there, I'd have tried to use it."

Chase didn't answer at first. He was trying to put everything together.

"Maybe it was Lomar?" Ryder said as he scrambled up the steep gradient.

"No, it doesn't seem like his style," Chase replied, not daring to entertain the idea that was playing out in his mind. "Let me ask you something, Ryder."

"Since it seems like now is the time you want to get everything off your chest, why not?"

"Seriously. What do you make of Alex?"

Ryder glanced back over his shoulder. Alex was around three hundred yards further downhill, brow furrowed as he tried to drag his skinny frame up the hill. "Not sure. He's quiet. Weird. Has a funny look in his eye. I can't quite figure him out."

"Do you ever feel like there's more to him than meets the eye?"

Ryder took another look over his shoulder, almost lost his footing, and then focused on the terrain ahead. "No, but I haven't spent as much time with him as you. Why? You think the skinny little shit is hiding something?"

"Maybe. Sometimes he says things that are just… I don't know. I can't figure him out."

"Maybe go talk to him about it. I don't know about you, but I'd rather save my breath for the huge fucking hill we're trying to climb."

Point taken, Chase fell back, letting Ryder go off in the lead. As his brain processed, rejected and reassessed information, he subconsciously let himself fall back so he was walking alongside Alex.

"Getting tired, Riley?" Alex asked, glancing at him.

"I'm okay," he said, hoping the lie was accepted. "I wanted to talk to you, actually."

Alex gave a brief smile and then focused on the way ahead. "You want to know why I cut the tyres on the truck, don't you?"

The directness of the question was a surprise, and Chase couldn't formulate an answer.

"I wondered how long it would take for you to figure it out once Ryder came back to the fold," Alex said, his tone conversational. "He was a convenient scapegoat."

"That could have helped us," Chase said, wishing he wasn't in such close proximity.

"No, it would have ruined the game."

"This isn't a game anymore. This is about survival. It does all make sense now, though."

"What do you mean?" Alex said, flicking another glance in his direction.

"How keen you were to be the one to face whoever was inside that truck. When we thought it was Ryder. It's the first time you've ever volunteered for something like that. You did it because you knew he wasn't in there. You'd already looked."

Alex glanced at him again and grinned. "Busted. Maybe I should have been a bit more subtle with that."

"This isn't some kind of joke, Alex."

"You don't have to tell me that," he snapped. "It would have been, though. You don't know how sick it made me to come out into that clearing and see that thing parked there. It would have ruined everything."

"It would have helped us."

"No," Alex shook his head. "It wouldn't. I saw it there, back doors open, that mess inside. I acted fast. On instinct. I ran over to it and closed the doors, then stabbed the tyres. I was sure one would do it, but I did three just to be sure in case there was a spare. I didn't figure about the flat grass thing, though. That was an oversight. Ryder was easy to blame."

"It makes no sense. I just... I can't get my head around it."

"This was supposed to be about killing. About who could be strongest. I like death, Riley. I always have. Do you have any idea what it's like to live with these urges and fantasies of hurting people and not be able to play it out?"

Everything clicked into place. Chase felt that tight, gnawing in his gut and knew that although every instinct told him to get as far away from Alex as he could, there was nowhere to run. The way ahead was where they were all heading together, the way back was already a dizzying distance below them down the steep, rocky terrain. He was stuck next to a man who he was starting to realise was potentially dangerous. He decided that his best course of action was to act as normally as he could. "No, I have no idea how that feels," he said, trying not to show his tension.

"Well, it's not easy let me tell you. Strangling cats and dogs only thrills for so long. Eventually, you need to move on to the next step, you know?"

"Have you... Killed people?"

Alex laughed. Up the hill, Ryder glanced down at them. To him, it would look like they were sharing a joke. Chase wished he knew just how unfunny the situation was.

"Weren't you listening to me?" Alex said, feet scrabbling for purchase on the loose terrain. "I have urges. Serious ones. Don't get me wrong, I've wanted to. A few times I was sure it was going to happen, but I always managed to restrain myself. When I saw this advertised, I wasn't interested in the game, or even winning. I did my research. It was the clause about anything being legal that got my interest."

"You told me that story. The one about your father…"

Alex shrugged. "Just words. Maybe I'm a pathological liar as well as a wannabe murderer."

"So why tell me all this now?"

"Because the game has changed. And because I know it's not being recorded now that we've ditched our equipment."

"Back at that watering hole… You were trying to kill Moses and me, weren't you?"

He didn't answer. He just flicked a look, the glint in the eyes and half-smile saying what the words didn't.

"You shouldn't be so surprised anyway, Riley. Isn't that the nature of the game? You come out here, kill a bunch of people for the entertainment of those watching at home, then are rewarded with whatever you want. Think about that before you shoehorn me in the murderer category. I mean, am I any more different from him?" he nodded up the hill to Ryder. "He pulverised a helpless girl's face in just because he thought he might win something. You don't know how envious I was of him. When I looked at what was left of her… I wished that had been me."

"Are you going to kill us?" Just asking the question felt insane, but it was nothing compared to the answer and the way it was delivered.

"If the chance arises, of course. I'm sure any of us will do the same to me."

"That's why you were trying to get me to kill Moses just before Ryder showed up. You wanted to do what you came here to do when it would be impossible for him to fight back."

Alex grinned again. The expression was horrifying. "You're good, Riley. Sharp as a tack. Don't worry, though, for now, we're good. I'll off the old man first chance I get. Until he's out of the picture, you can consider yourself safe."

Further up the hill, the ground had levelled out at the base of the cliff they would have to climb. Ryder was waiting for them, exhausted and drinking water. Chase and Alex arrived next, Chase still in a daze as Ryder and Alex made small talk. Some way back, Moses struggled to get up the hill. Chase watched him, zoning out the conversation between Ryder and Alex. He stared at the old man as he made his way towards them. A man who had saved his life more than once. A man who was dying and he had almost been talked into murdering. He glanced at Alex. Talking and grinning, acting like nothing was out of the ordinary. Chase considered why they were there. What they still might have to do. The cold words of Alex, telling him he was safe until the old man was dead, ringing in his brain. Moses was almost to the top of the mountain. He was coming up close to Alex. Chase moved closer, feeling sick with nerves, and tense with anger.

Alex started to reach down the hill to Moses, offering a hand. Chase acted without thinking. He also offered his hand, reaching that extra little bit further to ensure Moses grabbed it. The old man gripped Chase's wrist and scrambled to the top. Alex was staring at him, that ghostly smile on his pale face. Chase held his gaze, then with everything he could muster, pushed Alex as hard as he could and sent him back down the hill they had just climbed.

TWO

Alex tumbled and rolled, crashing off rocks and taking shale with him. It was painful to watch. His bloody, twisted body came to rest some six hundred feet below them, almost back where they started.

"What the fuck did you do that for?" Ryder said, shoving Chase into the cliff face.

"I had no choice. He was going to kill us. He's fucked up."

"So you kill him instead? Does that make you any better?"

"He told me he was going to kill Moses then us. What was I supposed to do?"

Ryder paced, running is hands through his hair. "You just shoved him. Look at him, you fucking killed him."

Alex lay on his back at the bottom of the hill, face and clothing a bloody mess, one leg twisted out away from him, arms splayed out. He wasn't moving.

"Then I guess that makes us even," Chase said, hating himself for saying it.

Ryder flinched and leaned on the cliff face, resting his head on his forearms.

"Believe me, there was no choice. He would have butchered us all. You said so yourself, he was weird."

"Weird is no reason to kill someone."

"He's right," Moses wheezed.

Both of them looked at the older man, who was sitting on the floor, absolutely spent. "Back in the cave, I heard him. He was talking about killing me. Trying to talk Chase into it. That boy was wrong. Sick in the head."

"We don't have time to talk about it anymore," Chase said, staring up the cliff face. "We're still being followed, remember? We need to make a move."

Ryder glared at him and then spat on the ground. "Fine. Let's go. Just keep your distance from me, killer."

"Same goes for you, murderer," Chase fired back. With exhaustion setting in and tension at breaking point, they started the long climb a further two hundred feet to the summit and whatever waited for them beyond.

STACKING THE DECK
DAY FOUR
INSIDE STATION THIRTY TWO
9:36 PM

Damien Lomar sat at the console, looking at the computer screens in front of him. Station Thirty Two was just one of over a hundred that were positioned at various strategic locations on The Island. Designed for both monitoring and giving veterinary care to the animals which roamed The Island, each station was kitted with an armoury, computer station, medical supplies and sleeping quarters. Over the years, he had used the stations for overnight sleeping when on one of his various hunts. While his terrified prey had huddled in the dark and tried to survive against the threat of the dinosaurs on the elements, Lomar was usually close by in one of his hidden stations, taking full advantage of the fact that, as a manmade island, there were certain privileges he had been afforded.

He stretched and took a sip of his coffee as he watched the group make their way up the cliff face. True enough, he could kill them. There was a way to the top of the hill to Station Thirty Five from this very chamber. A short walk down a hallway and an elevator ride through the central core of the cliff face would bring him out on top of the cliff. From there, he could lean over and pick them off with his rifle if he wanted to, and there was nothing any of them would be able to do about it. He wouldn't do it, though. He still had a television show to produce, and even with the editing team working around the clock to control what was outputted to the public, no contestants meant no show, no matter how good the digital wizardry might be. Also, part of him was curious to see how they progressed. This was a tough bunch now that the weak had been weeded out. He saw that they were nearing the summit, and decided how he was going to proceed. His bony fingers danced over the keyboard, bringing up commands, asking for and receiving his passwords granting him access to the secret set of menus. He selected the option he was looking for, was asked to verify h wanted to go on. He moved the pointer to the 'Y' button and selected it, then looked at the GPS map on his wrist. The red and yellow dots were joined by a series of green ones all across The Island map. Lomar referred to the map on the wall, a static one split into a grid. He found the coordinates of the sections he was looking for and typed in more commands. The green dots in the area the contestants had already covered disappeared, leaving just the remainder of The Island they hadn't yet reached. He typed in another command, hesitating as a second window flashed up on screen.

ACTIVATE PHEREMONE EXCRETION IN ZONES 39,40,41,42,43,44,45,46,47,48?

He selected yes, and waited as the system processed his commands, and brought up another message, this one in bold and surrounded by a black and yellow border.

WARNING!!
PLEASE ENSURE ALL PERSONEL ARE OUTSIDE OF SELECTED ZONES.

He pushed enter and waited. For a few more seconds. A chime told him he had been successful in his command.

PHEREMONE EXCRETION IN ZONES 39,40,41,42,43,44,45,46,47,48 NOW ACTIVE. DO NOT ENTER SELECTED ZONES UNTIL 12 HOURS AFTER PROCESS IS COMPLETE.

Lomar grinned. The pheromone excretion programme had been his idea. When they had first started to populate The Island with dinosaurs, getting them to breed had proved tricky. Not only was The Island large enough that certain species of the same animal might never encounter each other, sometimes there was a certain unwillingness for them to engage in reproduction. The solution had been quite simple. Baseline pheromones from all species of the dinosaurs on The Island had been taken and synthesised in the lab. These had been placed into steel rods which ran across the entire island beneath ground level. When activated, the chosen rods would rise from the ground and excrete the chosen pheromone, and in doing so draw the selected creature to a specific location. By using a series of rods excreting the pheromone in turn, it was possible to manipulate where the creatures would go at any chosen time. Some of the pheromones were for the purpose of breeding; others were designed to invoke aggression and to keep territorial boundaries between species. It was also useful if a team needed to go out into the field to perform maintenance. If such a thing needed to be done, the pheromone secretion system would draw any creatures away from the selected areas, allowing the maintenance crew to get in and do their work. It was the same principal Lomar was working on now. He was keeping the three act structure in mind for his production and thought the people might appreciate this next build until the grand finale. The public had been introduced to their characters and seen their individual motivations. They had witnessed their gradual breakdown as they had dealt with the trials of survival. What they hadn't yet experienced, was a full on attack by an aggressive pack of dinosaurs, all between them and the way off The Island. Even without his help, The Island was a killer. He would just give it a helping hand. He liked that idea. He was sure the public would love it too, so would the sponsors. One potential problem was that they knew he was involved now, and so might act differently. He was sure he could fix that. He would just have to wait until they reached the summit of the cliff. Once they had seen what he had in store for them, he was sure that he would be seen as the last of their worries.

TWO

Fingers numb, arms, shoulders and legs screaming in protest, Chase inched closer to the summit. He found a solid foothold and pressed his forehead against the rock face. He had been expecting to hear Moses scream out and fall almost all the way up the cliff, but he was still there. Still grimacing, still coughing, but just a little way below. Ryder was around ten feet higher. As Chase watched, he pulled himself up and to safety, rolling out of sight. The idea of a rest felt almost heavenly. With renewed determination, he resumed his climb, double checking every handhold, every position of the foot. If he fell, he knew it would be to certain death. Images of Alex filled his mind, ones which he quashed. He had done what he had to, and even if the others didn't understand, he knew he had done the right thing. He pulled himself closer to the top. Ryder leaned over. The cocky, arrogant man who had started the journey had gone. Now he was just another tired survivor hoping to live to see another day. Ryder reached down, and Chase took the offered hand. He was pulled up, Ryder's muscles bunching. He was as strong as he looked. Safely on top of the cliff top, Chase lay on his back, panting as he tried to get his breath back. Everything ached. He had been on the move without stopping for what felt like an eternity now and his body was desperate for respite.

Moses was next to be helped by Ryder. He too looked exhausted and lay on the ground next to Chase, his breathing sounding wet and ragged. Something inside him was definitely broken. Ryder was the only one who didn't seem to be exhausted. He crouched on the edge of the cliff, staring out over the plains.

"You better both take a look at this."

As exhausted as they were, the urgency in his voice compelled them to drag their weary bodies to where he was. They looked down at the moon-bathed landscape which stretched for miles as far as the eye could see.

There were dinosaurs. Countless species, all sizes. All of them were heading in the same direction they were. Ryder let his eyes follow the cliff. It stayed at the same height for around a mile, then tapered off into hills again. The dinosaurs were heading for this lower ground, s drawn to it by means none of them could understand.

"Where are they all going?" Chase whispered.

"Same place as us. South."

"Why?"

Ryder shrugged. "Who knows? Nothing in this fucking place makes any sense."

"It's like they're migrating, almost," Chase said.

"Birds migrate. Dinosaurs, I'm guessing don't. Whatever they're doing, it's not a natural thing."

"Can you all hear me?"

It was Lomar. They whirled around, staring down the rocky plateau and towards the trees which awaited them. All of them as one expected to see him standing there, rifle in hand. But there was no Lomar, no waiting party. Just rocks and in the distance, trees.

"You won't find me down that way. Look up," Lomar's voice said again.

This time, they zeroed in on the source. It was coming from one of the tree cameras. It had been strapped to a scraggy, half-dead pine. The black sightless lens stared at them, Lomar's voice coming from the tiny speaker below it.

"There you go. Do you see me now?"

They looked at each other, unsure how to react.

"Don't bother to reply, this isn't a two-way system. Instead, just be quiet and listen to what I have to say."

Chase glanced at the dinosaurs, which were still making their way across the plains some three hundred feet below.

"I'm broadcasting to you now on a closed private channel. This isn't being recorded for television. I wanted to speak to you in person. It seems one of you stumbled across my little hobby and has told the others. That, as I'm sure you are aware, changes things as far as this game goes. In my defence, those I hunted, the bodies that were found, were immigrants. I paid good money to own them. Like any animal, it was my choice to do with them what I wanted. If I choose to set them loose on my island then hunt them down like dogs, that's up to me."

Chase glanced at Ryder, who was staring at the camera, open-mouthed. Moses had his head down, staring at his boots. Lomar went on.

"That aside, the rules of the game have not changed. One of you will win the ultimate prize. You will win anything you want. Think about that. Anything. Are a bunch of stinking immigrants worth losing that prize over?"

He paused for effect, then continued.

"I'm prepared, under the circumstances to offer an olive branch. Now I'll admit. I came out here with the sole intention of killing you. All of you. We have footage of lookalikes being eaten by dinosaurs here that were pre-recorded. It would be easy to splice that footage into the feed and let the world believe you have met a gruesome end. Things, however, have changed. The fact is, you have reached further than anyone had ever anticipated. The world is inspired by your journey, and as I have a second season in mind, it would not be good business for me to kill you all over a misunderstanding. So, here is how it will happen. There will be no more interference from me. No more hunting. The three of you will go on and face the challenge of The Island without further interference from me. I won't bother you, nor will I hunt you."

Chase looked over his shoulder at the dinosaurs.

"One thing you will have noticed," Lomar said, "was the sudden movement of The Islands inhabitants towards your general direction. That is a very deliberate move to ensure that the public gets the finale they deserve. Instead of being spread about The Island, all of the creatures will be diverted to the southern quarter. There will be no avoidance. No strolling through valleys and skirting around watering holes. There will be constant danger. Constant threat. The fun ride is over. True enough, I'm not hunting you. But you will die. Rest well tonight, my dear contestants. Sleep in the knowledge that you won't be troubled. Tomorrow, everything that has gone before will seem like child's play. Tomorrow, the public will see death, and one of you will see freedom."

The speaker clicked, and Lomar was gone. The three of them stood there, dazed and confused.

"What do we do?" Moses asked.

Chase glanced at Ryder, who met his gaze.

"We make a fire," Ryder said. "Then we get some rest."

"You believe him?" Chase said.

"I think so. It's the perfect ending for him. Push all of the dinosaurs into a small area then make us go through it."

"We're in trouble, aren't we?" Moses said.

"Essentially, we're fucked. All that is for tomorrow, though. I don't know about you, but right now I could use some shuteye."

"Should we set up a watch?" Chase asked.

Ryder shook his head. "For what?" Everything on this damn island is going to be ahead of us and waiting for us to get there tomorrow. Make the most of it, Riley. Get some shut eye."

THREE

The small boy ran outside, legs pumping as he moved across the field, sun beating down on his face. The house backed out onto the glorious green Oregon forest. Creeks filled with salmon provided plentiful food for the brown bears which roamed the forest. The boy's father had warned him about going there, but he couldn't help himself. To him, the woods were a magical place, a place that was his alone. His secret. He plunged into the tree line, the temperature cooler here, that gorgeous smell of pine and tree sap filling his nostrils. He knew the way well. He had been here countless times. He wound through the trees, hopped over a small stream, and then made his way to his secret place.

The natural hollow in the woods was where he had been keeping the cat.

He had borrowed the plastic box they used when they had to take it to the vet. Nobody had noticed the box had gone missing, but they definitely noticed the cat as gone. His father especially loved that cat, and in the four days since it had gone missing, had even gone into town to put posters up in shop windows and on telephone poles offering a reward for information leading to the cat being found safe. Of course, nobody would ever find it and claim the reward.

He sat in front of the box now, looking at the ginger tabby as it cowered in the back. He poked a finger through the mesh.

"Hi Tiddles," the boy said. The cat hissed in response. It sensed the danger it was in. The boy smiled and took the gloves out of his pocket. They were thick gloves his father used when he was chopping wood for the log burner. Very thick, very durable. They would protect against most things, cat scratches included. The boy pulled the gloves on, savouring every second, wishing it could have been different. The fact was that his father loved the cat more than his own son, and in any world that was wrong.

He unclipped the latch on the door with his left hand just enough to fit his right arm in. He grabbed the cat. It scratched and clawed, but the gloves did their job. He didn't feel it. Once he was confident he had a grip, he opened the door the rest of the way and reached in with his other hand, closing his hands around the cat's skinny neck.

He had rehearsed this is his head countless times, but none of it compared to actually doing it. He pulled the squirming scratching cat out of the cage and squeezed with everything he could muster, watching as the life left it at exactly the same time he came to orgasm, wetting his underwear in a hot, sticky explosion as he broke the animal's neck.

He fell to his side in the leaves, exhausted and staring at the animal. It had been the family pet for three years.

Three years of coming second best to a cat.

The boy shook his head. No more.

He stood, wincing at the uncomfortably wet warmth in his underwear. He stood and grabbed the limp animal by one leg, picking it up and holding it at arm's length. He felt nothing. No emotion, no sense of right or wrong, just a pitiful black void.

He looked around his secret place and knew nobody would ever find out what he had done. He was too clever. Too smart even for his own family, even at just twelve years old. He reared back and tossed the cat into the woods, a gift for the animals, maybe a midnight snack for the bears.

Enjoy it, bears. It will make a nice change to fish all the time.

He scrambled back up the bank, looking forward to watching the mental suffering his family would endure until they realised poor little Tiddles wasn't coming back.

The feeling of what he had done was still fresh, still memorable in every detail, and yet, he still couldn't wait to do it all again.

At the bottom of the hill, under the watchful eye of the half moon, an eye opened from its bloody mask. As a tongue ran across broken teeth and assessed damage, a familiar rage started to build. No major injuries. He moved his hands, his arms. Then his legs. Sure enough, he had taken some damage, but it was all superficial, things that would fuel the beast that lived inside him.

Alex got to his feet and started back up the hill. More determined than ever to feel that elation at least one more time, and feed the demon which Chase had awoken.

ODDS ON
DAY FIVE
7:08 AM

As exhausted as they were, none of them were able to sleep aside from Moses, who continued to drift in and out of consciousness as the fever in him grew. They had awoken tired and angry. With no food and seemingly no chance of survival, morale was as low as it had ever been. Chase had been particularly troubled. Every time he closed his eyes, he saw snatches of Alex, the wide eyed look of realisation on his face which he knew would be forever burned into his psyche.

It had dawned on him, as he stamped out the small camp fire, that he had taken a life. Even though he had gone into the game knowing it was something he might have to do, the act itself made him feel both ashamed and nauseous. He wondered how it would be presented on television. How it would come across to his family and friends. He would look brutal and heartless. It came to him, as he stamped out the dying embers of their camp fire, that maybe Perrie had it right all along. They had ridiculed her and laughed at her for her lack of understanding, but she had been right. It was all a show. True, they weren't actors, but they were on a set. The output was being manipulated to be delivered to the public in a certain way. To them it was about survival, to everyone else, it was just a game show.

"You ready?" Ryder said. He looked jaded and haggard. Most of the mud had flaked away from his skin. It was hard to imagine him as the brash, cocky man from less than a week ago.

"Yeah, I'm good to go," Chase said.

"What about him?"

They both looked to Moses, who was struggling to pull on his boots.

Ryder lowered his voice. "We can't carry him forever. He's fading. It's going to get to a point where we have to make a decision."

"I think we both need to stop playing god and let fate decide."

"We don't have that luxury."

"You don't have to worry about me," Moses said as he struggled to his feet. He grimaced as he limped towards them. "I'm dying, not deaf."

He walked on towards the tree line. The others followed, wondering if this was the last sunrise they would ever see.

TWO

Following the storm, the new day was baking hot. As the ground dried, a light steam rose from it, giving an eerie backdrop to their slow journey. They moved through the scrub of trees, tense and waiting for something to happen.

"It's quiet," Chase whispered.

Ryder nodded. Even the birds seemed to have silenced. The only sounds were their footfalls and the moans and babble of Moses, who seemed to be flitting from coherent and aware to disorientated and ranting.

They went on, struggling with the humidity and waiting for the chaos Lomar had promised them.

"You think he's out there?" Chase asked.

Ryder glanced around, eyes scanning the trees. "Could be. Depends on how good he is."

"Wouldn't we see him?"

"You didn't see me," Ryder said, glancing over his shoulder. "I was as close as ten feet at some points. If you know how to use the environment, you can be invisible out here."

Chase stopped in his tracks, looking through the break in the trees. "Then what would you suggest we do about that?"

They had reached the opposite edge of the tree line. Beyond, was a marsh, the water filthy and topped with leaves and algae. Large mosquitoes zipped across the surface. There was no way around it. It stretched for miles in each direction. Forty feet across from them, a gentle bank sloped upwards towards firmer ground.

"It stinks," Chase said, looking both ways up and down the bank.

"No way to go around. We'll have to cross," Ryder replied.

Chase picked up a rock from the edge. "We don't know how deep it is."

"Don't," Ryder snapped holding a hand up. "Don't disturb the water. We don't know what might be in there."

It had never entered Chase's head. He dropped the rock on the ground and stared at the surface of the water. There was no movement, no hint of anything there. If Ryder hadn't been with them, he would have tossed the stone in the water. He felt suddenly like he knew nothing, and had got by on blind luck so far.

"So what do we do now?" he asked.

"We wait for a while and watch."

"For what?"

"Anything that might disturb the surface. Bubbles, ripples. Some animals, crocodiles and alligators, only need to breathe every so often. Usually, they wait under the surface or the water for someone to either step on them or throw stones in the water."

"It's not alligators I'm worried about," Chase said, ignoring the jibe.

"No, that makes two of us."

"How long do we wait?"

"Twenty minutes maybe. Just to be sure."

With nothing else to do, they waited, all three of them staring at the water. Fifteen minutes passed. Then twenty. Nothing moved apart from the mosquitoes, and nothing but Moses's babbling punctuated the silence. He had been indulged in a heated conversation with a family member, possibly from the past and one only he could see. For the past ten minutes, he had been repeating the same phrase, saying over and over again.

Why won't you let me retire?

Why won't you let me retire?

Why won't you let me retire?

It was infuriating to listen to, but Chase couldn't stop it. Moses was clearly starting to break down. For a moment, Chase considered that maybe he was the lucky one.

"Alright, it's safe to move," Ryder said, standing up and approaching the edge of the water. "Here's how we're going to do this. Chase, you go first. I'll follow ten feet behind. Moses, you bring up the rear, again another ten feet back."

Why won't you let me retire?

Why won't you let me retire?

Why won't you let me retire?

"You hear me in there? Do you understand?" Ryder repeated.

Moses nodded. He was shivering and rubbing his hands against his upper arms despite the stifling heat. Ryder and Chase glanced at each other.

"Alright," Ryder said, deciding it was best to move on. "Here's what we do. We go in slowly, quietly. We don't know how deep the water is, so we might have to swim. If that's the case, do it slowly. Remember, the aim here is to make the least disruption possible. If it's shallow enough to wade in, then again, keep quiet. Move slowly. Slide your feet across the bottom, don't be tempted to take big steps. You don't want to stand on anything down there."

"What about if we get in there and something comes?" Chase said.

"Then we swim like hell. It's only forty feet or so. Fifty tops."

"Great," Chase grunted. "Why do I get to go first?"

"So I can keep an eye on you and make sure you're not doing anything that might draw attention. It's easier for me to do that if you're right in front of me rather than behind."

"Alright, makes sense I suppose."

"You ready?"

Chase nodded, somehow managing to fight the urge to run.

"What about you?" he asked Moses. The old man stopped his incessant mantra, blinked and looked at him. "I'm ready, Simi. Just tell Father I'll be along soon, eh?"

"Jesus Christ, this is going to be a disaster," Ryder mumbled. "Come on, let's do this and hope the old bastard here understands what's happening."

Ryder turned to Chase. "The bank slopes down, so that should mean you can walk in. Remember, keep it slow. Take your time. I'll be watching."

Chase walked to the edge, by now getting used to fighting the instinct to flee. Keeping Ryder's words in mind, he inched into the water, grimacing as the cold, frigid liquid soaked through his pants. He waded in quietly; knowing that every step could be his last if there was something waiting to snatch him away. He the water reached up to his chest, then the depth stabilised. He managed to bob forward, fighting against the natural buoyancy of his backpack. He wished he had remembered to remove it before getting into the water, but knew it was too late now to backtrack. He wouldn't dare risk doing so now for fear of disturbing the water. From down at water level, it was even more frightening. He was aware that anything could be out there and he was powerless to stop it should it decide to attack. He paused and glanced over his shoulder. Ryder was up to his knees, moving slowly, eyes alert and flicking left to right with each step. Moses still sat on the bank, head low, arms on the floor. He looked like he was sleeping, his head flicking up every few seconds as his eyes rolled over to the whites.

Chase put him out of his mind. His own safety was the only thing that mattered to him. He focussed on what was there, on reaching out with his senses. The earthy, rotten stench of the water, which clung to him with its chilly determination, leaving a slick of green algae sticking to his shirt. His foot brushed something unseen, something solid. He froze, waiting for the attack, determined that the last conscious thought he would have would be the image of his wife and daughter.

But no attack came. He exhaled, and risked moving his foot again. The solid object was still there, but whatever it is was no threat. He suspected it may have been a root or some kind of underwater grass. He stepped over it and continued on his way, now almost halfway across. He risked another look over his shoulder. Ryder was now also up to his chest. Unlike Chase, he had remembered to take off his backpack and was holding it above his head. Behind him, Moses was also in the water. Inching forward into the cold, filthy water. It seemed that as delirious as he was, he was still lucid enough to have listened to Ryder's instructions.

He turned back to focus on the way ahead, and froze, his brain taking a second to register what was in front of him.

Lomar stood on the opposite bank. He was dressed in army fatigues, his rifle in hand, finger resting on the trigger guard. He stared at Chase, a wicked, small-toothed grin on his face. Chase stared back, time frozen as both men sized each other up. Lomar started to move, swinging his gun towards them.

He lied, Chase thought to himself as he prepared for the bullets to rip through him. He lied just to get us here.

He wondered if it would hurt as the bullets shredded his insides. He wondered if they would show it on screen, perhaps splice in one of the other contestants over Lomar. He hoped not. He didn't want his family to see him suffer.

He closed his eyes as the explosion of gunfire shattered the silence.

He wasn't dead.

The gun had definitely ejected. Six shots. He opened his eyes, looking at the ripples as they moved through the water.

"Move, move now!" Ryder said as he started to move through the water as fast as he could, Moses following behind as quickly as he could. Chase saw it coming towards them. A wake from further down the river, a rolling tide of water as whatever was beneath homed in on them. He started to move, wishing his legs would move faster, the backpack throwing him off balance. He lost his footing, and his head went under the water. He took in a mouthful of rancid water, the bitter taste making him retch. He threw his head up, coughing and spluttering. Lomar tossed the rifle into the water, then turned and started to walk away.

Chase coughed, as his feet found purchase. He glanced behind him. Ryder was stumbling along behind. Moses had abandoned his backpack and was swimming, his hair mottled with clumps of algae. He had almost caught up to Ryder. Both of them were around fifty feet from the wake which was drawing closer. As they watched, a great, grey-brown back broke the surface.

Chase was able to move faster now. The water was only waist high and his feet were able to grip in the soft mud. Ahead, he could see Lomar disappearing into the trees. Anger fuelled him, and he accelerated. He was free of the water, free of the mud and whatever was closing on them. There was no forethought. He put his head down and broke into a sprint, determined to get to Lomar.

THREE

Ryder saw the wake coming towards him and knew he was going to die. Moses was swimming, head down, arms slamming into the water.

The thirty-six-foot Sarcosuchus closed in on them, drawn to the noise. A relative of the common crocodile, the Sarcosuchus possessed a much longer snout filled with sixty-six teeth. At the end of its snout, a large bulbous protrusion called a bulla helped the enormous creature to lock on to the scent of its prey and hone in on it with deadly precision. The combination of scents from the two stranded men, sweat and the bloody mess seeping from Moses's boots, combined with their thrashing as they tried to flee, convinced the giant predator that this was a viable meal. It flicked its tail and closed in on the two men. Ryder saw it coming, but couldn't stop it. The creature opened its mouth; the soft, pink throat seemed impossibly large. He held his ground, and then at the last second lurched to the side. His intention was to make the creature miss allowing him time to flee, but he moved too early, and the Sarchosuchus reacted. It flicked its head in the same direction Ryder had moved. He saw it and threw up an arm, but the Sarchosuchus still managed to get a grip on his arm, its teeth sinking into the soft flesh of his upper arm.

Moses had reached the bank, and scrambled up to higher ground, he lay on his front, gasping and panting. He turned back to the water just in time to see the Sarchosuchus roll, taking Ryder with it into the filthy, black waters.

FOUR

Chase thought he had lost Lomar in the dense jungle, then caught a glimpse of him ducking under a half fallen tree. Another burst of anger fuelled his adrenaline, and he picked up speed, determined to get his hands on the man who had sent them to their own private hell on earth. Lomar tripped and almost lost his balance, but didn't fall. It was all Chase needed to close on him. Lomar half-turned, his eyes widening in surprise as Chase launched at him, tackling him to the ground.

"You son of a bitch, you tried to kill us," Chase grunted, grabbing at Lomar's throat. Lomar grabbed Chase's wrists, trying to alleviate the pressure.

"It's not what it seems…" Lomar said, choking and gasping for air.

"You set us up, you changed the rules," Chase grunted, feeling his fingers dig deeper into the old man's flesh. Lomar let go of Chase's wrists and pressed a series of commands on his wrist GPS display. The image changed, and Chase let go, staring and unable to comprehend what he was looking at.

FIVE

Ryder couldn't breathe. He clung to the nose of the Sarchosuchus as it rolled with him, trying to separate flesh from bone. He had seen wild alligators in Florida, but this was on an entirely different scale. He tried to keep calm, knowing that if he didn't, he would likely die. He tried to recall what he had read about surviving an alligator attack. He knew there was a fleshy palate at the back of the throat that was sensitive and might help him to free himself, but it was both out of reach and out of the question. The nearest thing to him was the eyes. He tried to reach with his free hand, but the way he was pinned made it impossible. All he could do was cling on as the massive creature continued to rotate. He needed to breathe, his lungs screaming for precious air. On instinct, he lashed out with a foot, catching the Sarchosuchus in its bulbous eyeball. It didn't let go, it simply increased the ferocity of its rotations, and pushed him down into the mud. He couldn't see, and had to squeeze his eyes closed as he was pressed into the soft earth. Mud started to encase him, entombing him. He lashed out again, giving everything he could the kick landed on target, and the Sarchosuchus released its grip, retreating into the dark. It was all he needed. He pushed himself to the surface, gasping in precious lungfuls of air, the agony in his arm unbearable. Ugly puncture wounds immediately filled with blood as he made for safety, scrambling towards the embankment, he ran up the bank and fell to his knees. Absolutely drained. The Sarchosuchus retreated back into the murky waters.

SIX

Chase blinked again and looked at the screen.

It was a dark room lit by a single overhead spotlight. Ashley was sitting on the floor, holding Elsie close to her. His frightened wife and daughter were afraid and wore almost identical expressions. Chase felt his stomach plummet towards his feet as he looked up at Lomar for some kind of explanation.

"Don't worry, they're not hurt. Think of it as an insurance policy. All the contestants are in a similar situation."

"I don't understand…"

"The nature of our business means we have to sometimes edit footage. We have our digital scans of you of course taken during the green screen vignettes you did back on The Island, but immediate family members can always tell the difference, so we hold them for a few days. They have no idea it's us of course. We send men in unmarked uniforms and take them to a featureless room. They are fed and watered and have a bed to sleep in, so don't worry, no harm will come to them."

"So why show me?" Chase asked, standing and waiting for Lomar to do the same.

"Because I want to let you in on a little secret while you are away from the others. See, you're the favourite to win this whole thing, Chase. The public like you. I like you. Don't throw it away by taking your aggression out on me."

"Why should I believe you?"

Lomar smiled. "Why should you believe them? You think they're your friends? No. They're your rivals. You should have seen how Ryder beat that poor girl to death. She was begging, crying. Did he tell you she didn't die straight away? She lay there burning under the sun and choking on her own blood whilst he watched her and did nothing to put her out of her misery."

Chase searched Lomar's face for a lie, but the older man was unreadable. "Why show me my family? Why put that pressure on me?"

"Because I want you to win. I want you to keep your eyes on the prize and remember why you took part in the first place. Of everyone, your story was the most compelling. You are the people's choice, and we like to give them what they want. Trust me, I've seen their profiles, I know their history. Those two people you want to consider as friends will stab you in the back the first chance they get. Keep that in mind, and remember what I showed you. I'll be watching."

Lomar turned away, ducking into the trees and was lost from sight. Chase stood there, shocked and trying to let everything sink in. He heard footsteps as Ryder and Moses caught up to him.

"What happened?" Ryder said,asked. His arm was a bloody mess, and he was holding it close to his body.

"He got away," Chase mumbled."I tried to stop him."

"Fucker tried to kill us," Ryder said. "My arm is all messed up. I'll need to stop for a while and strap it up. Here looks like as good a spot as any."

Ryder sat and opened his backpack, looking for his medical kit. Chase stared into the trees, not seeing the tangle of roots and leaves. All he could see was that spotlight Lomar had shown him with his terrified family inside. He had put them there, and there was no way he could ever shake the guilt of it, no matter what happened.

BROKEN
DAY FIVE
6:52 PM

The rain came in from the east, driving gusts which looked to be heralding yet another storm. They walked in silence, picking their way through the trees, which sloped downhill. Every half mile or less, they were forced to stop and hide or take evasive action. Their encounters with the dinosaurs were becoming more frequent, the creatures themselves agitated at being in such close proximity to their own kind. Although Lomar's intention had been to bring them closer to where the contestants were so that they would attack them, by making them share such a relatively small area, they were instead attacking each other, fighting for territory. The mostly silent jungles were a thing of the past. Now, everywhere around them seemed to be exploding with life. They stopped, ducking behind a mossy boulder as something large and unseen crashed through the undergrowth somewhere ahead of them.

Ryder had patched his arm up as best he could, but the bandages were already soaked with blood where the Sarchosuchus had bitten him. He was pale and sweating. Worse still was Moses. He was babbling again, and as they waited, he leaned over and coughed, bringing up blood which spattered between his feet.

"Keep it down," Ryder said, glaring at Moses.

He tried to silence himself, crossing his arm over his face and continuing to cough into the crook of his elbow.

Ryder glanced at Chase then back into the trees. "It breaks up ahead; we'll be out in the open."

"Any ideas?" Chase asked.

"No. We don't have any weapons. We're hungry, tired. The old guy is dying, I'm bleeding out. Looks like you might win this after all, Riley."

"I'm not thinking about that yet," Chase grunted. It was true; he was thinking about the haunting images of his family that Lomar had shown him.

"Alright," Ryder said, looking at them both. "It's safe to move on."

They jogged forward. The tree canopy above had kept them relatively dry, but as they exited the tree cover, the deluge hit them hard, soaking them in seconds.

"Fucking hate the weather here," Ryder said, glaring up at the sky.

"At least it looks clear."

"Yeah, come on," Ryder said, walking forward.

The long hip-high grass beyond was trampled down. It was clear that several large creatures had recently been there. Beyond the grasses, the ground fell away into a slope of loose dirt and rock, beyond which more grassland awaited. They walked towards it, Chase and Ryder well ahead of Moses. Ryder glanced across at Chase, then looked straight ahead.

"You know, sooner or later, we're going to have to make a decision."

"What about?" Chase said, knowing what was coming.

"Moses."

"I thought we agreed it wasn't our decision to make."

Ryder glanced at him again, then turned away. "That was before. He's costing us. Plus that cough...he keeps giving away our position. Eventually, it will cost us."

Chase glanced at the sorry, hunched-over man behind them, and then recalled Lomar's warning. "Let me ask you something, Ryder. Why are you here?"

"None of your business, Riley."

"Come on, why not? It's close to the end now. Why not share?"

"You first."

"Alright. I'm here because my kid has cancer. In the lungs. I want to put her right. That jab they gave me before I came here can guarantee her a life. I guarantee she's going to have a better one than I do."

"If you win."

"If I win," Chase agreed.

Ryder walked on in silence for a while. He was shivering from the rain. "There's not much to tell. I'm a thrill seeker. Adrenaline junkie. I came here to test myself. Of course, I didn't know what I was up against then, but you can't blame me for that. None of us did."

"No."

"What do you mean, no?" Ryder said.

"It's more than that. A thrill seeker wouldn't beat someone to death with a rock just to see if he was good enough. What are you hiding, Ryder?"

"Why do you care?" he snapped.

"I don't care. I just want to know."

"It's my business."

They reached the edge of the ridge. They could see the wall now, much closer than they anticipated. Between them and it, down at the bottom of the forty foot slope, dinosaurs of all shapes and sizes snapped and fought, ran and chased. It was a compact, self-contained example of the circle of life. Stretching between them and the end. There was no way they could avoid an encounter. Some of the dinosaurs were already dead, killed by their bigger, more aggressive cousins, and were being picked apart by scavengers. The larger species kept a wary distance from each other, not yet willing to engage in combat.

Ryder was staring open-mouthed at the sheer spectacle. Chase barely noticed. His mind felt overstretched, almost to the point of breaking. He couldn't shake the images Lomar had shown him out of his head.

"It's over. We can't get past those. Not without weapons. We'll never make it."

Moses had joined them, a limping, wheezing shell of a man who seemed to have wasted away in an incredibly short space of time. He glanced at the dinosaurs with little interest, then put his hands on his knees and tried to catch his breath.

They stood silent, rain driving down. There was nowhere to go. Above them, the night was almost complete, and with no moon to illuminate the way, seemed particularly imposing.

"We can't just stay here," Chase said.

"I'm all ears if you have any suggestions."

Before he could say anything, they were both distracted by the light coming from below. It was like some kind of illusion. They stared at the perfect square of light in the face of the large cluster of boulders below. As they watched, Lomar exited, closing the hidden door behind him. He hadn't seen them. He was crossing the valley, running in a half crouch, rifle thrown over his shoulder.

"What the hell?" Chase said, watching Lomar as he continued on his way.

"Of course," Ryder said, smiling. "This is all manmade, remember? Stands to reason that the slimy fucker would have little rabbit holes where he could go and resupply."

"We should get in there. See what we can find," Chase said.

"No, that's not the game. We need to get to the end."

"Are you serious?"

"Deadly," Ryder said, the aggressive note in his voice impossible to ignore.

"We should at least look. There could be medical supplies, maybe a way to contact the outside world."

"For what? You think that broadcast would ever go out?"

"Why are you so unwilling to even try?"

"Because that's not how this works. We go to the door, one of us walks out. I don't know how much more clear I have to be." Ryder was angry now and was squaring up to Chase. Even with one injured arm, Chase wasn't a physical match.

"Then maybe we should just go our separate ways. You go on to the end; I'll go see what's in that room."

Ryder shook his head. "No. That's not the game. Surely you remember how it goes?" he shifted position, a subtle gesture but one which got the message across. Ryder had put his palm on the handle of his hunting knife.

"So we go with you, try to survive then let you kill us?"

"Way I see it, we're the only ones left anyway. The old guy is on his last legs. May as well get to the end first and then fight it out there."

Chase thought of his daughter and his wife, sitting in that cold room, neither of them knowing why they were even there. "Looks like I don't have a choice," he said, lowering his eyes.

Ryder grinned and relaxed. "Good. I'm glad we–"

He never finished the sentence. Chase was still thinking of his wife and daughter, and no matter what, he wasn't about to let them die there. He lurched forward, then, just like he had before, shoved Ryder as hard as he could over the edge.

TWO

Ryder tumbled and rolled, crashing down the steep slope, rocks and stones following him down. He came to rest with his feet in a narrow creek, bloodied and groaning. Lomar heard the commotion and flicked his head around. He saw Ryder first, groaning at the bottom of the hill. He then flicked his eyes to Chase and Moses, then back to Ryder. He started to approach the creek, pulling his rifle into position, the expression on his face one of betrayal and anger. By finding the pit of bodies, Ryder had almost cost Lomar everything, and the billionaire was determined to eliminate this particular threat. He fired, the gunshot rolling through the air, a shower of rock and dirt exploding inches from Ryder's head.

Ryder lurched to his feet, half-stumbling, half-running back under cover of the forest. Lomar gave chase, breaking into a run, not willing to give up the hunt yet.

Chase turned to Moses. "Can you walk?"

Moses nodded.

"Come on then, let's go."

Chase helped Moses down the slope, both of them half-sliding, half-falling to the bottom. Moses was moaning again, his eyes glassy. Chase threw the old man's arm over his shoulder and helped him to the cluster of rocks. With an approximate idea of where to look, finding the door was easy. They approached it as two gunshots echoed out from the trees beyond the creek.

"What's that? Are they shooting at us?" Moses mumbled.

"No, not at us. It's something else."

Before Lomar could come back and find them, Chase opened the door, wincing at the harsh light, shoved Moses inside and followed, closing the door.

BEHIND THE SCENES
DAY FIVE
9:20 PM

Chase blinked, taking it all in. The bunker was laid out much like the others around The Island, this one, Station Forty Five, was smaller than Station Thirty Two, but still possessed the essentials. An armoury, a bunk, a cabinet with medical supplies, and an array of television screens showing camera views from around The Island. Chase walked Moses to the bunk and sat him down, trying to think what to do. There were several handguns and rifles on a steel table in the centre of the room, as well as a half-finished cup of coffee and a plate containing the fleshy remains of a ham and cheese sandwich. It seemed Lomar had stopped by to grab a drink, a bit to eat, and to resupply whilst they had been fighting for their lives. Chase grabbed one of the handguns, verified it as loaded and slipped it into his belt. He looked at Moses, who was rocking on the bed, and turned his attention to the medicine cabinet. Bandages and plasters, painkillers and morphine. It was a well-supplied cupboard, with more than enough to treat any injury. Chase wasn't sure what to give Moses. He was looking for antibiotics, and wondering how much he could take with him.

"Are you allergic to anything?" he said, calling over his shoulder.

"Moses, I need to know if you have any –" he turned and then stopped talking.

Moses was standing by the table, pointing one of the remaining handguns at Chase. He was still wheezing, and his eyes were still glassy, but they still shone with the desperate determination to survive.

"I'm sorry it…had to…come to…this," he said, each wheezing breath coming in a wet rasp.

Chase held his palms up. "Look, you don't have to do this. It's not what you think. Lomar is playing us all."

"No, it's not… It's not what you think."

"What are you talking about, Moses?"

"I'm not who…you think I am." He tried to smile, but it came out in a grimace which forced him to stifle a cough.

"I don't care what you did in the outside world. You're a good man. You proved that more than once. Let me help you, we've come so far."

Moses tried to chuckle, it came out as a wet rattle. "I was never a part…of this. Not as a…contestant like you."

Chase waited, unable to take his eyes from the black eye facing him which could end his life before he could do anything about it.

Moses was catching his breath now, his speech returning to normal, wet rasp aside. "I've worked for the Lomar family for years, my father before me, his before him. I used to drive Lomar's limo. Can you believe that? I was so scared of him. So intimidated back then. You think any of this is new to me?" He waved the gun at their surroundings, then trained it back on Chase. "This is my fifteenth game on this island. Fifteen. My job is to make sure you people go the right way, to make sure you don't go wandering off into places you shouldn't be." He coughed, and Chase eyed the gun, wondering if he could close the distance and grab it, but quickly dismissing it. The table was in the way. He would be dead before he took three steps.

"Why would you do that?" Chase asked, trying to buy time to think.

"It pays well. I need the money. Usually, it's not so hard. I make sure Mr. Lomar always knows where you are. That all changed when Ryder found the body pit and made us ditch all of our GPS trackers."

"But the illness…"

He shrugged. "The illness is real. New boots started it. Pneumonia will finish it. I suppose it was only a matter of time. I wanted to retire. Begged him to let me, but he wouldn't, no matter how much I asked him."

"But people will see you. They will know you're a contestant from last time."

"Will they?" Moses said with a grin. "Go to the console. Type show world feed."

Chase did as he was told, hand shaking as he keyed in the commands. "It's asking for a password."

"Type Aweyo-fifty-seven."

Chase did it, watching as the password was accepted. The largest of the screens came to life with images of The Island from the various tree cameras.

"This is going out tonight. Yesterday's show," Moses said.

Chase watched, feeling his stomach tighten as the package aired. It was completely out of context. Chase had been painted as the heartless hero determined to win for his family, with Ryder as the eye candy who was the true leader.

"You see me on there anywhere?" Moses said quietly.

Chase watched. Moses was there, or at least in body. His face had been digitally altered. The man on screen was young, maybe in his twenties with a short goatee beard. It was absolutely flawless.

"Meet Simi. My digital alter ego. He's named after my cat."

"But how…"

Moses shrugged. "Technology. It's surprisingly easy. Moses Aweyo doesn't exist, not to them. Out there I'm Simi Rayoro, illegal immigrant taking part to provide a better life for my family, much like you. They have used my illness, of course, it's too good not to."

"This makes no sense," Chase said. "Why would Lomar go to all this trouble to set this up and then change how it goes out?"

"What does it always come to with rich people? It's all about money." Moses smiled, then stifled a cough. Chase watched the gun, hoping Moses didn't pull the trigger in the midst of a coughing fit, but he managed to hold it together. He went on. "There are betting rings. Of course, there are ones out in the streets, those are small time, though. There are private rings, ones where hundreds of millions are staked on people like you. Lomar likes to wager, but he doesn't like to lose, so he makes sure things go the way he wants it to go."

"What about the prize?"

"Oh, that's real. Someone has to win. You shouldn't have found out a lot of the things you did. They will fix that for next season, though."

"I think I understand," Chase said. He took a step towards Moses. "I think you said too much."

"Stop, stay there. Don't make me shoot you."

"You won't shoot me," Chase said, closing the distance. He was now standing on the opposite side of the table. The gun was less than three feet from him, pointed at his chest. "See, I spoke to Lomar. I saw him out there in the woods when you and Ryder were in the water."

Moses frowned and shifted position.

"He told me I was the favourite. His personal pick to win. That's why I know you won't shoot me. You can't. You're not allowed to kill the favourite, not if Lomar has put money on it."

"Stop, I'm warning you," Moses stammered.

Chase reached out and took the gun from Moses. "I think I'm starting to learn how this game works," he said, turning the gun on Moses. "What if I decide to shoot you? What do I have to lose?"

Moses didn't look afraid, just tired. "I saved your life. More than once."

"And I saved yours. You just didn't know it."

"I don't think you will shoot me, Riley. People out there, the public like you because you're a good man. You won't pull that trigger."

Chase pointed the gun at Moses, finger poised over the trigger. He knew just a little pressure, and it was all over. Moses would be dead. It was conceivable that Ryder was also already dead. He had heard the gun shots. Maybe Lomar had killed him already.

One in two at worse.

Maybe one in one.

Good odds.

Very good odds.

He stared at Moses, who looked back. There was no fear in him. Chase held his breath, telling himself he had to do it. He squeezed the trigger, wondering when it would kick back and spray Moses's brains all over the wall. He let out his breath and lowered the gun, slamming his fist on the desk.

"Shit!" he screamed, then sat in the swivel chair by the console, head in hands. Moses returned to his bunk and sat down. The room fell silent, only the hollow sound of the rain clattering on the outer imitation rocks for company.

"What happens now?" Chase asked.

Moses shrugged. "No matter what, I'm done. I can't go on. I have pneumonia, and my feet are destroyed. I'm going to wait here and rest."

"So it's just me?"

"And the dinosaurs," Moses said.

"And you swear you won't come after me and kill me?"

"Trust me, if I was allowed to kill you, you would have been dead the moment I picked the gun up."

Chase nodded and walked to the door. He paused and turned back to Moses. "Thanks for saving my life."

"Thank you for not taking mine."

Chase opened the door, and turned to step outside, then was shoved back into the room. Caught off balance, he sprawled to the floor. In the doorway, covered in blood, Ryder stood, his eyes alive with fury. He dived onto Chase, clawing and scratching at his face with his good hand.

"You fucking tried to kill me," Ryder grunted. Chase struggled to fight him off, but Ryder was incredibly strong. Moses crossed the room and grabbed him, but Ryder shrugged him off, sending him crashing ribs first into the table and tipping it over. He was a man possessed. He closed his hands around Chase's throat, muscles bunching as he squeezed. Chase couldn't fight it, he felt the air squeezed out of him, and his vision started to dim. He saw his family, his beautiful family who he had put himself through hell to try and save, and as now going to fail at the last hurdle. Chase looked up into the furious, bloody face of Ryder, then it was gone. It drifted away, disappearing in a shower of blood.

The pressure eased as Ryder slumped forward, splattering blood onto Chase, who could at last breathe.

Moses had saved him again. He was sure of it. He wiped the blood from his eyes, shoving Ryder's body aside with one hand.

Something was wrong.

Moses was still on the floor by the table, clutching his ribs. Chase flicked his eyes to the door.

Alex smiled, lowering the gun to his side. The crust of filth and dry blood on his face gave him a monstrous appearance. He stepped into the bunker and kicked the door shut.

SHOWDOWN
DAY FIVE
9:54 PM

Lomar opened his eyes, blinking through the blood and trying to unscramble his mind. He was face down in the dirt. He winced and shifted position, shifting position from the tree root which was jammed against his ribs. He sat up and leaned against the tree, trying to recall what had happened. He was dazed and bloody, but otherwise okay. He took a moment, allowing his brain time to settle. He noticed that the GPS tracker in the sleeve of his jacket was missing. The entire lower portion of the sleeve had been cut away, leaving a few superficial cuts on his tanned forearms. For the first time he could recall, Lomar felt panic. He was confident as long as he knew where the dinosaurs and contestants were. Now that his information had been removed, he was in as much danger as any of them. He let his mind go back, trying to piece together how he had ended up bloodied and face down in the jungle. He recalled leaving the bunker after a short resupply, and then seeing Riley shove Ryder over the edge of the ridge. He recalled how he couldn't believe his luck that the one man he had to make sure died had been presented to him.

He had taken off his gun, but his first shot was rushed and went wide. It had been enough to send Ryder running into the trees, and him in pursuit. He forgot in his anger and determination to eliminate this one particular problem that, like him, Ryder was a keen survival expert. He knew all the tricks. Lomar had stalked through the woods, looking for the tell-tale signs, perhaps in some way made complacent by the clumsy movements of the others. Ryder, however, was a completely different story, and even wounded, wasn't about to be taken so easily.

He recalled seeing it out of his peripheral vision. He had been less than five feet from Ryder and hadn't seen him. He had camouflaged himself with mud and leaves and launched out of the forest like a wailing demon.

He had tried to swing his gun around but was too slow. Ryder had grabbed it, and it had gone off, blasting into the trees. Lomar pulled away, and tried again to level the weapon, and almost managed to get it on his subject when Ryder had thrown a kick at it, knocking the muzzle up and sending the second shot into the air, bringing down a fluttering rain of leaves onto them. Lomar spotted the bandaged arm and swung the butt of the rifle at it, Ryder screaming as it connected, giving Lomar a little breathing space. Hands shaking, he tried to reload the gun. But Ryder wasn't to be denied. Fuelled by adrenaline, he had launched himself at Lomar, driving the older man backwards into the trunk of a tree. Winded, Lomar had reacted, bringing an elbow down onto the back of Ryder's neck. It was to no avail; Ryder reached down and grabbed Lomar's legs, pulling them up and sending him to the ground hard, the back of his head connecting with the tree.

That was when he had started to beg and plead for his life, knowing that he was no match for the younger, stronger man. He knew what Ryder had done, what he was capable of. He had seen the footage of the brutal way he had murdered Perrie and knew he was next. Ryder dragged Lomar to his feet and stared at him. Eye to eye nose to nose. With his mud and blood mask and the wild glare in his eye, Ryder looked terrifying. Lomar was about to offer him money, even a free pass off The Island, when Ryder launched his head forward, making a perfect connection between forehead arch and Lomar's face. It was then that the lights went out, and Lomar had awoken, bloody and in pain, but still alive. Either through mercy or by accident, Ryder had let Lomar live.

Lomar struggled to his feet, wincing as he touched his face. He had a broken nose and a chipped front tooth, but the engine was still running. He still breathed, and he still had a job to do. He found his gun in the undergrowth. The ammo had been removed. He tossed the weapon into the jungle. It didn't matter. There were more weapons back at Station Forty Five. He would go back there and resupply, then kill them all. He had grown tired of the game.

SURVIVOR
DAY FIVE
10:08 PM

Time was suspended. Alex stood there, a broken, bloodied mess. He was filthy, and his eyes glimmered with absolute fury. Chase was sure he was dead. There should have been no way he could have survived, and yet, there he was, standing in the entrance to the bunker, calm and emotionless despite just murdering someone. Chase wanted to speak, but couldn't think of a single thing to say.

"You look surprised to see me," Alex said, still calm. "Nothing to say?"

Chase tried. Words and responses spun around his brain, a cyclone of possible responses, but the connection from brain to mouth seemed to be severed. Instead, he sat on the floor, covered in hair, brains and skull. Moses stood, holding his ribs. He looked at Alex, then at Chase, and at the mess on the floor that used to be Ryder.

"This isn't the game you think it is, we…"

Alex shot him. Calm and clinical. He simply raised the gun and shot him in the face. Like Ryder, it left a mess. Moses Aweyo was no more. What was left of his head was spattered all over the screen still playing the television feed, his digital alter ego now all that remained of the man.

Alex turned back to chase. "I wanted to take my time. I don't like guns," he said, sighing and looking at the weapon. "You forced this on me. Two people I've had to end quickly because you betrayed my trust."

"You told me you were going to kill me. What else was I supposed to do?" Chase stammered.

"I am going to kill you. Nothing has changed. This could have all been avoided. I liked you, Riley. I was going to do you quick, maybe slit your throat in your sleep. Now, I'm going to take my time. Now I'm going to make it slow and painful."

"Why?"

"Because I want to. I have to. I don't know if you understand. I tried to explain it to you before. I have these urges. These desires to want to hurt people. Do you know how that feels? I have a daughter, she's seven. I have urges to hurt her too. Do you know how it is to live with that, having to fight against the desire to put my hands around her delicate little neck and snap it?"

"You need help, you shouldn't be here," Chase said.

"I cheated the psych evaluation. I read the answers to the questions they ask online. You people didn't do your research, did you?"

"Look, I have a daughter, she has cancer."

"I don't care," Alex said. "You and your family mean nothing to me. I don't do the whole emotion thing, Riley. I don't do the happy family stuff. I'm broken inside. Most people are warm and empathetic. I'm a cold black void. This is the only place I've ever felt at home. Here with the savages, with the beasts."

"What about after? You think those urges will go away if you kill me? They won't. They'll just get stronger. There's a word for people like you. Serial killer. You can't stop."

Alex considered it. "Maybe. Maybe not. See, my plan is to go to town on you. I want to gut you, hollow you out, take all the insides out and break them down to their most basic elements. There will be nothing left of you, Riley. Nothing for your family to bury. Nothing for your wife to cry over. Just blood and mess. Now get up."

"No."

Alex smiled. "Don't test me. You don't have any comprehension of the things I'm capable of."

"There are monsters out there. Fucking dinosaurs. You need to look at the bigger picture."

"They are animals. Dumb ones at that. We're so close, Chase. So close to the end. It's only right that I do my work in front of the cameras of the world. I want to show them what I can do. I'm hoping that when it's over, I will burn out that desire that's in me and I can go back to a normal life."

"You're insane."

"No, I'm not. This isn't the movies, Chase. I'm not the maniacal super villain. I'm just a man who knows he has a problem and was gifted a way to fix it. Now get up, or I'm going to shoot you in the hand. Believe me, you don't want that pain. Do you know how many nerve endings are in the human hand? Trust me, there are a lot. Now get up."

Chase did as he was told. He knew he had a better chance of fighting back if he was on his feet. He looked at the bloodbath surrounding him, Ryder face down beside him, a pool of blood expanding underneath him. Moses splayed against the wall, the top of his head missing. He didn't even react anymore.

"Come on, let's move," Alex said. He ushered Chase outside. The rain was incredibly loud. It pounded the ground around them. There was just a single large valley between them and the wall. "We'll do it down there. Near the exit," Alex said, breath hot in his ear. He smelled of dirt and blood.

"We can't go that way, just look."

There were three tyrannosaurs in the valley. The two largest were twenty feet tall, their greenish bodies covered in a light down of reddish feathers. They looked different to how they had always been perceived in books and movies. The smaller, juvenile rex was still imposing at almost fifteen feet, and moved around with more grace that Chase expected to see, head bobbing slightly like chicken which also reminded him of the man who was about to butcher him on live television.

"They'll kill us. Both of us. Look at them," Chase said.

"They won't attack unless we provoke them. Go."

"I can't do it."

Pain. His shoulder exploded with it. He saw the explosion of blood as he was thrown forward. Alex had pressed the gun into the back of his shoulder and fired. The bullet had gone straight through, but had left a mess. Shattering the humerus bone near to the shoulder joint. He screamed, and his legs buckled, but Alex grabbed a handful of hair before he could fall, dragging him upright. Blood soaked through his shirt, staining it a deep maroon.

"The next one will go in the other shoulder unless you start walking. Go straight ahead. We're close enough not to bother them. We should be fine if we keep our distance."

Chase staggered on, the agony unbearable as he walked into the valley, the point of the gun jammed into his back. Seventy feet away, the largest of the tyrannosaurs caught the scent of blood from Chase's injured shoulder on the wind. Sensing that its territory had been invaded, and having not eaten for ten hours, the predator lumbered closer to investigate.

TWO

The high-pitched whine was almost unbearable. Everything was dark; everything was still apart from that maddening noise. That smell. Copper coins.

The smell of blood.

Consciousness slowly came back. Displaced memories falling into place.

Ryder opened his eyes.

He knew he had been shot. He remembered the sound, and then nothing. He tried to will himself to get up, but his body was unresponsive. He turned his head, opening one eye. Blood and steel. Everything swimming in and out of focus.

He should be dead. He knew that. Somehow, he had been shot in the head and survived. He suspected he knew why. He moved his arm, his reactions slow, and every motion making him nauseous. He touched the back of his head, the mess of flesh and hair. He could feel the steel plate in his skull underneath the skin. Placed there after a car crash when he was a teenager, it had saved his life now for the second time. The bullet fired by Alex had hit the plate, slid over it and skimmed his skull. Sure enough, it had shredded the skin to a pulp and he would lose some hair, but his brains were still inside his head. The force of the impact had knocked him out. It was no surprise they thought he was dead. He must look a mess. He tried to push himself up, but a wave of nausea killed that idea dead. He suspected the force of the impact of bullet on skull had still scrambled his brains pretty badly. He looked around, using only his eyes, not yet willing to move his head. He could see the overturned table and a single muddy boot protruding from behind it. There was somebody else in here with him, but he judged that they were dead. The pool of drying blood around the foot seemed to confirm so. He tried again to get up, ignoring the nausea, pushing up to his knees. He stayed there on all fours for a while, willing the nausea to pass, watching the blood pour from his skull and patter on the floor. There was a lot of it. The nausea passed eventually, and his vision sharpened. Using the leg of the overturned table, he pulled himself up using his one good arm. The pain in the other seemed almost secondary now. He was getting blood everywhere. As he pulled himself up, he was dripping blood all over his hands, his arms, the floor and table. He saw what was left of Moses, sitting against the wall. He didn't want to see that, so he stared at the TV screens, waiting for his vision to clear. He saw what he was looking for. He shuffled over to the cabinet. The bandages were strewn all over the console from where Chase had been looking for medication for Moses. They couldn't help him now, but Ryder thought he could benefit. First things first.

The pain.

It was borderline intolerable. He saw the morphine bottle on its side, a pack of syringes next to it. That would help. He pulled out the largest bandage he could find, tearing the pack open with his teeth. There was a small mirror in the cabinet door. He looked into it and immediately wished he hadn't. Everything above his eyes was a bloody mess. The skin was split and seeping blood, the top of his head and his hair was puffy and matted, shredded by the path of the bullet. He had to keep looking. Using his wounded hand, he touched the clean end of the bandage to his forehead. It changed colour, soaking up the blood greedily. Using his good hand, he wrapped it around his head until it was used up. The blood was still soaking trough. He found a second bandage and repeated the process, wrapping the entire upper part of his head. To hold it in place, he used the surgical tape. He pulled it as tightly as he could, wrapping it around and around his head. He took another look in the mirror. He looked like a soldier who had been wounded at war. Dirty and bloody.

The pain was still a problem. He retched and dry heaved. If he had eaten, he was sure he would have thrown up. He waited until the next wave of nausea passed, then used the syringe to give himself a shot of morphine, following the instructions on the bottle. He had just survived a gunshot wound to the head and didn't intend to give himself a lethal dose of morphine and die at his own hand.

He expected total relief but didn't feel any different following the injection. The pain was still there. It seemed his entire body was riddled with it. Also still present was that maddening high-pitched whine. He hoped that was just a side effect of the gunshot wound and would fade in time. His immediate future was centred on revenge. He staggered towards the exit, pausing to pick up one of the handguns which had been tipped off the table and onto the floor.

GAME OVER
DAY FIVE
10:28 PM

The three tyrannosaurs attacked as a pack. The larger of the two adults came straight for Alex and Chase. The second adult flanking around to the rear and cutting off any hope of escape. The smaller juvenile cut off the way ahead. There was no rush to their attack; they were slow and methodical, taking their time. Chase was terrified.

Alex was laughing. "You can't buy this kind of thrill, Riley. God it feels good."

"We're going to die out here."

"Everyone dies," he replied, shouting to be heard over the wind and rain. "It's how you go out that's important."

The tyrannosaurs were wary. They had experienced humans before, and some had possessed the ability to hurt them. The largest of the three took a step towards them. Alex laughed and fired at it, the bullet hitting it in its massive underbelly. It roared and lurched away, frightened off by the sound, its kin following suit.

"We need to get somewhere safe," Chase shouted.

"We stand our ground. I'm the alpha male on this island, not some animal that was too stupid to avoid extinction."

He fired again, two of the three bullets hitting the larger male, making it back off even further. "Let's keep walking," Alex said, shoving Chase forward. The dinosaurs kept a respectful distance but didn't fully back away. Keeping within close proximity to their potential meal.

"They're gearing up to attack. We need to run for it," Chase said.

"Run where? Look around. We've got nowhere to go!" Alex laughed again and fired as the larger male considered attacking.

This time, it didn't back away, it moved closer, lowering its head and snapping at them, still not ready to commit.

"See? They're stupid," Alex said, grinning. He pointed the weapon at the large T-rex and fired, his smile fading when the hammer fell on an empty clip.

There was no time to think. Chase knew this was his only chance. He was tired but didn't see another choice. He started to run, grimacing against the pain from his shoulder. He remembered reading once that tyrannosaurs were said to be slow, but also considered that those books were based on speculation, and so it was either a case of right or wrong.

"Don't you run from me!" Alex screamed, setting off after Chase.

Trusting their millions of years old instinct, the tyrannosaurs saw their prey fleeing, and gave chase.

They were able to keep their distance from the adults. They were slower and more lumbering, the effort of chasing such a small meal outweighed by the energy it would waste. The smaller, lighter juvenile, however, was more than up for the chase. He closed the distance easily. Chase glanced over his shoulder, watching as the dinosaur approached Alex from behind. He prayed for it to attack. But the dinosaur moved past him. It could smell the blood on Chase and wanted it.

Chase changed direction, doing it suddenly and shearing off at a ninety degree. The much larger tyrannosaur couldn't change direction as quickly. It scrabbled for purchase, its three-toed clawed feet kicking up the slick dirt. It fell down hard on its side, buying Chase enough time. He changed direction again, making for the opposite side of the plain and the wall. Lights had been set up across its upper perimeter, no doubt in preparation to greet the winner. He wasn't thinking that far ahead yet. For as much as the T-rex couldn't change direction as quickly as him, Alex could. He was now close, eyes wild, a manic fixed grin on his face.

Chase focused on moving forward.

The juvenile tyrannosaur saw the distance from its prey, and gave up, changing direction and lumbering down the valley after its larger cousins, who had spotted a herd of stegosaurs and were moving closer to investigate.

The relief lasted only seconds. He was tackled to the ground by Alex. He landed on his wounded shoulder, white light exploding in front of his eyes. Chase threw an elbow back with as much force as he could muster, Alex grunting as it connected with his ribs. Chase scrambled up. He was close now to the wall. He could see the doors looming ahead, the yellow glow of the spotlights on the walls making a pool of artificial daylight.

"That's where we'll do it," Alex shrieked from behind. "Right there in front of the world. I'll show them how talented I am. I'll show them what I can do."

Chase wasn't sure how much further he could go. He was tired and in pain. It was then, as he was trying to think about what to do, that his foot folded under him, his ankle exploding in agony as it twisted. He went down hard, screaming out and clutching his foot with his free hand. Alex stopped running and grinned.

"Close enough I suppose," he said as he stood and caught his breath. He reloaded the gun, popping a new magazine into the bottom of the handgrip. "This will have to be close enough judging by how you went over on that foot. I was going to shoot you in the knees so you couldn't run, but I don't think that's necessary now."

With his free hand, he took out the knife. "I'd tell you this won't hurt… But I'm pretty sure it will."

Chase rolled over onto his back. He was done. There was no escape, no way he could flee. He was unarmed and immobilised. He wondered if his wife would ever understand what he had been through. He supposed not. She would see what the corporation wanted her to see. That troubled him. He wanted her to know how much he loved her, how sorry he was.

No.

He wouldn't just roll over and die.

Alex was close, a little too close and over confident. Chase kicked out with his good leg as hard as he could, connecting flush with Alex's kneecap.

He screamed and pitched forward, knife still in hand. Chase caught him and tried to wrestle the knife from him, engaged in a battle he knew he had to win if he wanted to survive.

TWO

Ryder crouched in the bushes forty feet away. The morphine had kicked in, and he felt a little less like he was on fire. He was still in agony, but it was bearable. He watched as Alex and Chase wrestled on the ground. He looked at the gun in his hand. He could win. He knew he could do it if he could just find the courage to do what needed to be done. He crept forward out of the long grasses, approaching the pair as they fought, completely oblivious. He held up the gun, hand trembling. He was crying and didn't know why. He didn't want to kill, but he also didn't want to die. He had been through so much already, and the end was so close. He was ten feet away from them now. Alex was on top of Chase and trying to drive the hunting knife down into his chest.

He wondered if he should let the battle play out and off the loser or just go all in and kill them both now. He pointed the gun at the pair, trying to decide.

"Don't."

Lomar put the knife to his throat from behind. "Don't pull that trigger."

Ryder glanced to his left, seeing Lomar's bloody face. "I bet you thought I was dead."

"You should be," Lomar replied.

"You should have done a better job when you shot me. I'm tougher than I look."

"You think I did that to you? If I'd shot you, you'd be dead."

Ryder tried to recall what had happened. The last couple of hours were still a blur, however. That particular section of his brain still scrambled. "This is the game. Why the fuck do you care? I can win this right now."

"No. You don't get to win. Not now. Not knowing what you know," Lomar said.

"About the bodies? Yeah, I know. Everyone else will too."

"You don't get it do you? You could have won. You should have won. You had been handpicked for it. Then you fell and everything changed."

"They both know. What's the difference?"

"One of them doesn't care about it. The other is only interested in doing right by his family. You...you don't have anything I can use to bribe you with. You're a loner, and that makes you dangerous."

"You can't stop me before I kill one of them"

"But you do and I'll slit your throat. You die, one of them wins. Either way, it's the perfect ending for me."

Ryder considered it. There was no question about if Lomar was bluffing. He knew he wasn't. He focused the gun on Chase and Alex, who were still wrestling for control of the knife.

"You know, I came here prepared to die. I'm happy with it."

"If you put the gun down, I can make sure you live. We can smuggle you out, give you a new life. Tell people you died here. Money. Cars. Everything you want."

Ryder flicked his eyes towards Lomar. "Who is your money on?"

"What?" Lomar said.

"Which one don't you want me to kill? It's obviously important enough to you to throw the idea of a new life at me. Who's your winner, Lomar? Who is it you've handpicked to be your champion?"

"That's not how it works," Lomar said.

Ryder didn't reply. He could hear the agitation in Lomar's voice.

"I think you hate not being in control here. How much do you stand to lose if I off the wrong person?"

"Ten million. Wired to an offshore account. It's yours. You'll be set for life. Just put the gun down."

"Can I say something first?"

"Quickly," Lomar snapped.

"Fuck you."

He fired, Lomar pulling the blade across his throat at the same time. Arterial blood sprayed in a wide arc, as Ryder fell to the ground, finally succumbing to the death he had avoided so far. His shot, however, had been true. It had hit Alex in the back of the skull. With no metal plate in there to protect him, it had been devastating, ejecting his brains out of a fist-sized hole in the front of his skull. He pitched forward, face down in the dirt.

Silence.

Chase lay there, trembling and covered in blood and brains. He was absolutely spent.

Lomar approached. He too looked like hell, but somehow found a smile. He stood above chase.

"Congratulations. It looks like you're the winner."

Chase couldn't move. He stared up at Lomar, trying to come to terms with what he was saying.

"Come on. It's just a short walk from here. You need to do it yourself."

"Why me?" Chase mumbled. "Why me over the others?"

"Right place right time. Just accept it for what it is. Come on. Stand up."

Chase got to feet. He couldn't put any weight on his right leg, and his shoulder was still destroyed, but he was alive. He started to hobble towards the pool of lights ahead.

"What about my family?"

"Freed. I arranged it back at the station. They will never know who took them and why. I'm sure you will keep it that way. You don't want them blaming you."

Chase nodded. The exit was just fifty feet away. It all seemed too surreal. "Should you be coming with me?" Chase asked.

"I'll be edited out. Don't worry," Lomar replied.

He was calm now and relaxed. The main threat was over.

"What happens now?" Chase asked.

"Now you go free. Your daughter will receive her treatment; you will probably be inundated with interview requests and the like. The Lomar Corporation can assist with those of course. Get you a P.A; make sure you say all the right things."

"Yeah, message received," Chase muttered. His mind was swimming. He didn't consider winning as an option. Now it was about to become a reality, he wasn't sure how to react. He stopped walking, staring at the wall.

"Problem?"

"No, not really. I was just thinking about the rules."

"What rules?"

"The rules about how only one person can walk out of here alive."

Lomar's expression changed. He watched as Chase pulled Alex's gun out of his belt and pointed it at the billionaire. "I still count two."

Lomar threw up his hands and smiled. "I gave you this, made sure you won. You owe me everything."

"No, I don't. You put us through hell. You broke me. I'll never be the same. Nothing can fix that."

"I'm not a contestant. It will be murder!" Lomar said.

"No. We signed disclaimers. Until I'm outside of the gates, everything is legal. Besides, like you said, they'll edit you out. You were never here."

"You haven't thought this through, you're overtired. Exhausted. We can talk it through, we can–"

Chase shot him.

There was no scream. Lomar went down, the hole in his forehead spilling blood onto the ground.

He felt nothing. He squinted up at the wall. On the top of it, he could see tiny faces staring down, their cameras rolling. He dropped the gun onto Lomar's lifeless chest and shambled towards the gate. There was no joy, no celebration. He was quite sure he would never be able to celebrate anything ever again. The Island had broken him, but he had beaten it.

The gate opened as he approached, the pale round-faced television executive staring at him open-mouthed as he shuffled past. Chase paid him no attention. He walked out into the light, unsure what the future held but knowing it could never be worse than the experience of the last few days. It was only when the south gate was closed and locked behind him did it hit home. He walked out into the thunderous chorus of cheers, and then he fell to his knees and wept.

CHECK OUT OTHER GREAT DINOSAUR THRILLERS

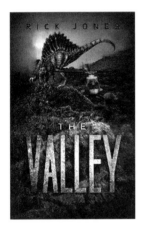

THE VALLEY
by **Rick Jones**

In a dystopian future, a self-contained valley in Argentina serves as the 'far arena' for those convicted of a crime. Inside the Valley: carnivorous dinosaurs generated from preserved DNA. The goal: cross the Valley to get to the Gates of Freedom. The chance of survival: no one has ever completed the journey. Convicted of crimes with little or no merit, Ben Peyton and others must battle their way across fields filled with the world's deadliest apex predators in order to reach salvation. All the while the journey is caught on cameras and broadcast to the world as a reality show, the deaths and killings real, the macabre appetite of the audience needing to be satiated as Ben Peyton leads his team to escape not only from a legal system that's more interested in entertainment than in justice, but also from the predators of the Valley.

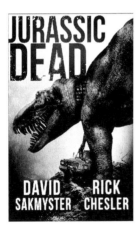

JURASSIC DEAD
by **Rick Chesler** & **David Sakmyster**

An Antarctic research team hoping to study microbial organisms in an underground lake discovers something far more amazing: perfectly preserved dinosaur corpses. After one thaws and wakes ravenously hungry, it becomes apparent that death, like life, will find a way.
Environmental activist Alex Ramirez, son of the expedition's paleontologist, came to Antarctica to defend the organisms from extinction, but soon learns that it is the human race that needs protecting.

CHECK OUT OTHER GREAT DINOSAUR THRILLERS

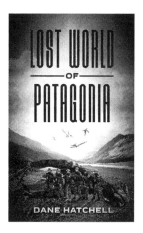

LOST WORLD OF PATAGONIA
by Dane Hatchell

An earthquake opens a path to a land hidden for millions of years. Under the guise of finding cryptid animals, Ace Corporation sends Alex Klasse, a Cryptozoologist and university professor, his associates, and a band of mercenaries to explore the Lost World of Patagonia. The crew boards a nuclear powered All-Terrain Tracked Carrier and takes a harrowing ride into the unknown.

The expedition soon discovers prehistoric creatures still exist. But the dangers won't prevent a sub-team from leaving the group in search of rare jewels. Tensions run high as personalities clash, and man proves to be just as deadly as the dinosaurs that roam the countryside.

Lost World of Patagonia is a prehistoric thriller filled with murder, mayhem, and savage dinosaur action.

SAVAGE ISLAND
by Alan Spencer

Somewhere in the Atlantic Ocean, an uncharted island has been used for the illegal dumping of chemicals and pollutants for years by Globo Corp's. Private investigator Pierce Range will learn plenty about the evil conglomerate when Susan Branch, an environmentalist from The Green Project, hires him to join the expedition to save her kidnapped father from Globo Corp's evil hands.

Things go to hell in a hurry once the team reaches the island. The bloodthirsty dinosaurs and voracious cannibals are only the beginning of the fight for survival. Pierce must unlock the mysteries surrounding the toxic operation and somehow remain in one piece to complete the rescue mission.

Ratchet up the body count, because this mission will leave the killing floor soaked in blood and chewed up corpses. When the insane battle ends, will there by anybody left alive to survive Savage Island?

Printed in Great Britain
by Amazon